M000189811

The Garden of Earthly Intimacies

Meeka Walsh

The Garden of
Earthly Intimacies

The Porcupine's Quill

CANADIAN CATALOGUING IN PUBLICATION DATA

Walsh, Meeka
    The garden of earthly intimacies

ISBN 0-88984-184-5

I. Title.

PS8595.A588G37 1996   C813'.54   C96-931401-9
PR9199.3.W35G37 1996

Copyright © Meeka Walsh, 1996.

Published by The Porcupine's Quill, Inc., 68 Main Street, Erin, Ontario NOB 1TO, with financial assistance from The Canada Council and the Ontario Arts Council. The support of the Department of Canadian Heritage through the Book and Periodical Industry Development programme and the Periodical Distribution Assistance Programme is also gratefully acknowledged.

This is a work of fiction. Any resemblance of characters to persons, living or dead, is purely coincidental.

Represented in Canada by the Literary Press Group. Trade orders are available from General Distribution Services.

Readied for the press by John Metcalf. Copy edited by Doris Cowan. The cover is a detail from a painting by Wanda Koop, *Untitled, (Cattellya Orchid and one Brazilian Hummingbird)* 1989, acrylic paint on plywood, 8' by 8'. Typeset in Ehrhardt, printed on Zephyr Antique Laid, sewn into signatures and bound at The Porcupine's Quill.

This book is for Sherri and Zach.

Contents

The Garden of Earthly Intimacies

You know, there's a lot to learn about intimacy and the
way it operates. I see ours as a burl nut. Started out as
a seed, maybe a germ, maybe like a grain of sand in an
oyster. Maybe that's a better way to say it. Now we're a pearl, a
beautiful pink-tinged globe-of-a-coming-together, a jewel, a
precious, round, milky sphere desired by the very thin Duch-
ess of Windsor for her stringy neck to put in that scooped-out
place that even she'd wanted kissed, and warmed there in its
skin nest in the hollow near a pulse and turned from milky to
cream when the pale-eyed Duke played cards with her alone
at night behind brocade curtains and they listened to Wagner
playing softly on the gramophone, just the two of them with
the creamy, milky pearl of how they'd learned an intimacy
that suited them.

But ours is different, our pearl grown large enough to cup
in your upturned palm and yes, you're quite right, formed
from an irritant, sometimes, yes – the ooze around an irritant
– but not so much any more, you're right there, too, we're
much better now, more pearl less sand, or like I said about this
woody nut much prized by carvers – all swirls and whorls and
rich, veiny graining. Something you can shape and polish,
and hard at its core as all-get-out, fine-pored and dense, like
molecules packed tight in there, adhering to each other, clan-
nish wood specks clinging together and glowing, burnished
under a caressing, polishing hand, rosy with intimacy. Us.

Remember when you and me and Nicholas travelled
through Germany on that tour and all the stops in different

cities where we spent sometimes no more than one night and part of the next day or once even just a half day?

The whole thing was absolutely right for my sense of an intimacy that moves beyond the usual. Think of it. Trains: close, small spaces lengthened into a tail, attenuated cells, whipping curves curling back out behind you like swimming, and you flutter only your feet, just a little, to keep your legs from dragging down, flit, flit, white feet flashing like little fish and you look back to see if it looks like it feels, the train back there and stretching out before, too, thin white arms stretching forward, green-white under a skin of water, the train a long arced body stretching through the water, cutting water, especially at night. At night a phosphorus trail in dark water. So how could something that happened mostly on trains not be intimate, I ask you.

We'd been travelling then for about five days and had stopped to do readings and give talks, in three cities. Each of the stops had been good. We agreed. Remember in the East, being met everywhere by student protests and seeing all the changes, all the turmoil, the churning, a country growing back to its own self. We were stirred. Remember how we were always eating meals at odd times and that what we were eating was often the wrong food for the time of day. The three of us had such energy; we were excited by our adventure – you and me and Nick. Wasn't Nicholas amazing – how much older than us and still with the same energy. He was always game. He was like us – he couldn't see enough. And the weird hotels, the dingy guest houses, none of that got him down. However early we'd get up he'd already have eaten his breakfast. Remember those breakfasts with the almost hard-boiled brown eggs barely warm. That was kind of intimate. Well – eggs – you know. But the way they were served, in a basket wrapped in a heavy linen napkin. And knocking off the cap of the egg with a spoon but they never gave us small spoons. It was always soup spoons and you'd dig around through the congealed white and there would be this custardy orange centre. You'd fill the spoon to get the white and the yolk and some of the pepper and then you'd have to open your mouth wide and almost push the whole spoon in because you couldn't sip it like soup. Well, sitting in those odd breakfast rooms which were always furnished like old parlours because, come to think of it, that's probably what they'd been before, in those guest houses – that was kind of intimate – opening your mouth wide in public. Even at the dentist's it's sometimes odd.

So there were the trains. At the end of a day or early in the morning, going into the train stations. In the big cities they'd be like cities themselves. A whole world. Busy, crowded enclosed spaces, things to buy that had to do with being closeted away – sandwiches, bottled water, fruit, liquor in small bottles, pastries, perfumes, tissues, newspapers, books, scented soaps, combs, the kinds of things you needed to please yourself or people you were going to be with in a close space.

Or the stations in the more remote cities – small central spaces without colour, just a couple of ticket booths and a clock and wooden benches. Sometimes a sort of lunch room, cafeteria-style, and then the low dark tunnels to the trains – just concrete or tiled like hospital bathrooms. No shops, only a few people who'd set up small tables or laid out a blanket – selling scarves and soap, some heavy watches and plastic combs. I guess everyone needs a comb for a long train trip no matter where they start out. So even the stations suggested a kind of familiarity and you knew you had and hadn't been there before.

Remember how we'd get to the big stations and kind of split up to shop for the trip? It was never arranged, not even the first time and after that it worked out so well we just carried on. Nick went for the oranges and other fruit for breakfast. You'd go for the vodka or brandy and mix and most of the time you remembered plastic glasses. I went for chocolate and pastries to eat later in the morning. Then we'd meet at the board to figure out which train was ours and suddenly we'd be hurrying to get a compartment all to ourselves, so we could read and eat and drink. We were pretty skillful too, or maybe we just looked formidable, two big guys, one woman, stacks of luggage and a kind of private look about us.

You knew, didn't you, that in an entirely innocent and inevitable way I loved Nicholas. You can't not. How long have we known him as friends, and you longer than me, and all the time he holds off, slips away, keeps himself apart.

But there we were, two weeks in a train, just the three of us, everyone around us speaking a language we didn't know, our communication with them limited to menus. Three people who like language and no one to share it with but each other. I've got you now, Jack Fish, two hands on your long body, both hands on your skin. We'll swim along together, the train splitting the water for us and I'll find out some things about your remarkable head, Nick Fish.

Dip your hands in water before you touch a fish if you don't plan to keep him. Lets him keep his smooth, slippery jacket whole, and off he flicks unmarked, into the dark stream.

I had no plans to keep Nick or leave my thumbs on him either. You and me and our warm pearl bead is all the intimacy of that sort I want anyway. But there *was* something.

As I said, in the big cities, the train stations – a harlot's closet all feathers and glitter and scent, high heels and leather, powder and layers of paint. Comfortable and not, like a toilet cubicle in a public place. Someone leaves it and you walk in, usually in a hurry – between acts or before a plane – and it's warm and there's someone's perfume. Not unpleasant, just startling and you feel you've learned more than you should. A real secret because, what's there to tell.

The train stations and the trains, focused and singular, like making love – one goal in mind, one destination – to get – there. And we'd all get on the train. There'd be the movement, the sound and feel of it; all the special things we'd bought for each other. Always books, art books in a language we couldn't read but with pictures to remind us of what we'd seen that day. And the three of us, alone when we were lucky. It was so good I wanted to stay on trains that way forever. On the move like that we were cheating time and all of us, unavailable to the world, were slippery fish, the sun flecking the colours on our skin, arcing in the light and then gone.

That was the best way to travel, three people in a space for six and maybe only by chance we'd never met real crowds. But Frankfurt to Berlin was different. 'Take the night train to Berlin and save time. Give yourself the full weekend in Berlin. It's the best way.' they said. And they made the arrangements for us. What did we know, three fingerlings, fish out of water, babes when it came to that kind of travel.

And the Frankfurt station. We went crazy. Lychee nuts, *eaux-de-vie*, almond pastries, Dutch chocolate, oranges the size of Chinese lanterns, bags of food for the night train to Berlin.

Our little compartment would be a cube of light as we moved through the night landscape. Someone, up late, fatigued, worried, would lift a window shade in a flat by the tracks looking for dawn and they'd just see our lights and the silhouette of three glorious travellers as the train slid quietly past. They'd catch the outlines of three arms raised in a toast to trains and motion and the intimacy in which we were all suspended. Not that we ever spoke of it. I mean, here I am telling you about it and you're looking at me funny as though it were something only I was feeling.

Well, maybe, but I don't think so.

Remember on the Berlin train how we had to move sideways along the aisles of the train because there were people
and bags and our arms were full of parcels of food and we
struggled with our suitcases and finally found the car that
was ours and the compartment was dark and full of people.
We looked in and this small space was like the inside of a
kitchen cupboard with shelves lining both sides, and people
lying down under blankets. Three shelves were empty. We
looked at our bags, at the parcels of food. It was hot. People
were hanging out the windows in the alleyway. We had to
push our bags under the bottom beds. You and Nicholas were
on the bottom across from each other. I was in the middle,
above you. Across from me a young woman with long curled
hair was already asleep, in spite of the crowds and the noise.
An American woman was above me. A net was stretched
across the two top bunks so that no one would have a serious
fall in the night. You couldn't stand with the net strung up
and remember how surprised we were in the morning, to find
someone else up there. It was like he'd hatched overnight.
From those big brown eggs.

You went to find the conductor to tell him we had to move,
to tell him we were too big for the space, to explain to him
how it was with us when we travelled by train, how we needed
room and that we had lychee nuts and *eaux-de-vie*. You came
back and said the train was full, there wasn't a single other
place.

We put away our food and drink because we couldn't sit up
in our beds. Nicholas went out and stood by a window and I
found a bathroom and took off my suit and put on jeans and a
T-shirt and washed my face and brushed my hair and touched perfume to my neck and the insides of my elbows and
between my breasts and thought that a night in a small space
with six people, well, I figured only five until I knew better in

the morning, I thought a night with five people in a small space when I knew only three counting myself, was more intimacy than I was prepared for. All that breathing, the night sounds people make, being party to someone else's dreams, a small dry cough, weight shifting, the kinds of things you only know when you live with someone. And then in the morning would we look at each other's faces and not speak about what we'd learned? Was there an etiquette for night travel with strangers?

You'd taken off your shirt and were lying on your back. You had turned on the small light near your head and you were reading with one arm folded behind you. The American woman couldn't see you but if the girl with the thick hair had been awake she would have seen your beautiful chest and maybe she did.

I lifted up into my bed and propped myself on my elbows as high as the bed above me would allow. No one spoke. We had the window open in the compartment and the train was moving.

Nick came in and bent to his bed. He unbuttoned his shirt and took it off. I realized that in all the years I'd known him, even at the lake, I'd never seen him without a shirt.

His skin was very white and even. He looked thinner than he did dressed and I didn't notice the small belly he'd sometimes pat with both hands and make fun of. He lay down, turned on his side and pulled the blanket up around him, leaving his shoulders uncovered. There was a wonderful full wind at the window and I wondered if his muscles would chill and ache in the morning. Then I lay back and closed my eyes. It wouldn't have been appropriate to look more and I wouldn't have touched him.

I did sleep but I woke often and each time I seemed to be the only one awake. Outside, the fields were heavy with mist that lay close to the ground like a dense wood smoke. It looked thick and viscous and in my half sleep I remember thinking it might slow the train's movement and I wondered if we'd lifted from the tracks because there seemed now to be no sound at all.

There was one time when I woke that I sensed you were also awake and I leaned to the side of my bed. Do you remember? I reached down to find you and you reached up first with one arm and then with both and we stroked each other's arms soundlessly, playing a mute harp. Then we slept.

A couple of days later, in Berlin, when we were eating lunch at that lovely outdoor restaurant Nick said that on the train he'd opened his eyes for some reason and he'd seen us reaching for each other. Remember he described it as a beautiful web of arms but he hadn't said anything at the time.

It seemed this whole trip we were somehow prevented from sharing a bed. All those narrow, chaste spaces, thin mattresses wide enough only for boys or narrow-hipped girls. We'd played a siren's song with our arms, a high, inaudible keening for the separations that were always being forced on us at night. I'd stroked the silk fur on your arms, feeling its dark colour in my fingers, you made a ring of your thumb and forefinger and slid the soft circle up and down the length of my arms. Nicholas saw all of this.

When I woke in the morning I felt we'd come through something remarkable, like waking cool out of a fever. We'd passed a night close by one another, not spoken about it at all but when the porter brought the coffee we'd ordered the night before, I was happy, almost giddy with pleasure, and Nicholas too, seemed to have let something go.

Argue with me if you want that this has nothing to do with intimacy.

The guest house in the last city in East Germany was an amazing place, the whole city was. I loved the colour of it and remember the morning after we arrived, we had some time and we walked into the centre of town and found, of course, a bookstore. Neither of us had a decent camera and we'd been so charmed by our walk through the city the previous night that we'd wanted a picture book and we'd found two – one with photos taken when things started to open up and one with reprints of the city as it had looked in the twenties. Both were black-and-white and we couldn't distinguish between them. That was wonderful. Ever since I was little I've wanted to go back to see how things were – not like H.G. Wells in a time machine to the ooze stage, just a hundred years or less. I wanted elegant and familiar signs, not confrontational brutality and creatures that snorted. So seeing the city trapped in amber by government neglect was perfect. Maybe not for the people who'd lived with it for decades but marvellous for me. I hope they don't ruin it when they begin the fixing. Even the colour was right. In the sun, a kind of sepia; probably in the rain a mould grey, but it was sunny when we were there.

Weren't you surprised by the guest house that belonged to the university? It must have been grand before the war, Gothic revival, and inside, Art Nouveau curves and carved door panels. I guess there'd been a lot of money in the city. And our rooms up on the third floor. Poor Nicholas. His room must have been a cupboard for linens. Remember how he pressed the bed and said he'd sleep on the floor. Poor back. You know, I wondered how he managed in that narrow little room. There wasn't a space on the floor for the mattress. I meant to ask later but he was great the next morning, wasn't he?

Do you figure the whole of the third floor would have been for the servants? Must have been – all angled ceilings and narrow halls and our room tucked under the eaves, with its yellowed fleur-de-lys wallpaper and brown linoleum – but clean. You were disappointed with the beds, weren't you? –

two singles end to end, but still, everything else we needed except a bathroom. I kind of liked the room. We each had a reading light, the windows opened onto a street lined with trees and I could smell lilacs and the sill was wide enough to lay out my panties when I washed them – you said they wouldn't dry but they did – and a little cupboard with six hangers and a clothes brush on a hook. Remember the small mirror right next. I don't think I saw myself full-length the entire time we were away. I knew my face; my body was a secret and maybe that was why intimacy shifted, why I recognized it isn't always the stuff you expect. Like the night in the train and that morning in the bath. Yes, that morning in the bath.

You were settling our bags into the room and I explored the halls. The 'Ladies,' as they say, or 'Damen,' actually, was right across from our room which was fine but it had only a toilet and a laundry tub with a single spigot and again, a tiny piece of mirror.

The bathroom, the room for the bath, was around the corner and quite near the stairwell, tucked in under a sloped roof. You almost hit your head against the little window, an oval in a recessed portion of the ceiling. We couldn't find any electrical wiring, not a switch or a pull. The window was translucent, pebbled yellow glass and the light seemed to leak through it. Again that yellowed light. Do you remember what was in the room? A low wooden chair and a deep, footed tub. A wire basket was hooked across the tap end and there was a piece of soap in it. On the bottom was a rubber drain. The floor was unpainted concrete. On it, beside the tub, was a coarse fibre mat. That was it. Everything was clean but unless you were first in you'd be using someone else's tub. There was no shower and nothing to clean the tub with.

We've teased about loving each other's dirt, calling our bodies sweet, accepting everything. I'd share your tub. I wasn't prepared to share anyone else's. So when I came back to our room I said we'd have to be up by five so I could be first in.

We slept past five, drugged by the lilacs, and woke instead an hour later. There were no sounds. It was okay. I pulled one of your big shirts around me for a robe, the way I always do, and picked up the towel, my shampoo and scented soap. Then, a soft slapping sound in the hall outside our door.

'Who's that?' I remember panicking and you opened an inch of door and looked out.

'It's Nick in a towel. He must have had a bath,' you told me.

Nicholas. A bath. But only Nicholas.

In the bath room the sun was just high enough to touch the yellow window glass. There was that much light and no more. The narrow radiator was on and the room was warm. The water had been hot and the room was very warm. The house was still. Moisture showed on the glass, puffs of it breathed at me while I prepared for my bath.

I set the towel on the chair, the shampoo and scented soap in the wire rack, my hair brush on the towel. I dropped my arms behind me and your big shirt slipped off. I hung it on the door knob, bent at the waist and brushed my hair down from my neck. It fell in a warm cowl around my face. Traces of perfume flicked off the brush with each stroke. I could feel my face grow warm. I set the brush down. My feet in my bronze leather slippers, the grey concrete floor, the rush of my red-brown hair. I raised my hands to the back of my head at the base where it curves to my neck, the part that you say breaks your heart to look at. I stroked the smooth hair from my neck down its length to the end. I combed my fingers through it for tangles. I moved my hands through, stirring its warmth and scent, took off my slippers, lifted one leg and then the other over the high sides of the bath and stepped into Nicholas's tub. He had been there minutes before. It was damp and still warm from the water he'd used. He couldn't have known that for me, in the barely lit, yellowy room he was fully embodied, palpable, shaped and weighty, the room filled with his breath and heat.

I knelt, leaning back against my heels and the warm porcelain sides were high around me. I could smell his soap and how it had mixed with his skin and the room was very warm. The radiator ticked.

That morning, so far as he'd known, he'd been up early and alone and had taken a quiet bath in this almost-dark room. I don't expect he gave any thought to who would follow him there and so far as he knew he left nothing behind, only those things he couldn't take with him – his scent, the warmth he caused, and some moisture.

A shadow could barely leave less.

Mexican Island Quartet
1. Sand

She'd travelled a fair bit. Caribbean islands had collected in her memory. Winter vacations, a warm caramel on the tongue, a soft shape, up under the palate, a round shape dropped hot onto the snow in February or March, settling on the surface then dropping down into memory, melting a spot in the cold and sinking almost out of sight. This one in Jamaica, another on Martinique, two weeks in the Florida Keys, a spa on the Dead Sea, Nice, Cannes, California for a time – everywhere sea, sand, heat.

She'd thumb the pages of fashion magazines, travel magazines, read with care the pictures advertising sun creams, scan the bodies not for shape but for surface, interested not in the skin but in what sat on it. This was all done casually, not as an obsession, just genuine interest. Not even a hobby, just a matter of interest, but it went on for years. And in this time, which now extended to probably twenty years, she became something of an expert. She could comment with authority that tans came in a number of colours: gold, rosy gold, a real brown like fine polished wood, or a yellow brown which seemed perhaps unhealthy.

Some tans were deep, colour staining the skin probably down to the bone, the whole cross-section of skin like you see in ads for rejuvenating cream, epidermis, dermis, follicles, fatty tissue – she'd imagine it all coloured brown. 'Get a deep tan' the ads would read and in her mind's eye the cross section visuals would extend to the bones and they'd begin to colour like the brown crispy ends of a standing rib roast.

Some tans were barely a stain resting lightly on the surface, a thin wash of colour applied with a sable brush. Those she liked the best. A tint of rose suggested body warmth, colour generated from inside under the skin, just showing through, the skin's response to pleasure, tickled pink, a very private joke, lowered lids, a blush – toe tip to ear tip.

Still, it wasn't actually tans in all their variety that interested her. It was what sat outside the tan, on top, against the skin. Once more there were choices. Oils that rolled over the body filling in surface abrasions, making the skin even and tight like a very shiny, close-fitting surgical glove; or sweat, real or simulated, beads generated or applied to indicate warmth or healthy exertion, maybe even sex. Sometimes it was a combination – an oiled body emerging from the sea, ocean, pool – water beading on the slick surface like rain pearling on the hood of an expensive car.

Still this wasn't it. What she looked for, what caught and held her, what provoked genuine longing, was sand. Single, individual specks of sand on the skin – course-ground pepper, sweet paprika, minuscule mountains, tiny fractured boulders, small individual grains of sand flecking, powdering, dusting the skin, clinging to oil, sweat, water, each one individual, notable, like crystals of salt clinging to the melted butter glistening on the lip of someone in a darkened theatre watching a movie, mouth open a little with desire.

She'd look at the magazines and travel brochures, at photographs blown up for posters and she'd long for the moment when the shutter opened and closed, want to be the woman on the beach, skin moistened to wear the fine sand stipple. Driving down an ice-rutted street in December her head would swivel to the window of a travel agency and her eyes would cling to the images pressed against the glass, eyes would cling to the image, to the glass, the way she knew the sand clung to downy, oiled skin, for those photographs.

Over the twenty years of her looking she'd gone to beaches. She'd oiled her skin, always using the right creams, creams which promised to protect her from the sun. She'd covered herself meticulously, shielding her very white, very fine northern kind of skin. She'd worn hats or scarves against direct sun on her head, never went without dark glasses to protect the delicate skin around her eyes, to guard against the fine lines that squinting would etch. She was careful and it paid off. The skin on her body would finally tan just the colour she liked, a light rosy brown, more water colour than oil paint. She took care and the skin on her body remained smooth and unmarked, never losing the elastic give that young girls have. It was soft and smooth and supple like a fine, very thin, pale chamois, the kind you'd use for buffing and never want to put down, the kind you rub between thumb and forefinger without thinking.

So given all of that she never could just take off her hat, set aside the book and bag she often took with her to the shore and lie out directly on the sand. She thought about doing it. Wherever she went she'd seek out the best sand, judging its qualities comparatively, making intelligent informed assessments, testing with her toes and fingers, gauging, considering, then moving on. There were lots of beaches that would have been almost perfect but always she moved on.

At home the photo enlargements, the travel ads, the sun cream promotions continued to draw her eye.

Several years passed without a winter vacation. Her life had changed, the kind of changes that come with a divorce – suddenly not enough money, suddenly too much work, suddenly the trimming away and paring down and redefining, suddenly the terror and excitement. The right creams, a hat against the sun, perfect sand, ceased to be issues in her life. Now there was someone new and one year, just before Christmas he said, 'I need to find you. I can see best in the bright sun. We'll go to an island.' And that winter they did.

It was a small island, a modest place without lush vegetation. There were no tall trees, no plantations, no sudden red bleed of poinsettias as there'd been in Martinique, no fluorescent bougainvillaea like in California, no hibiscus, red and yellow and pink velvet horns with long pricked stamens like Jamaica. This was an island of coral rock and sand, quiet along one length, wild to the sea on the opposite side. So wild on this side and open to hurricanes, rising, wind-lashed water, sharks and undertow that no one lived or even swam there except at the farthest end, which had a lighthouse.

Each day they rested at the pool, she under the shade of a thatched cabana. At four o'clock they drank Scotch with ice, on their balcony, and watched the light change on the sea, watched the water flatten under the fading light, watched the colour turn from turquoise to hazy aqua and then disappear in the night. They'd take a taxi into town for their evening meal, wandering up and down the streets until they found the restaurant that was right for that night. They were slow and relaxed and the heat and the soft damp air made them quieter with each other than they usually were. They'd eat, most often fish, they'd look at each other's faces, they'd be still, waiting. Then they'd walk slowly back to the hotel, along the sea, quiet except sometimes giddy for no reason, silly, like when he would pick her up in his arms, carrying her crosswise and run down the road and she'd scream and laugh and he'd stop and bend on one knee as if he were about to propose marriage in a fairy tale and he'd help her to her feet, setting her gently to the ground and they'd walk the rest of the way back to the hotel. They made love quietly too, their movements slow, held in the warm, heavy air.

In the mornings they'd be up early, sometimes early enough to hear, far below them, the kitchen staff preparing the tables for breakfast beside the water. They ate huge quantities of fruit and attributed their love-making to the Mexican cantaloupe.

'It's the melons. They make you sexy.'

'No, it's the mollusks. It's because we're eating seafood all the time.'

'Actually, it's the limes. Did you ever see such big ones?'

And they made believe that whatever caused the limes to grow to the size of hardballs, whatever was the chemical that made the skins acid green, was also an aphrodisiac. Libido limes, they'd say to each other as they pressed the green skins in their fingers, covering fruit, fish, chicken, avocados, everything they ate with the pale, astringent juice, letting it run down their wrists, rubbing it into their forearms like eau de cologne, watching each other, smiling.

One day they rented a jeep.

'You can't get all the way round to the other side of the island without a jeep. The road stops and it's just a sand trail,' the people at the hotel told them.

When they set off they knew it would be good. She couldn't wear a hat because the jeep was open and when they bumped along with the open sides and sitting so high up she had to hold on and couldn't hang on to her hat too. At the beach she couldn't wear it either because of the wind on that side of the island.

They were alone on the road, no cars either direction, only the occasional truck loaded with sand. The paved road stopped and the jeep dipped onto the sand tracks. He drove with concentration. She watched him, his brow lowered as if against landmines, quicksand and crocodiles. The seat was set back and he drove with both hands on the wheel, arms stretched out high at ten and two and she admired the fine dark hair on his very brown forearms, the slender wrists and elegant fingers, always for her a surprise on this big man.

They were very careful about the spot, stopping six or eight times, getting out of the jeep, pacing the beach, looking for a private place, a protected place where no one had ever been before. They found it. It was a circle of sand cut off from the rest of the shore line by rocky outcroppings. If anyone were walking along the shore they couldn't get to it without going far into the water or climbing through low prickly shrubs and over porous rock. It didn't invite casual walkers.

There were no footprints, no beach debris, just wind and rocks, low scrub, a high bluff shielding them from the road, the sharp porous rock protecting them from walkers, sharks patrolling unseen twenty feet offshore, and water, light, heat and sand.

The sun shone white, the sand was white, the wild sea was blue, with white. They spread their towels and unpacked what they'd brought for their lunch. He handed her his Swiss army knife. She took an avocado. With the point she picked out the stem end. Then top to bottom, sliding the knife just under the skin she peeled it, split it top to bottom, separated the two halves, easing her fingers into the crevice to separate the parts. She did this three times. Her hands were green and slippery. She walked to the water and pushed her hands into the spongy sand at the edge, sliding them in to the wrist several times to rub away the creamy fruit. She walked back to the towels, cut the tomatoes in quarters, the avocados into long thin wedges, stripped the onion and cut it into flat wheels and then into halves. She cut the limes in half. She picked up each piece, held it to his nose, to hers and then squeezed it over the salad. Finally salt. They ate everything – the salad, the radishes, first wetting the magenta surfaces with their tongues and then pressing them into a gather of salt on their plates, the brown rolls, the sticky pastries and the small sweet bananas.

When they'd eaten she lay back on her elbows and looked out at the sea. The wind had picked up and the waves were blue-green walls rising and holding vertical for just a fraction of a second, then rolling under their own weight, spreading white and foamy onto the spongy sand where she'd washed her hands. She watched for a few minutes, then reached into her straw bag and took out her blue bathing suit, the one he liked, with a deep V in front. She stood up, untied her shirt and dropped it off her shoulders. Always interested, even after all the time they'd been together, he rolled from his back toward her and lay on his side watching. She removed her shorts, stepped out of her panties and, suddenly shy, pulled the blue suit on quickly.

She'd always had a good body, well proportioned, slight, with long legs. Her muscles were tight and she'd taken good care of her skin, the pale chamois skin. She had an ease with herself, never dressing for show or to be revealing or provocative but never uncomfortable about being naked either, in private. But his interest, his fascination which had grown to something more, was different again.

He'd bought a Polaroid camera and photographed her all the time, showing her in art books and books by famous photographers how her body was the same or better. Together they'd studied the images and commented on shadow and light, on the subtleties of contour. Alone, stepping out of the shower she'd look with interest at her body, as though it were other, belonging now to both of them – hers to move through space and of course for pleasure, his for looking at, photographing and for pleasure too.

How odd, she thought, after all those photographs, all the admiring study, their increasing intimacy, how odd to suddenly feel shy. And working back in her mind the way she did, she tried to track the cause. Why had she felt the need to hurry into her bathing suit or even put it on at all? Well, one thing, a change or anything new always made her a little anxious, even momentarily, and she'd never been naked on a beach before. And the light was so direct, so white and insistent. There was the intense heat too. And the wind, a hot tropical wind, too intimate, too familiar on such a short acquaintance, touching her everywhere. And the sand, fine and white as fruit sugar, warm and even and deep and unmarked. Her unease, she realized, came from feeling not entirely alone with him.

Lying out on the spongy sand she let the water roll over her. She could see now why people cautioned against the undertow. Even here on the shore the water sucked at her when it drew back and would have pulled her in if she'd offered no resistance. He came down to the water, lay out in it and they linked arms. He'd hold her fast. She closed her eyes and allowed herself to be pushed and pulled.

Maybe a half hour, maybe less, and they returned to their beach towels to read. She lay on her stomach, her book propped at the edge of her towel. To the left and right and top of the book was the fine white sand. She lowered her chin to the towel, licked her lips and found them salty. She looked closely at the sand now inches from her face, read it closely, moved into it slowly. She was travelling in space, into another galaxy, travel measured in years; she'd be old when she got there, dead on the return trip. Into the warm sand, slipping between the grains, slowly pushing forward – she slept.

She woke with a start, sat up confused by the midday nap. He was there beside her reading.

'Let's make the spot over there behind the boulder, up on the bluff, the toilet,' she said and she slipped on her sandals to walk over the scrubby ground. When she stepped out from behind the rock and looked to where they'd settled, she realized she'd climbed probably thirty feet up. She looked out over their spot, over the sand to the sea. Holding her blue suit in one hand she picked her way deliberately down the bluff, over to the towels, dropped her suit, walked out of her sandals and into the sea. She stood thigh deep and waves broke over her, soaking even her hair. He came to stand beside her, also naked and they moved in waist deep. The water was warm and foamy and it swirled around them, twisting away from the rocks of their little cove. She faced the waves and watched them come toward her. She turned and faced the sand and the bluff and let them pummel her unseen. A little to the left of where they'd settled for their picnic was a small crescent of white sand surrounded on three sides by the porous black rock. It was raised a little as though it were a large stone dish filled with confectioner's sugar. She looked up the beach and in the other direction. She turned and faced the sea, dipped once to her neck and walked out.

With great care, placing each foot deliberately, lifting each one so there'd be no drag, she walked to the edge of the sand-filled stone crescent. Then with one movement she lay flat out, face down in the sand. She moved her shoulders and hips slowly, settling into the sand. Against her cheek it was fine and soft. Against her body it was soft and warm.

He came to stand near her but not too near, understanding the containment, the suspension of the moment. He didn't speak. Then she rolled over onto her back propping herself up on her elbows and they both looked.

Each contour, every pore, all of her, was dusted with white sand. The fine bones at her shoulders and neck picked out, her breasts round discs of sand; nipples small stone sculptures; over her belly, the bones of her hips, the rise of her sex, the rounded parts of her thighs, knees, the long leg bones.

Then he did it, rocking lengthwise on a spot of his own – front, back, and they looked.

They stayed till the light changed then they washed at the

sea's edge, rubbing each other to loosen the sand, their skin growing pink and shiny under the fine abrasion, the sand a loofah under their hands.

She probably wouldn't stop to read vacation posters any more; magazine ads for sun oil and tanning creams wouldn't draw her attention. She knew about sand now – under the hands, hot on damp skin, fine against a warm cheek. All those years she'd been concerned with surfaces. Looking from the outside was what she'd been doing. Now she was inside and the stippled carapace was her own. She'd wear it when she liked.

2. Chicken and Ribs

She wasn't given to large hysterical gestures; flamboyance in others made her pull back; extremes of behaviour seemed stagy and insincere and she found the stories people told about fantastic aspects of their own lives or the unusual conduct of family members too bizarre for anyone who could hold a job, wear clean linens or own a car and pay school taxes. They left her incredulous. They were making these things up, she knew. The flat house facades she passed each night when she walked her dog weren't concealing the things people described to her. If such stories were true the city simply could not function; it couldn't work without reasonable people collecting garbage, repairing streets, erecting light standards, designing traffic patterns, supplying safe water, ensuring that services worked, that there were the necessary police, fire, ambulances, hospitals, all with little violence or disorder apparent to an ordinary person. It couldn't work if the things she heard or read about really did happen. What was needed was the routine, the expected, the unexceptional dailiness of things in order to pull it all off.

At the same time, she subscribed to the snowflake theory of individuals – each of us different and special, unique in our own way. She'd look around her in queues or waiting rooms or pushing a cart in a supermarket, suspecting that she wasn't just like everyone else with only a small distinguishing difference. At the checkout counter she noticed that even the contents of her cart separated her from the people who'd unloaded their groceries onto the turntable in front of her. Packages of frozen, breaded fried chicken and fish, bags of peas and corn and carrots, tiny pieces each separate from the other, frozen, fixed, clattering to the counter; snack food, fried and puffed and salted, soft drinks in huge plastic containers, never cold enough and always flat before they were emptied, bags of sandwich cookies filled with jam or cream; spaghetti in shapes in cans, noodles with flavouring that doubled or tripled in size when mixed in a cup with boiling water. Her cart had sweet peppers, ginger root, brown rice, oranges, garlic, olive oil, raw chicken breasts and coffee beans. The carts weren't interchangeable. The lives weren't interchangeable.

But while she acknowledged differences, she preferred to think of the dangerously exceptional as obvious. If someone's behaviour were aberrant wouldn't it show, she wondered? Was it really true that a serial killer could dandle a neighbour's baby on his knee – ride a cock horse to Banbury Cross – and not have a revealing tic or wild eyes or, from time to time, a rage at work?

Well, she knew that wasn't true. The theory about the banality of evil confirmed that and teachers interviewed on TV after a former student shot up a restaurant, murdering dozens of innocent diners, always remembered the chap as helpful, friendly and soft-spoken. So yes, it had to be possible that an otherwise ordinary person could house one small variant, one unusual characteristic and still be just fine. The mail would continue to be delivered if she allowed that she, for instance, had tied herself to someone who wasn't like anyone she'd ever known or wanted before.

They'd gone to an island in Mexico, small, not yet spoiled but set to provide visitors with anything they could want. Hot and dry all day. Hot and windy, the air always moving, a flat place close to the surface of the sea around it. No shade trees, no splurges of colour, just a steady, even heat all day, a gentle, soft-furred heat at night – a cat-in-the-lap warmth – some weight, some heat, and late at night, rain.

They needed a vacation, a real holiday, not the usual work-and-steal-an-extra-day kind of trips they always took. This was to be a real holiday. Nothing to see, nothing to assess and store. This would be just for the two of them, as they were together, for now, and no further. Still, the days would be long, they knew, and if they felt like it then maybe they could bring a small project with them and in the afternoons, come in from the heat and work, if they wanted. But not, they agreed, for the first few days. They'd just play and be attentive to each other. 'What we'll do,' she said, 'since you can't ever not work is work at vacationing. Then there'll still be some tension to keep us afloat, right?' So they agreed. They'd do what everyone else all around them did, for a time. Nothing.

Now ordinary and regular as she was she'd still always found herself drawn to men with a certain spark in the eye, an edge in the voice, a hard bony ridge of spine. Nice guys bored her. Before, she'd misread the edge, had taken it for toughness, strength, a man in charge and she'd been wrong. They were soft or weak, one she'd really loved wasn't tough and strong at all, just smart and mean.

So she was wary now, wary but apparently hooked. Inextricably bound, she'd tell herself melodramatically, tied in some irreversible way to this sometimes beautiful man. This man, more than twice her weight, they'd figured, who finally filled her arms full when she held him, who in turn held her attention the way no one ever had before.

Sometimes just the fact that he was twice her weight frightened her. Twice as big, he'll diminish me by half, she'd calculate in a panic. He's bigger, darker, heavier, louder, stronger. I'll vanish under him. He'll press me flat to the ground. Passersby won't know I'm there, won't see me. I'm gone. I'll vanish, and once she'd done what the Hulk had done on TV week after week, his strength amplified chemically, hers augmented by fear. One night when he pressed against her she'd tossed him off. Just like that. When it happened, that first time, they were both shocked. 'You flipped me like I was weightless. That's remarkable,' he said, his eyes round as an otter's.

He was big and dark and he described his changing moods as 'black-ass'. She never knew quite what that meant but it seemed to identify the turns of temper that moved in quick as hail and then out just as fast, leaving surfaces pebbled, dented and bruised. Sunny again, those eyes otter-round, he'd grin and stride off. Usually she'd match him and they'd move off together. Knowing she could flip him if she found herself pinned down made her taller, lengthened the stretch of her legs and squared things off a little.

This island with its cat-fur nights was new for them. She'd brought long soft skirts to wear for dinner and thin bare tops. She had silver ballet slippers for evening and they bought her an armful of bracelets set with turquoise and onyx and malachite. At night after dinner when they walked through the town and along the sea her skirts moved against her bare legs, against his bare legs. The silver shoes made no sound on the pavement but the bracelets clacked and rang like small bells.

Everything slowed under the heat and she wondered, after they'd been there a week, if she could still flip him, if she had the strength in this air and resting as she was, without the tension of work. Maybe in this soft damp air it wouldn't be necessary. Maybe she could just let it go.

Early one day they'd rented a jeep and gone to the wild side of the island where there were no people and they'd taken off their bathing suits and dipped at the edge of the water letting the waves fold over them, folding themselves over the breaking waves and then she'd pressed herself full out onto the very fine, unmarked, white sand and rested there quite prepared to stay forever. Maybe there, on the wild side of the island, on that unpeopled stretch, on that soft, perfect, fine, white sand he could press his weight up and down the length of her, cover her and make her invisible and there it would be all right. She could stop, they could rest. There'd be no tension to support them but they wouldn't fall.

Most nights they ate in the small restaurants that served local kinds of food. They loved the sweet onions chopped with hot peppers and tomatoes and cilantro. Almost every night they ate fish and lime soup and wedges of avocado. But one day lying on the patio of their hotel she overheard one couple discussing meals with another couple. The first couple went on about the dinner they'd eaten the night before. Chicken and ribs. All you could eat, with the best sauce they'd ever tasted. They described meals they'd eaten on vacations all over the world and this one, it seemed, had been the best.

'That settles it,' she announced, leaning over to him in the sun, 'tonight we'll have chicken and ribs. It'll be a nice change.'

Their usual restaurants were outdoor patios with just a thatched roof and some brick half walls separating them from the street. The floors were paved with terra-cotta tiles that had gained a soft patina from feet slapping over them, from plate spills, weather and straw brooms. Usually the few walls were white stucco and the spaces were filled with green, the line between inside and outside indistinct. Furniture was unmatched. Table linens were rare. When they ordered the same drinks they often came in different glasses. They'd eye

[35]

each other's drink and then one of them would say, 'You got mine,' and make a move for the larger glass. The food was perfect, fresh and hot and simple.

The chicken and ribs restaurant was different. The floors were covered with flat, floral-patterned carpeting. The room was brightly lit and filled with blond Scandinavian furniture, the chairs upholstered in green and blue stripes. Pub-style mirrors advertising American beer reflected the spinning fans that alternated with the hanging light fixtures. On each wall there was a giant TV screen and each screen showed a different bikini beach contest. Enormous women with elaborate hair and perfect teeth, their browned skin jiggling, pivoted on stiletto heels while men in T-shirts spilled beer on them and each other and hooted the women on, offering encouragement and praise, jumping toward them legs apart, jumping up and down on the sand, jumping to face the camera, making beer waves in their glasses, jumping off-camera, cheering and whistling. The mirrors reflected the screens; in the darkening night the windows of the restaurant reflected the screens and the mirrors.

She ordered the rib platter and decided on rice. He wanted the chicken and ribs combo with french fries. They smiled at each other and their eyes strayed to the screens. They sat across from each other at the blond wood table and watched TV, which they rarely did. His eyes lifted to a screen. She watched a blurry performance in the window. Drinks came, they lowered their eyes, raised their glasses to each other, drank and shrugged at this odd, un-Mexican kind of place. 'What a strange spot,' she said. 'Who do you think owns it? An expatriate American, some old triple-by-passer looking for an island retreat? I mean – whose idea could this be? It just doesn't look very Mexican.'

'Well,' he said, 'this'll be over soon. Someone will pick winners and they'll shut them off.' But there was no discernible pattern and if the contests ended they began again without pause. She began to feel a little anxious. How long before dinner would come? To avoid the circling fans, the flickering in the window, the screens she could see if she turned just a little left or right, she lowered her head and looked down at the grain on the pale wood table. Service was slow. In spite of the fans the enclosed room was hot. He ordered another drink and another.

'You're sorry you came, aren't you?' he said.

'Yes,' she said. 'This was a bad choice, my fault. Sorry. Tomorrow I'll kick sand in that couple's pina coladas.'

'No. I mean you're sorry you're here on the island with me. You wish you'd never come. You hate it here. It's not nearly posh enough – just a tacky, flat, hot little island with no god-damn flowers.'

'Wait a minute. I love it here. You're just hungry,' and on cue their waitress tripped over with dinner.

Splitting one rib off the rack with her knife, she picked it up in her fingers and started to eat. He stared at her.

'You're crazy,' he said. 'We're through and you're eating.' She smiled at him, amused by his goofiness.

'Try the ribs. They're good,' she said.

'You're out of your mind. How tough are you? You're pushing food into your mouth, filling your stomach and the most significant relationship we've both ever been in is over and you're eating. I was wrong about you. That's clear. You just came down for a good time. You don't love me. You're no different from the women on the screens. I'm leaving tomorrow. I'll get a flight out and you can stay on for the second week. This was a really stupid idea. Another one of your tedious middle-class ideas – a winter vacation. Well, you bore me.' Now he was shouting and people sitting around them stopped, ribs in mid-air, mouths open, eyes wide.

'Please,' she said. 'Don't shout.'

'Right,' he said. 'Well, that's another boring, bourgeois idea of yours – don't make a scene.'

Her eyes filled. She lowered her head. The tears fell onto her plate mixing with her rice. Chewing slowly, hardly able to swallow she looked up and across at him. He was holding a rib, one hand on each end. His lip was lifted showing very white teeth with red sauce riding up along each tooth. God, she thought, he's just killed it and it's still bleeding. He moved quickly up and back, his moustache a ridge of fur along the bone. Then he went at the chicken, tearing it with his teeth. She imagined feathers, a warm stringy neck. Terrified, fascinated, she stopped crying and watched him. As he ate she could see the rage recede, slipping down from his hot brown forehead, down the high pricked cheekbones, down along the jaw, relaxing it a little, the mercury dropping in its glass pipe – all clear, easy now. She watched. He loosened his grip on the bone and grinned. Red showed between his teeth and there were small flecks of chicken.

'Good, huh?' he said. 'Why aren't you eating?'

She wiped the almost dry salt trails from her cheeks and separated another rib from the rest. 'It is good and you're out of your mind. You may even be capable of murder but I love you and I can probably still flip you if I really have to,' and she ate.

They wiped most of the sticky sauce from their hands with the paper napkins and asked their waitress for finger bowls. She shrugged, walked off and came back with the bill.

Outside the restaurant he turned and faced her. He pressed his hands together and made to pull them apart, tugging and grunting, showing her they were stuck as if for all time. One final pull and they separated. 'I'll race you back to the room,' he said, dimpling, and sandals smacking on the pavement, ran off, dodging strollers on the packed boulevard.

For just a second she thought she wouldn't follow along

after him. But what she'd told him was true. There were times when she thought he could be dangerous, no one she could live out her life with. It was also true that she loved him. She just wouldn't love him in a quiet, even, oily-surfaced kind of way. Theirs would be troubled waters and finally that was what she wanted. If sometimes she was rocked and ill with the slide of it, well, that was okay. Recovery came quick after and she welcomed the sweet gulps of air that followed when the nausea had passed.

With some persistence she alternately jogged and walked the three miles back to the hotel, finding him nowhere along the way. She was tired and a little dizzy with the effort so soon after eating and in the heat and all.

The doorman opened the door for her. She nodded in response to his *buenos noches* and climbed up to the room.

He was on the bed in the dark, his white teeth showing a grin in the light from the balcony. Only the rise and fall of his nicely furred belly showed he was at all out of breath.

She fell in beside him. He held her facing sideways, very close, firm but not tight. She leaned in to him, content, relaxed, breathing the smell of chicken still warm on his moustache.

3. Island Domestic

'Look,' she told him, 'it's not likely to work. You can't go back. You know that.'

'Of course I know that. I'm not interested in recovery. You're the one who's keen on elegy. I'm just saying – it's not finished yet. There's just some things I'd like to do. I want to go back to the same place and build on what we had there last year.'

She looked at him, his fine, solid face, the brown-to-yellow eyes – young and wolfish. He was asking her.

The island in Mexico interested her, too. Something about its plainness meant that things could happen; the spareness of it could be seen as a kind of generosity; it offered the basic elements – heat, sand, water, time and left the rest up to you. It was an invitation. Okay. She'd accept.

'And let's not get weird about not going back, okay? This is a small island. There's only so much ground you can cover.' He was tense.

They were sitting at breakfast, eating melons beside the sea in their hotel's outdoor dining room. Okay, yellow eyes, she said to herself. You've got something in mind. Something's been cooking for a year now since we were here last. But the thing about this island was you could wait. The air breathed slowly here. Things unfolded. She'd wait.

So the first few days they stayed close to the hotel, absorbing the heat slowly, sitting in the white light, she under a palm thatch cabana, he out in the full sun. They filled with heat, their winter bodies warming, rounding, until there was no difference in temperature between them and the air they rested in. Two soft-skinned lizards taking on their surrounds, thinking if they didn't move no one would see them.

On the fourth morning he left her with her breakfast coffee. Thinking he'd gone to collect beach towels she settled in the shade and waited. He returned with the hotel's big blue-and-white towels but his gaze was distant and he seemed remote; he'd journeyed to places she hadn't been, had pictures in his head she wasn't seeing, there was that sense about him even though they'd been apart no more than twenty minutes. When they lay out for their morning read he kept shifting, turning, staring out over the water and she watched him.

'What's up?' she finally asked.

'I've rented a jeep. Let's go to the other side just to see what it's like now,' he said.

The ground rules being they both understood you can't go back – still, the place they'd stopped last year, the isolated little cove, hidden from the rough road by a small cliff and saved from easy beach access by the sharp, almost volcanic rocks all around, had been so blessedly perfect, with its sugar sand, that you were helpless not to want to go back. Three times they parked the jeep and hiked down to the water to find it. Finally, everything looked right. The rock against which they'd leaned their backs, the rise of land behind them, the black rocks, pitted and porous and sharp underfoot and the white sand, unmarked by footprints, showing only the hieroglyphs of bird tracks on its surface.

'The water's higher this year but this is it for sure. I know this is it,' he said and he told her they'd come back.

'I've got the jeep until tomorrow night. We'll do our shopping early and spend the day.'

He paced the beach with authority, almost pushing her aside when she came down to walk near him. Like a buyer about to make an offer on a piece of land, he seemed to be measuring it off in strides.

Well, she thought, next he'll pee on all the corners to mark off what's his. But he kept on pacing, looking out for something, bending to lift beach debris, pushing at driftwood with one foot and walking on. Leaning against the rock, she put her hands behind her and watched. When he'd walked some way down the beach, as far as the sharp rocks would allow, he turned and walked back. He was dragging four bamboo posts, slender, hollow trunks. Panting a little, he deposited them at her feet and showed his white teeth.

'There,' he said. 'For the house.'

'House?' she asked.

'Yup. We'll need some shelter. From the sun. We'll buy blankets. I'll make a lean-to.'

His sentences became rudimentary to match the architecture he was planning. Two of the posts looked to be about four feet long. The other two were longer. Somehow he'd managed to find two almost even pairs. The shelter would be higher in front. It would slope back to the rock. It would work. Yes. It would work.

He became more assertive. They needed certain things. Two blankets – one for the roof, one to sit on, rope to tie the blanket to the posts, a cooler, some plates or bowls for their picnic – he wanted her to make the same avocado, onion and tomato salad she'd made last year and they'd see what else they needed when they shopped.

Usually he loathed shopping and teased her when she was domestic, making clucking sounds and pretending to search for the eggs she'd just laid. But he'd promised this trip was not really about going back and certainly he was breaking new ground with all of this.

That night, after dinner in town, they walked up and down the close, partly lighted streets, stopping at open shops, looking for his blankets. The people who lived on the island were small and their buildings low. Often, doorways were set down into the ground and it was necessary to duck on entering. Whatever interior courtyards or gardens there were were behind the public face of the houses and in the absence of much light the whole town seemed a single dwelling. She remembered being startled one evening to find her arms wet with a light rain, having forgotten she was outside.

She happily trailed him in his search for the blankets and liked the ones he finally chose – two identical woven cotton squares with uneven stripes of white, brown and black.

'Like the sand and the rock and harder to pick out that way,' he said.

By whom, she wondered, having seen no one there on any of their visits.

In the morning he moved with such assurance, seeming to keep to a prearranged schedule, that she again found herself trotting along after him, falling behind, hurrying to catch up, feeling maybe twelve years old, a child, or that just behind him was her real place. What had been amusing was now a little annoying. And she couldn't say, Wait up, all your rushing is silencing my voice, or, Your pace isn't allowing me my right place, or, I have an opinion and want to be consulted, because she didn't have an opinion, or anything she wanted to say, now.

At the picnic spot he continued in charge. 'I'll unload the jeep. You just carry the blankets,' so she headed down the slope and began to pick her way across the rocks. The surface was treacherous and she concentrated hard on making her way safely. Feeling she'd been given a lesser role she wouldn't accommodate some notion of herself as incompetent by tripping and turning an ankle so she didn't lift her head until she had cleared the rocks and was standing on the white sand of their beach. She moved toward the boulder against which he'd build their shelter. When he came over the rocks he'd see her there and their partnership would be reaffirmed.

There on the boulder, facing the sea, outlined in blue sky, his body the colour of corroded metal, the surface oxidized into scales, was an iguana. Pushing up on his arms, elbows bent to right angles, chest lifted off the hot rock surface, small quick head shaped like a flattened shot casing, his body long, long, sloping down from the raised elbows, down to a long tail, thick and heavy as metal ship's cable, following after. His head clicked toward her. Nothing else moved. He shifted the thought in his eye from water to her. She flicked the picture in her eye from shelter to lizard. He took the time he needed; with everything arranged for her, she had time. They looked fully at each other. The rock was warm and smelled like dust. The sky, too hot for sea birds, was empty. The sand was fine salt and it gave under her foot. There was no wind and the hard green plants growing around the rocks were still. He filled his neck with air and pumped it. Then turning on his left arm he drew his tail around behind him in an arc. Its weight pulled it vertical. Still raised up on his elbows he looked again to the water. The tail clicked over the hot stone. The vines growing around him opened, quivered in the white light and closed behind.

'There,' he said. 'That's everything.' And he set the cooler and straw bag on the sand near the rock.

'Did you see him? Did you know they were ever that big? Did you see the length of his tail? The tail alone must have been over three feet long,' and she went on. 'He was there on the rock, sitting, facing the water. I saw him in profile. He was like a Chinese bronze, solid and heavy. Nothing moved except his head and then his neck and he disappeared over there into the vines, like he was drawn on tracks. I don't think his legs even moved.'

'What? What was there?' he asked her, looking at the vines where she pointed.

'The iguana,' she said. 'The iguana was there because he was a sentinel. He was guarding the spot in case someone else took it. He was waiting for us and then when we came he could leave. Or maybe this is his place and we're not supposed to be here.' She looked around her. 'Maybe he was trying to warn us away.' For a moment the emptiness of the place seemed less inviting.

What could it mean, really, the iguana here on the rock? He hadn't been there before and they'd always come this early in the day and the days had all been the same. Why was he there on the rock this time? Surely it must mean some particular thing and what she wanted to know was – should she be alarmed or reassured? She'd think about it later after they'd settled in because now he wanted her attention and her help.

'We'll stand the posts in this way,' he said pushing each one in turn into the sand and hammering them down with a solid section of log he found on the beach. 'Then we'll drape the blanket over and secure it on each corner with clothes line.' He pulled out the Swiss army knife he'd bought at the duty-free the year before. He sawed at a section of line while she held it taut. His concentration was perfect, complete. A man who never missed the smallest sound she made, who could detect a change in her breathing while she slept and was immediately awake, who responded to her slightest shift or movement – now he was lost. He'd walked into the place in his imagination that was the wild side of the island and for now at least, had closed her out. Okay. She'd wait. The room had only one door. He'd come out the way he'd gone in or he'd reach out and bring her inside.

He looped and knotted the line around the blanket on each post, spread the second blanket underneath, pushed the cooler into the shade and unfolded the big hotel towels against the rock. She crouched down and looked in. At the higher end she could almost stand. Toward the rock at the back the roof would comfortably clear the top of her head when she sat up straight. She crawled in, turned and sat back against the towels. He brought her straw bag to her. He squatted for a moment on his haunches looking in, could see she was in shade, knew it would be late afternoon before the sun would be low enough to show below the blanket roof. Then he straightened, brushed the sand from his hands and walked off toward the water.

She reached into her bag for a book and the sun cream. The cream was still cool from the hotel room and it smelled like the fine department store it had come from – faintly of gardenias. She thought of wrist corsages and small boxes lined with green tissue slipped into refrigerators late on summer afternoons.

To her arms, neck, chest, shoulders. Cool gardenias with fleshy petals. She was protecting herself and he protected her and there he was prowling along the water's edge, bending, knees flexed in a form she recognized. Against the light reflected from the water he'd become a featureless silhouette so it was only gestures she could read. His feet must have been sinking in the wet sand and his shoulders sloped forward when he walked. A few strides would bring something to his attention and he'd reach a long arm into the shallow water and bring what he'd found close to his face. She thought of clam shells smashed open with a stone to provide lunch and she remembered they'd brought things for a salad. But she thought – what a short distance we've travelled – the man patrolling on the beach, the woman safe and quiet in the shelter.

Now there was time to think about the iguana but she wasn't sure how. He belonged on this island but not with her. He wasn't a pet, not a dog or a songbird. He hadn't seemed threatening but then she hadn't challenged him either. He'd been waiting, that much she decided and if you waited it was for some reason. She liked the idea that he'd been keeping the place for them. Did he expect they'd build a shelter for themselves? Had he hoped they'd settle, she in the shade, the man patrolling the shore? Or had he hoped they'd spread a single woven rug where the sand was soft and unmarked, that they'd take off their clothes and be lovers in the full light, that they'd be as big as he was, that their soft-skinned bodies would rub, but not clatter like his would, and that after, they would wash the sand from each other at the edge of the water, dip their light bodies into the blue-green sea, take on the turquoise colour and emerge bright and glittering? Was that what he'd expected. Would they do less than he wanted?

She looked out into the light from her shadowed spot. The beach was deserted. He must have moved along the water and was out of sight. He'd come back with his hands full of the pieces he'd gathered – shell fragments, bits of coral and stories of how the sand had been under his feet, of what he'd seen over there beyond the rock arms of their cove. And he'd be hungry.

Under the leafy scrub, under the dark vines that grew along the rocks and close against the sand, their iguana was sliding and lifting and watching. Somewhere, beyond where she could see, the man was walking and stopping and looking. For now, she could rest and read.

Their lunch would be a salad made from the vegetables they'd bought that morning at the market, and bread from the small bakery near their hotel. It would be enough. Their big meal was taken in the evening in town when it was cool. With his knife she peeled and separated chunks of white onion, quartered the small tomatoes and peeled the avocados. The flesh lifted easily from the pit and she sliced big segments into each bowl. Here, the avocados were big and solid and buttery and she gave them each a whole one for lunch. She crawled out of the shelter on her knees, her hands greasy with the pale green flesh and she walked to the water to wash. She could see him a hundred yards or so down the shore and she waved her arms over her head, flagging him in a mock semaphore. He responded in the same way and began to walk toward her.

She returned to the shelter and with his knife cut the giant limes in half and squeezed a full one over each bowl. The juice would keep the avocados green and sweeten the onions. She could see him at the shore just in front of her. He was laying things out on the rocks. Then he stepped into the surf up to his knees and bending, washed his hands and arms. She sprinkled the salads with salt and opening out the paper bag, broke the bread into chunks and laid them out.

He crouched low, crawled onto the blanket and leaned his hot face toward her. She tasted salt on his mouth.

'It's wonderful out there,' he said, looking over his shoulder and swinging his arm wide.

They ate the salads and the bread and drank the bottled water they'd kept in the cooler. They had small bananas and chocolate and more water. He walked over to the flat rocks at the water's edge, brought back the things he'd gathered and spread them out on the blanket. They bent together, looking close. There were shells, broken pieces and perfect whole ones in shapes and colours they'd seen only in specimen cabinets.

Not knowing their proper names, she told him they had contained unguents and scent for a princess in Venice, that the shelves in the inner rooms of the doge's palace had been lined with them, that the doge would dip into them with the finest point of the filed nail on his last finger and spread the scented cream in the place between his lover's breasts. She also told him about the gondolas on the water and that after dark the sky would be the same mauve as the shells he'd found.

'That's right,' he said. 'All that.' And now his mouth tasted of lime and salt.

The sun dropped below the edge of the blanket and they were no longer in shadow.

'It's time to go back,' he said.

She packed her book and the sun cream. He unknotted the loops of line that held the blanket to the posts and coiled them around his hand. They folded the blankets and rolled up the towels and gathered the remains of their lunch. Then using a half tube of bamboo as a scraper he scooped bits of debris that had washed near their spot. Stepping away from their place she gathered pieces of Styrofoam, a rubber sandal, some tangles of torn fishing net and they put all this into a bag they'd brought with them. When they left, the place was perfect, unmarked. Only their footprints showed there had been anyone there. The last thing he did was pull the posts out of the sand and push them high up out of sight into the scrub that grew behind the rock.

With the cooler on his shoulder and the blankets under his other arm he set out for the jeep. She was carrying the straw bag and she walked slowly, a few paces behind him, pushing her feet into her sandals as she went. The sand was soft and warm and as she slid each foot the sand mounded, then trickled off. When she got to the flat, broken rocks she turned to look back to the boulder that, for the day, had been home. She wanted the iguana to have reclaimed it, to have stretched himself out on its baked surface. They'd left the place better than they found it and part of the finding had included him. But he wasn't there.

'We'll come back again in a couple of days for another picnic,' he told her. 'I'll get the jeep again. The posts are there and we've got the blankets. Same menu. Some things can't get better.'

She looked out over the baked red hood of the jeep as they drove, at the scrub and bushes, very green and growing close by the narrow road. The wind pushed her hair back from her face. He was right.

Several times during the days that followed, sitting under the thatched roof of a cabana at their hotel she'd be startled to find the iguana on the pages of her book instead of the close black type. In reflection she knew no more about his presence on the rock than she'd known sitting under the shelter. He was just there – a picture in her mind, a silent lizard on a boulder. They talked about when they should go back and he rented the same jeep. They varied their picnic only with the addition of a box of foil-wrapped Swiss cheese triangles. 'Protein,' she said.

Attentive to the care the rocks' sharp, pocked surface required, she picked her way over them to the sand without speaking. The boulder's crown was bare. Neither of them mentioned the iguana. Knowing exactly how he'd do it, he set up the shelter quickly. This day the wind was strong and off-shore and the water, pushed back, had revealed a perfect half circle of rocks, like a basin. The floor of it was white sand and together they lay back in it and let the water wash over them to their necks.

'Before the water comes in it's like an enormous bowl of Bird's custard powder,' she said. 'I'd always found it more appealing to look at and touch than to eat and now here we are lying in it.'

'Well,' he said, 'that's not the first thing that would have come to my mind but whatever it is we're wriggling down into, it's gorgeous.'

They had their lunch and he told her he would walk along the water in the other direction today. She rinsed their salad dishes beside the sand-bottomed basin and took the bread that had been left over from lunch, and stepping up onto the rocks that protected one side of their beach she broke it into chunks and spread it out for the gulls. Then she settled back under the shelter to read.

Even in the shade it was very warm and she could feel herself drift for seconds into sleep. Lifting her head with the start that comes on waking out of those quick sleeps, she was sure she'd seen something moving to her left. Leaning forward she scanned the rocks where she'd put the bread. Nothing moved and she could pick out no new shapes. Again. And she knew she'd seen something. Crawling out of the shelter she moved to the edge of the rocks to see a small, fawn-coloured animal crouching off near the scrub.

It's a gazelle, she thought, never having seen one and thinking of Yeats, 'Two girls in silk kimonos, both beautiful, one a gazelle.' It must be one of those tiny deer that live in warm places. I didn't know they had any on the island, and she climbed up onto the rocks for a better look.

Frightened, the animal stayed low and crept off, looking back over its shoulder as it went. She could see it more clearly now.

It was a dog, a small dog with a fine, narrow head and very thin legs, and she whistled and called softly to it, crouching down herself so there'd be less difference in their size. The dog stopped, lowered itself to the rock and looked back at her.

'Come, now. Here, little thing. Here, to me,' she cooed and sang softly. 'There, it's okay. I couldn't hurt you. Here, now,' and she edged toward the dog, ungainly in her squatting, offering her clumsiness as evidence of good will. She picked up a piece of the bread and rolled it across the distance between them. She stopped where she was, reeling the dog

[51]

toward her with her voice and the bread. Still low, the dog turned and with legs bent, crept in the direction of the bread.

Each of her ribs was distinct and her shoulders and hip bones pushed up against the honey-coloured pelt that rolled loosely over her frame when she moved.

She's a nursing mother and she's starving, she recognized, and the dry bread seemed, suddenly, a mean gift.

'Here, here. We've got biscuits in our shelter. Come here to me,' she sang softly and she thought of the very yellow butter cookies they'd brought and was sure they were coloured by the bright egg yolks she'd seen at breakfast in their hotel. The dog should eat those splendid cookies.

'Eggs and butter and sugar.' She ticked off the ingredients and the dog edged nearer, seized the bread and ran off a way to eat. She rolled another piece and moved back, still singing to the dog's small-boned frame. She came for the second piece but this time ate it where she was.

'There. Now we can see each other nearer. Pretty mom, lovely lady, good girl, here, here,' and the dog edged nearer.

'Yes, that's right, here, here where I am,' and this time she rose a little and still facing the dog, began to step back down to the shelter.

'Yes, come with me, here out of the sun. Come to the biscuits. Yes, that's the girl, good mom,' and with her voice she wound her nearer, pulling her by will into her shelter.

'Just wait. See what we have here, sweet cookies for you and your pups,' and, afraid to startle the dog with any new sounds, felt in the straw bag for the package.

She reached with her forelegs in the shade of the shelter but, still wary, didn't settle in, her body quivering with her readiness for flight.

'Here now. Have this,' and she broke off a piece of cookie and let it lie on her fingers.

Thinking of her babies and with her belly folded in on

itself, she reached for it with small white teeth.

Close now, she could read her face. Yellow eyes ringed in black. Long, narrow muzzle – fawn turning dark just around the nose. The nose perfectly black and flat on top – the nostrils thin and lifted. A few distinct, stiff, glossy black whiskers stuck from her muzzle, evenly spaced. Her eyes were clear, her nose wet. She carried her ears well back and flat to her head and they lifted and turned, responding to any new sounds. She'd been taught to be still or she'd learned it on her own. She waited for more cookie.

'Here's more. Have this and there are more. They're yours.' What she wanted was to see him coming back along the shore. They needed more food.

'Wait. There's cheese. Wait now, I'll find it,' and she found the round package in the cooler. Two triangles left. 'Here, we'll have cheese,' she told her. 'Wait to see what we have,' and she fumbled with the red pull on the foil and picked the paper off. 'Here now, try this.' The nose worked while her fingers fumbled and the small mouth closed around it at once, her little sharp teeth just touching the woman's fingers, while she eyed the second piece.

She looked around and there he was, walking toward them. She hoped he'd see the small dog and be careful in his approach. The dog raised herself up and backed out of the shelter, moving off to the rocks, but she didn't go farther.

'Look what's here. This lovely, dear dog. She's nursing pups. She came for the bread I put out for the gulls and I've been giving her what was left of our lunch.'

'She'll need more than that,' he said, but they had no more.

'Look, you keep her here. A couple of miles back there's that beach stand with beer. They'll have something.' He took his wallet and the keys for the jeep out of the straw bag and worked his way over the rocks.

She urged the dog back into the shade with more cookies and fed her the second piece of cheese. The hand that she held out to her was empty and wet from the dog's mouth. She slipped it under the narrow jaw and brushed the chin lightly with one finger.

'You poor dear thing, you lovely dear creature. Wait with me and we'll feed you.' She lifted her hand to the side of her head and knuckled one ear. The dog's head tilted that way and for a moment the yellow eyes closed.

'Yes, quietly, here,' she said. 'You're fine here.'

He'd gone off with the jeep. She'd seen no one around. He seemed to be taking a long time and she thought – where was the iguana? In the same way that the sharp broken rocks made it difficult for anyone to approach, it would be impossible to run if she needed to. She and the dog sat quietly in the shelter but now she was aware of her heartbeat, and the dog's ears turned, even while she lay there. Where was he?

'Where are your babies, little thing? Where in the heat and the scrub have you tucked them? But wait for a bit. He'll be back. Wait to see what he brings,' and she stroked the round cap of her fine head. The dog heard him first and started to lift.

'It's all right. He's back and he's brought you something good.'

He was carrying a plastic plate covered with another one. 'They'd just caught grouper out behind the stand and were starting to fry it when I came by,' he said. 'I told them it was for a dog. I think they understood when I gestured and bent down like I was patting something. They laughed but here it is,' and he lifted the top plate off and showed her a dish with fried grouper, rice and peas.

They held it out to the little dog and coaxed her forward again. With each interruption she'd become timid, doubting her welcome.

'See, here mom. For you and your babies,' she half sang. 'See what he's brought for you,' and she pushed the dish toward her. The dog dropped her muzzle to the plate and ate the two fillets and the rice and peas without lifting her head.

The woman's chest hurt. To be so hungry and still wait and be gentle. Would she wait like that? She wondered how it would be if the bones of her pelvis pushed right to the skin, if her shoulder blades almost broke through, if her elbows were sharpened by hunger – if she'd be so quiet and fine. If she were desperate could she be so mannerly? She'd want to be that way if she were the dog – or otherwise.

When she finished eating she flicked her tongue around her muzzle, looked to each of them and moved off to lie down near the broken rocks. She was civil and well-mannered, sociable in her way.

They lay again in the water, at the edge, and she watched them, getting up to look and then settling, a curl in the warm sand.

The woman herself felt quiet, the ache in her chest easing with the easing in the dog's belly. One good meal wouldn't do it but it would help. The thin body could give more to the pups if something had nourished it.

Where were they? she wondered again. How far? and she lay back in the sun.

She lay back in the sun and the weight of the food in her belly felt good. For now, at least, she wouldn't need to think about food. In the heat, everything was still. It was good here but she could feel her teats pricking. It was time. Rising quietly she walked to the water, stood for a moment and looked. Then she turned, and climbing up onto the rocks began to make her way carefully. She lifted each small, long-toed foot and set it down on the intermittent smooth parts of the rock. Up and down, circling around the sharpest sections, looking left and right to be sure nothing followed her, she headed off to the spot where they waited. Those small fawn creatures, none even the size of a cupped hand, all of them waiting. She looked left and right and once, back over her shoulder where they still lay out in the water.

'I'm so glad we could feed her,' she said. 'This could make the difference,' and she lifted on her elbows to look round at the dog.

'She's not there. She's gone,' and scanning the rocks she picked her out, making her way over the scarred surface to the open sand beyond. 'There she goes. She's trotting up into the scrub. That's where they are, hidden up in the bush.'

She was tired, panting now and one foot throbbed – cut when she'd slipped into a sharp pocket in the rock. The pups were waiting. She'd go on. It wasn't something she'd decide. They were just there and that's where she'd go.

They packed up knowing they wouldn't be back, working slowly, deliberately, taking care to leave the place unmarked. Now she thought maybe she understood. She hadn't been able to think why the iguana had been there on the rock that one time and not again and it had troubled her. He was totemic. She read his presence that way; he was an iguana but couldn't he be more? She knew he'd had something for them. Then he'd been replaced by the little dog. They'd been offered a simple choice. Iguana – big, wild, not for holding – and fawn dog, at first mistaken for a gazelle, then taken for the dear dog that she was.

They'd come to this spot, come back to this spot. They could stop there briefly, lie out like lizards, rustle and brush and thrash and leave, their bodies printing their haste in the sand, or they could do what they'd done – make a shelter, stay, be slow and return. The iguana and the small dog. They'd chosen the one that fitted them best. They weren't quick and hard. If there were scales and layered, hard skins, if they'd brushed and glanced off each other early on, they weren't like that now. They'd learned other ways.

They could please the iguana but only inside the frame of the shelter they'd built for each other. The man would prowl the beach, protecting her and bringing her the treasures he'd find. She'd wait and tell him stories about the things he'd bring. The iguana would slide close and listen.

4. Windward

That night, late, sitting alone on the balcony looking out over the wild sea, the tails of the hurricane still wrapping around the island, she tried to recall if there had been a way to anticipate any of this. The morning began as it had each day of their holiday. The sun had risen over the water. Far below them breakfast things were being arranged in the large, thatched, open dining room and they could hear the clink of dishes and indistinct voices, people calling up and back to each other in short phrases. They'd rolled toward each other on the white surface of the bed, made love in the languorous way the island's climate encouraged and then, as they liked so much to do, read, legs tangled together.

Afterwards they'd settled themselves on the hotel's small sand beach, she under a thatched cabana, he just beside her in the sun. They read for an hour or two, then dressed and walked into town. It was the last day of their holiday, the end of February and the beginning of the local Mardi Gras celebration and enormous papier-mâché heads had been pulled down over the large plaster finials that lined the sea wall.

They'd moved down the boulevard photographing each other beside the heads, clowning for the camera and for the day, anxious to enter the event. It was very hot now, midday, and a silly time to be out in the sun but the streets were crowded, people moving about, everyone welcoming Carnival.

They'd looked out over the flat blue sea, noting the darkened horizon line, lifting their eyes up from the seam of sea and sky, and they'd scanned the hard blue cup that was the sky over their heads.

A small wind had come up, lifting her hair from her neck, moving the sleeves of her linen blouse against her arms. The perfect domed sky seemed flatter now, its even, Persian blue interrupted by horizontal bands of white. They were flecks really, just smudges and they stirred with the white clouds before hurrying on. We haven't seen a sky like this before, she'd thought and turned to ask him if he remembered anything like it.

'No,' he'd said. 'Not like this. This is faster. Everything's picking up for Carnival,' and he'd pulled her toward him, twirling her around and around, insinuating his leg between hers. 'Do you tango, miss?'

She'd spun, loving him in the heat, closing her eyes against the dizziness, comfortable on the crowded walkway, smelling the sea, the oily exhaust from the boats skipping around the bay, the quickening wind pulling a little at her hair, her hem, the unbuttoned neck of her blouse.

It's so hot and I'm so dizzy I hear music, she thought. 'I hear music. I do hear music,' she'd said. 'Stop twirling me. Where's it coming from?'

A grassy boulevard with its shrubs and stubby trees divided the broad road that followed the sea into town. On the other side of it an old flatbed truck was moving down the street and they stood beside the white seawall while she strained to see the truck. He'd lifted her onto the wall and she'd braced herself against his back. An amplifier mounted on the hood poured out mariachi music.

Brassy and golden. Sound has a taste and this tastes good, she'd thought, honey and corn syrup sweet on my tongue, a tongue to my ear. Following the sound was a trailer hooked to a dented half-ton and on it was the real spectacle. As dense as a street crowd, the floor of the trailer was packed with dancing women. Raised up they were eight feet tall. They wore satin and ruffles and flounces. They showed shoulders and legs. They were gilded and feathered and silver-finned, landed mermaids hardly more mobile in their narrow sequined dresses. Draped and painted, exotic and improbable, they existed nowhere else but on that rolling platform under a swirling sky, in the heat, with the crowds, beside the sea. One man, his hair pomaded into a foothill on his forehead and soldered into his silver lamé chaps and red satin western-style shirt, mimed a rock tune on a pink guitar.

The truck drove slowly past them and the crowd closed the space behind it, moving to the music that fanned in its wake. The sound became small and what remained was scattered by the wind gusting in from the sea.

'Was that all of it, do you think?' she'd asked, 'or will there be more?' They looked down the tunnel of space the truck had cleared and out of which it had, just moments before, appeared. A few people moved slowly at the edges of the emptied street.

'See. There is more,' and as she said it they could hear the music and it moved nearer. The same flatbed truck had turned when it reached the centre square and was moving back down the road toward them.

Again the crowds danced with it, still the same energy, the colours gorgeous in the sun, the women, the feathers, the glitter and the country rocker's sculptured hair. She'd leaned against the white wall, the sun hot on her head. The wall pressed its heat along the length of her and the wind pushed and picked at her hair, her loosened clothing.

They watched the single truck and its music and dancers and the crowd that followed pass them again and again. Finally she said, 'Now it's been a parade. That was long enough to have been a parade. Let's go back.'

The water was dark blue and for the first time there were small waves flecking its surface like uniform white parentheses, little brackets of foam on the face of the sea.

'That's a pretty happy sight, don't you think?' he'd asked, 'Except the colour of the water's a bit off. Too serious for the Caribbean. The ads promised turquoise waters and this is a rather stern military blue.'

They were hungry and anxious to get out of the sun. Still, they'd kept stopping, turning to look out at the water and up over the sea at the sky which was filled with heavy clouds, rolling and churning – the sky now more cauldron than cup.

'Let's have beer and then a hot dog with onions and tomatoes and mustard and chips and more beer,' she said, 'and let's hurry. I'm hot and really hungry.' But they'd looked at the sea and moved toward their hotel at the same pace.

When they arrived he arranged two chaises under a cabana and together they collected their beer from the bar and then their food from the beach vendor. They kept their eyes on the action in the bay. Occasionally a wave would hit the shoring on the decks and flare up, scattering small globes of water that held solid for a moment in the sun and then broke on the planks or fell further forward onto the sand where lunchers lounged and ate.

They finished their hotdogs, decided to share a second one and he signalled with his fingers for the man at the bar to bring two more beer. The action, this play of weather, had seemed confined to the space in front of them, unreal, distant, like at a movie. But now, when the wind gusted it carried a brief chill.

'You have my second beer,' she offered. 'I'm fine.' It occurred to her, sitting cozy on a chaise in the shade hoping to see the spectacle of a tropical storm if she couldn't see all of Mardi Gras, that a storm isn't something you watch. This wouldn't be sharks and eels on the other side of a glass wall at the seaquarium. If she were going to see a storm on this island it would likely be from inside it.

'You know,' she said in a conversational tone, 'this isn't a very deep island. I mean, it's long and narrow. There really is no inland here, is there?'

'That's right,' he said. 'It's just two coasts with some scrubby swamp in the middle.'

'So,' she went on, 'if it really blew up, if the water started to rise there would be no place to head for.'

'Right,' he said. 'No one will say let's head for the hills. There aren't any hills to head for.'

Now the clouds were more grey than white and as they looked around them they noticed that almost everyone else had moved inside. A few big drops splashed on the sand, sizzled on the surface for a moment and were absorbed, leaving intermittent, greasy dots.

She pulled her towel around her knees and hooked her arms over them, prepared, in the face of no alternative, to be a sport. The waiters and hotel people moved calmly about and she figured if they were okay it must be okay. More rain fell, no longer big slow drops – now narrow hurried ones – closer together and cold.

'Let's sit for a bit in the dining area. I'll buy you a drink,' he said and they packed their beach stuff and ran the fifty yards to the spot where they always ate breakfast.

'We'll watch from in here. I'll have a Scotch,' he said to the waiter. 'Just ice, please.' She ordered one too, feeling she needed some interior warmth.

He walked to the sea edge of the patio and stood with his back to her, looking out. Waves rose against the deck and lifted in points. Some of them broke on the planks. Most rolled back out to sea and careened off the next incoming swell and both accelerating ridges of bottle-green water rushed against the deck.

Two become four become eight and we're under she thought, as she watched from her seat in the middle of the room.

'Scotch is here,' she said more to herself than to him, barely hearing her words in the howl of the wind but he turned and came back to the table. Still standing he drank it down. His face glistened. The fronts of his T-shirt and shorts were soaked. Drops of water, caught in the hair on his arms and legs, glittered.

'Let's go,' he said. The patio was slick with rain and they skittered across it as they ran for the hotel. They took the stairs up to their room, surprised to find water covering their sandals. The marble stairs and open corridor were treacherous. They slid along, afraid to lift their feet. She felt as if she were under water. It's happened, she thought. The whole island is submerged. This is drowning.

They found their room and he turned the key and pushed. The door didn't move.

'It's an airlock. Stand back,' he said, sounding like someone else. He lowered his shoulder to the door and pushed with all his strength. It gave way, they fell inside and the door slammed behind them with the suddenness of a guillotine.

If they stood two feet back from the balcony's railing they could see out and stay reasonably dry. Below them the hotel people were running, pulling patio tables back under the roof, sections of which lifted, pulled loose and flew off, small thin fingers of straw spiralling in the chaos. Waves broke under the deck and some of the planks lifted and fell back with each rush of water. No one sat outside. Over the wind they thought they heard someone banging on their door.

'Close the balcony doors so I can get the hall door open,' he told her.

They recognized one of the waiters from breakfast. He was soaked. She could see the outline of a sleeveless undershirt through his wet cotton jacket and his chest rose and fell with his quick breathing. With the authority of a combat officer he instructed them to bring their patio furniture inside the room, stay off the balcony and keep the doors closed. Then he was gone, banging on the door of the next room.

'I would have suggested we toast this adventure with a Scotch and soda but we can't get down to the bar,' and he flopped onto the bed and picked up a book.

Chilled through, she stepped out of her still damp clothes, folded back the spread on her side of the bed, made a narrow place for herself between the sheets and with the wind shaking the glass patio doors on one side and whistling under the door on the other, she slept. In the same way that some people sleep so well on trains, the endless clacking assuring them of the continuation of things, she slept on, drugged by the points of rain driven against the glass. When the wind slowed and the rain stopped hours later, she woke up.

'Well,' he said, leaning over, 'I'm so glad you weren't frightened. You slept like a baby and the worst of it's over. Let's shower and dress and get out of here.'

'Are you quite crazy?' she asked, now entirely awake. 'First of all, I slept probably out of terror, and second it's still blowing out there and raining. No doubt roads have been washed away, buildings down, hydro out. We're lucky to be alive.' Then realizing she might be overdoing it she added, 'Maybe we should just eat in tonight. What do you think?'

'No. Our last night.' he said. 'We'll go out to that place we loved where we had the chicken and chilies. Remember, really hot food?'

The word hot was persuasive. They dressed and took a cab into town. Water had pooled in low places on the roads and some palm fronds lay across the boulevard but there appeared to be no real damage anywhere. The sea was close and high behind the seawall. Waves clapped against it and scattered over the sidewalk. Some of the papier-mâché heads were tilted. They looked quizzical, waiting for answers to questions that couldn't be heard over the wind. Awnings in front of shops and restaurants flapped and she noticed as they drove past that some were ripped and swinging free of their iron frames. There were cars on the road and other taxis but no one was walking.

'Isn't this fantastic?' he said. 'Look at that sea and how about the wind. It's pushing the car sideways even in town.'

The taxi pulled up to their restaurant. He almost flew out, clearing a large puddle, telling her to wait where she was. Then he whisked around the car to her side, scooped her up, carried her over the wet sidewalk, pushed the door open with his foot and set her down just inside. Like most of the restaurants they liked on the island this one was half indoors, half outdoors and the room felt cold.

'It's fresh,' he acknowledged when they were settled, 'but I'll take care of that,' and he disappeared. They'd eaten here several times before and agreed it was the best – best food, best music. In minutes he was back with two giant, pale green margaritas.

'Cold in the hand, warm in the belly. Madame, your health,' and he lifted his glass.

The two young waiters who had served them before and laughed when they'd found them snuggling each time they'd brought food to the table, appeared now with tortilla chips, guacamole and a big dish of salsa. He was right. The drink was good, she was warmer and sure they'd spiked the salsa with extra chilies. She felt great, perfect. And the wind that hammered the wooden shutters behind her was an old friend. There were people in the restaurant but not as many as other nights and the owner came over to greet them.

'My friends,' he said, 'tonight is special – the evening of the day of the hurricane. Let me feed you. I'll arrange everything,' and he took the menus they'd just picked up.

There was soup, then plates of fish. Meat with vegetables, stacks of yellow tortillas and more margaritas followed. The young waiters, the owner, the chef, all in turn, sat with them. The music started. Four men with drums, flutes and a guitar. Sweet singing like birds – notes that sounded green and hot. They toasted the musicians who joined them from time to time and glasses were raised.

I know about tequila, she thought. Two's my limit and she held the third drink and only sipped a little from it. But he continued to drink and he smiled and his face shone with heat from the food and with pleasure and excitement.

'Your health,' he said to each person in turn as they joined the table. Now the owner brought the narrow, heavy-bottomed shot glasses and a bottle of tequila and the trick was to down it neat while everyone chanted and clapped.

'You're wild tonight,' she said. 'I love you. Everyone loves you tonight.'

There was something about him. All night he'd been getting up from the table and moving around – talking to people, sometimes just stopping at a table and smiling, folding his big hand for a moment over the shoulder of one or the other guests or disappearing into the kitchen to say how good the food was. He'd had a lot to drink but that wasn't it. He wasn't drunk, just excited like horses get when it's windy and warm and they run toward something and find it isn't there and wheel and run the other way, spinning on their quarters, ears pricked, nostrils lifted, picking at a scent to find the way.

'Okay?' he said. 'Enough? We'll go.'

For their last night she'd put on the long, peacock-blue silk skirt and a small sleeveless silk top in deep violet. Against the wind and the cold she had a printed wool shawl shot with silver. Wasn't she his lady of the draped silks and white plumes after all, and wasn't he her courtier, stronger than anything?

A storm was of no moment then and she'd dressed for him.

'We'll walk,' he said when they were outside and it did seem calmer, until they turned onto the road that ran beside the sea. He meant to cross the boulevard and walk beside the sea wall.

'No,' she said. 'The water is still coming over the top. We could be drawn back into it. I can even feel the spray on this side of the road.'

She was right about that. The wind was lifting the spray and carrying it across the road. If they walked next to the wall they'd be wet but probably not in any real danger. Still, she said no. 'This is close enough.'

He was walking very fast, taking long strides. Her skirt blew tight around her, tangling in her legs so she couldn't stride out to keep up with him and her shawl worked like a sail pushing her along for a bit then emptying of wind and flapping at her sides. She wore soft leather slippers and they were wet through. There was no one else on the street.

'This is just grand,' he said when she'd caught up with him. He pulled her in close and with his arm around her waist hurried her down the sidewalk, her feet touching the stones only every third step.

Locked like that, compressed by the wind into a single unit, they blew up to the hotel. With the flourish of a matinee buccaneer he rounded her through the hotel lobby, up the marble stairs and into their room.

'I'm off,' she heard him say and the door closed behind him.

It was two hours. He was gone for two hours. She knew because she'd looked around the room wanting to see him there and she'd noted the clock beside the bed. During those two hours she'd gone down to the lobby three times. She'd checked the bar, the patio, the stairwell.

He's dead, she told herself. They'll find him tomorrow or in two days or never. He went to the seawall. The water reached up and sucked him over the top. It's Mardi Gras. The rest of one of those giant green heads grabbed him and choked him and threw him into the sea. The nice men in the restaurant poured something into one of his drinks. They've drugged him and rolled him, stolen everything and pushed his body into the swamp. The birds have picked his bones clean. There's no way to identify the remains. There'll be nothing to drape and take home in the cargohold of the plane.

There was a quiet knock at the door. She knew it was the police. They'd found his body and enough remained to be identified. They'd come for her to confirm it. She opened the door.

He stood there wearing his white undershorts and holding his clothes. 'I lost my key,' he said. Big as he was, he looked like a small boy and she reached for his hand and with some firmness drew him inside, directing him to sit down on the bed.

He explained that in the same way she thought he seemed bigger on the island, he felt bigger, and tonight – biggest. Like the water rising under the wind, he'd risen under it too, had lifted to it and felt he'd wanted to respond somehow. He'd been stirred, excited and here on this island, as unlike home as any place he'd been, he'd felt a kinship with the wind and wild water, somehow a part of it all.

'You know, like I'd had something to do with it. You'll laugh, but this afternoon when we spotted those first few wisps of grey in with the white clouds, when I grabbed you and spun you, I was wishing for a storm that would turn and turn around the island and we would be the centre, we'd be the pivot, the wheel. And then when it seemed to happen I was spooked but really excited, too. I felt huge like you're saying I am here, so at the restaurant all those people *were* friends and I drank with them all. But when we got back to the room it wasn't finished.'

He told her he'd walked again down the seaside road into town but this time he'd walked first beside the wall and then on top of it and the waves had almost knocked him over but hadn't. Then, when he'd come to the small park beside the harbour he'd gone in and stretched full out on his back on one of the stone benches and looked up at the sky and watched the moon speed behind the dirt-coloured clouds and then finally there were no clouds and the moon stopped rolling and the stars came out and stood still in the sky, nailing it in place. He'd felt quieter then. He'd wanted to swim, he told her, but the sea had turned squid-ink black and he knew if he swallowed any of it, it would be salty and dark as olives, so he'd come back to the hotel. He'd walked through the yellow light in the lobby and no one was there. There was no one on the patio and no one in the pool so he'd taken off all his wet clothes and he'd floated in the warm pool face down and then on his back, not wanting to interrupt the pool's surface which looked, he said, like corduroy, in the wind. He thought he'd been in the pool for maybe half an hour and then he missed her and he'd come up to the room.

She was still wearing the long peacock-blue silk skirt and violet top but she'd dropped the shawl when she'd come back to the room. Her feet and arms were bare. She raised her thin white arms over her head and slowly wrapped the fingers of one hand around the wrist of the other.

'So,' she said and he watched, sitting naked near the pillows on the big bed. Slowly she began to circle, pivoting on one leg. The blue skirt lifted. She moved faster and the long skirt pushed out around her legs. She spun, fixing her eyes first on one side of the room and then the other and when she stopped she was steady.

'*My* gyre. *My* centre,' she said and she walked over to him, pushed him gently back against the pillows, pulled the covers around him and picking up her shawl went onto the balcony to look out at the still wild sea.

Rose Toast

I'd say she was a more or less regular person. I mean, there was nothing weird about her except she liked things to be special. Small things. For instance, she never went out without perfume, every day, and good perfume, too – on her wrists and elbows and the backs of her knees.

'Knees. Why your knees?' I asked her and honest-to-God she said, 'So there'd be a trail of scent when I walk by.'

And no fake fabrics, please. She wore only linen, or silk, or cotton, or very soft wool but no angora because it made her nose run. And no packaged food either, only fresh.

She once told me she ate flowers on her Hovis toast. 'What does that mean?' I asked her. 'Just exactly what are flowers on toast?' I remembered peas on toast from Home Ec class and was that awful, if you can imagine, so please – flowers on toast!

And like her feet never touch ground when she walks she says, 'Yes, well, you pick the petals from wild roses and you rinse them with care so as not to bruise them and you cook them with sugar in a small copper pot and when it's thick you spoon it gently into fat glass jars and once it's set you can only serve it with a silver spoon or the colour is ruined and you spread it on cold butter on thick Hovis toast and it's pink like pearls but soft on your tongue and then it's not only butterflies who eat flowers.'

She'd say things like that and I'd have to stop and look at her because wild roses grow in ditches everywhere and anyone can pick them and sugar's plain stuff but no one else I knew put them together with toast.

One day I remember, I called on her and she was wearing a blouse, light blue, cotton of course, but the colour was really nice and I said to her by way of conversation and, I have to admit, because I liked her answers, 'So what kind of blue is your blouse? It's barely a colour at all,' and I thought, God, I'm starting to sound like her, and she said, 'It is nice, isn't it? It's a straight-through, rain-washed-sky blue and old as clouds.'

So she'd say things like that from time to time but not everything sounded that way. Anyway, she got married and I heard it didn't work out and we lost touch and years later I bumped into her buying doughnuts and coffee, which wasn't exactly roses on toast or whatever and she looked fine and I said how are you and she did look fine and she said my life is totally different and I'm happy. I'm writing now. Let's talk one day but I've got to run. You know how this stuff is only perfect when it's really fresh and off she went.

She's right, you know. From the time they put the dough-nuts into a bag you've got about twenty minutes to eat them before the taste changes. It occurred to me how much I'd liked those ideas of hers. She used to think about things and have these little theories about them. She'd tell you what they were when the subject came up and you'd think – oh for Pete's sake – and then right after you'd realize she was right.

Anyway I thought I'd like to see her again but I didn't know what her name was now – if she'd changed it when she married, or where she lived, but a couple of times when I was in the neighborhood I went in for doughnuts and this one day she was there again and we sat down with coffee and that's when she told me this story.

Understand – it's a simple story but I was so glad to hear it because it took me back and made me feel like we were girls again walking on the street in the light, wearing cardigan sweaters and that was a time when things were still right enough and something small like the way your rubber soles felt on the sidewalk could make you happy. I mean, not the story itself, but that she was telling me something that I could settle with and think about later.

Anyway, it turns out that she's working now and living alone but she's with someone good she tells me and when she has time she writes. I remember she'd said that in the dough-nut shop the first time I saw her after all that time but it didn't mean anything to me. So when she says she's writing I think back to being kids and I think of pen pals and chain letters so I miss that this is something important. And she says to me, like it's got sparkles on it or something – 'I'm writing now.' But she's not, you see. She's drinking coffee with me at a For-mica table and I smile because I'm waiting for roses on toast. You know, one of her little stories. We were never very touchy but she reaches out and with her knuckles she pushes for just a second at my hand on the table and she says, 'I write stories and people pay me and they print them.' And she might just as well have been wearing her sky-washed, rained-on blouse because she looked like that same kid.

'How did you come to do that?' I wanted to know and she tells me about the guy she's with who thinks her life has been fascinating and courageous, she says, and that whenever she'd talk to him he'd say 'That's remarkable' or 'Astonishing, you should write it down' and she said that for a long time she couldn't figure out what he meant because so far as she was concerned it all seemed pretty unremarkable to her, pretty much everyday stuff. But one day after work she'd made her supper and cleaned up and taken the dog for a long walk and still felt that she needed to do more and she'd sat down and written a story and when he came over a couple of days later and asked her like he always did, so interested, what she'd done, she told him about the story and he said, so read it to me, and she thought she'd just as soon not but she did anyway and he told her it was good and hearing it with him in the room she liked it too.

Anyway, they took a trip together and he introduced her to friends of his who were writers and she said she'd been terrified because she'd read their books and who was she but it worked out so well and he'd said to her, these people are your friends now and boy was he right, she said, because that was where she met this guy.

He was a famous American writer who lived in Canada and he was, for her, like the idea of leaving a trail of scent was for me. What do I mean by that? I mean not the usual stuff.

She met him but she didn't say much to him. Mostly they talked to his wife or she listened but she observed him, she said. He was long and thin and he was wearing white pants and a white dress shirt. His hair was white and longish around his ears and straight. He had a narrow face and a narrow nose and she said – get this – that every time he spoke she saw those ceiling fans that circle slowly. Now usually I didn't interrupt her stories but like it was when she said she was writing, I figured I'd missed something. So I had to ask her what did she mean and she said he had a slow way of talking – 'mouthful of magnolias' she said and I thought – eating flowers again and then I realized she meant he had a southern kind of drawl. Also, he was wearing black socks and he had very long, thin feet.

Anyway that was essentially it, she said. That was all there was to the meeting and there was nothing more except he'd been very kind and polite and interested in an off-hand kind of way.

When they got home her guy said to send some of her stories and he kept asking her if she'd done it and finally she did and it turned out that man liked them but that was all.

When she had time and felt like she needed to do more than she usually did with work and all she'd write a story and her guy would hear it from her and he'd tell her to send it and she did. Here she got this look on her face like we weren't eating doughnuts and she said she would come home from work and start up the walk and she could see right from the gate if there was anything in her mailbox and she loved the time it took to walk to the stone steps and up the steps and over to the mailbox. There was always sun there even in the winter. Practically everyone she knew lived in the same city with her so letters weren't what she expected but she said she knew from the bottom step this one day that she had a letter in her box. One of those blue tissue airmail envelopes and on the back it said Hotel Sacher, Vienna. On the front was her name and address and a forty-cent Canadian stamp.

She said it even sounded foreign the way it crinkled and was so thin and she couldn't think who would be sending her something from Vienna and she had to check the address again and it *was* for her and she opened it. Now here, if it was me telling the story I would have had a duke who was her long-lost relative finding her and asking her to move into his castle and inherit all his lands but no. She said it wasn't that but just as good. The letter said something like 'Your stories are fine. Keep writing. All best.' And she told me she could hear his voice and see the circling fan and she remembered his long feet. She said when she got that letter, for the time, there was nothing more she could want. Figure that.

'So what then,' I asked her. 'Did he call or write again?'

'Oh yes,' she told me. There were more. About four months later another letter is in her box when she comes up the steps and this one is a heavy envelope – creamy like an official document where the paper had to support a wax seal, she tells me. 'You know the kind,' she says, like we both do, 'where the red wax is thick enough to take an impression from a signet ring with your coat of arms in reverse and you press the stone into the wax and the soft wax oozes up around the seal and then the message can't be forged,' and what can I say but yeah. So she says this envelope was good paper and on the back in raised gold letters it said Grünwald, Venice, and again on the front was her address and a forty-cent Canadian stamp.

'What did he say this time? Was it personal?'

'Yes, it was,' she tells me. "I should have written before this but I've been working. You too, I trust. All best." And she says she hears his voice and thinks of the long feet and sees them placed carefully side by side in brocade slippers resting on a pillow settled deep in the bottom of a gondola and she's so pleased that with all that travel he's taken time to write.

'Yeah, but what was so personal about that?' I asked her and she told me she hadn't realized right at first but what he was doing was making her a very special gift of those places and by just having her think about a faraway city it came alive in her mind. And here she gives me another picture. She says – 'Remember pinball machines where each time the metal ball hits a post the light goes on and stays on?' and I did remember. 'Well, now Vienna and Venice are lit like that for me – cities of light and the real city of light, too, because there was an envelope from the Bristol in Paris and later from Berlin and Jamaica.'

'What did they all say?' I had to know and she shrugs, well, not so much shrugs as lifts her shoulders and settles into them like she's wearing fur and she says, 'Wonderful live things, so special, like the one from Jamaica – "The sun is a fish and flashes on the water. I take ginger with my tea. All best."

And she says, 'Each time he writes a letter I write a story and sometime later I send it to him but now I'm finding the travelling a little tiring and anyway with all the unrest he's staying home more.'

[76]

Then she leans toward me and she lowers her voice, like all the people in the doughnut shop care or can even hear and she says, 'Here's the really remarkable part. It took me maybe two years to figure out that all those letters had been written and mailed in Canada, right here in this country. He had this cache of hotel stationery in this polished walnut cask lined in bottle green velvet and fitted all out in brass with small cut crystal bottles for inks and he pulled all of those places out of the box and gave them to me in envelopes, a different one each time and each message was a line from a song and each one rang with its own music.'

And she says to me, 'Now if that isn't the most wonderfully fabulous gift to give to someone you think one up and tell me.'

Like always, later, I figured she was right.

Choker

The dog was a Great Dane. Fawn with black markings – black ears and muzzle, a rectangular white patch on his chest the size of a flip-top cigarette pack. All fawn, one skin, right to the end of the long, coarse-haired tail that finished in a twist of black wires, a calligrapher's brush I once dipped in water colours and drew with on newsprint.

We ordered him. Searched for him. Wrote to breeders all over Canada and the States, had in mind a certain dog, both of us wanting him to be big in our lives. I had settled on the breed years earlier, succumbing to an ad. Me, always holding back from what everyone else ever wanted, whatever was being sold to everyone else, me falling prey to an ad. In the ad a girl with dark hair like mine, but long and straight, an American girl not a Canadian, but a girl with dark hair like mine and red lipstick, the same colour. A girl my age sitting behind the wheel of a red sports car, top down. Beside her, taller and better looking than any guy, was a big dog. Without ever having seen one I knew it was a Great Dane and I knew I'd have one. He sat there tall in the seat, flat tan hair lying neat, eyes big, chops long and dark, firm pricked ears, easy brow, broad chest. A real guy. Quiet. But game.

It was a billboard ad for 7-Up. I didn't drink it then. Still don't. But I bought the dog.

The man I bought him with was my husband. Not just right then but not so many years later, either. When we were married we agreed on the dog, both of us searching him out, both needing him to finish things off, like a fourth for bridge.

Actually, Clyde was a little like the dog. Also six feet tall standing up. Same colour hair but Clyde's eyes were a flat, light blue. Dog's were the same as mine – brown with green and orange.

When we got him he was a pup. Came by air freight in a wire cage, his ears newly cropped and held up by plasters joined across the top of his head with a string. He had big feet, the toes humped like arthritic knuckles. The skin was loose on his frame, folds of it settling like upholstery fabric each time he sat. He was awkward and unsure and Clyde and his family laughed, making him out ridiculous and dumb. But his eyes were bright and the dog and I looked directly at each other from the start. The bones were there. The frame would carry a big male dog and the skin would pull tight across his back when he became the size he was meant to be.

Clyde's frame showed promise too. He took a big suit coat. His shoulders were level. He had big wrists, big hands, a well-shaped head, flat ears. But his chest was almost hairless and his body was soft, smooth and unmuscled. It never took a definitive form. Even now, years later, I guess he could still develop it if he wanted to. But the dog is dead and Clyde, I expect, wants everything soft and easy.

Clyde took the dog to obedience classes in the basement of a church. I'd come along sometimes. The programme started in the winter. Naturally, we didn't enter via the sanctuary. We used a side door that led off the ground level behind the kitchen. For just a moment there'd be the smell of candle wax and floor cleaner. Then we'd be in the lower level and there would be other smells. Hot water heat, old boards, men's black foot-rubbers, chalk dust, and dog urine.

Clyde was serious about the course. The dog would learn, would respond to single-syllable commands. Sit. Stay. Come. Walk. Man to man they'd trust each other, know their limits. The familiarity and mutual respect would make them friends, equals, buddies. Between church basement sessions they practised in the school playground near our house, marching the perimeter of the field. After supper they'd head out. I'd finish the dishes, pull on my sheepskin coat and walk over. From across the street I'd see them in profile, two dark silhouettes trotting, stopping. They'd pause, then push off, jogging along the edges of the lot. One night in early spring they'd finished a particularly satisfying session. Dog was off the leash moving easily on his own over the flat, brown ground, snuffling intermittently at the occasional tussock of grass. He was coming along well, filling out, gaining height and weight. The plasters had come off his ears and they held erect on their own, two perfect silk-velvet, isosceles triangles gesturing the sky. Clyde and I stood watching.

'You know,' Clyde began, 'you know why girls don't have hair on their chests?' I thought for a moment, looking out over the field in the fading light. A little wind hiccuped some papers across the ground in front of my feet and pushed them up against the chain-link fence. 'Why don't they?' I asked, sensing a riddle, maybe a joke.

'Well,' he said thoughtfully, having spent every evening for two months in the school ground coaching the dog, 'do playgrounds have grass?' He pushed me with his shoulder, pleased with himself, with the night's work, with our stable camaraderie and he whistled for the dog to join us.

Do playgrounds have grass? Will I live my whole life out lying next to a man who asked that question, who could see a flat, scabbed playing field and think of a woman? I thought of the fine-textured white skin on my chest, of the network of blue veins that show through the thin skin, of the small, winged collar bones that stretch the skin and draw it fine, up from my belly, over my breasts, up my long, thin neck. Do I lie next to this man for all time?

The dog was doing fine. We fenced in the back yard. Clyde built a good solid, high fence. I painted it white. Dog cleared it at will. Approaching it like a hunter jumper with no rider on his back, seeming to stop just in front, then tucking his forelegs up under him he'd push off from behind, clearing it by inches but jumping clean, a clean round each time. We'd run through the gate calling after him, trotting a little down the lane, far behind him, then shrugging, return to the yard, close the gate and wait in the house for his return. He came back each time to the front door, never jumped back in, the jumper course working in one direction only. I was never easy until he came back. A key player was missing and we were a nice threesome.

Dog was an athlete, a real sport. In the summer at the lake we'd set up a badminton net. He'd pick a side and jump for the bird. It was hard to manoeuvre if he was on your side. His big tan body spread itself across the net. His eye was quick. He stood, quarters lowered, compressing his muscles, ready to spring. In his enthusiasm for the catch, in his total concentration, he'd be unmindful of anyone around him and more than once he knocked me to the ground. Springing to the bird he'd catch it in his jaws and then wait. He'd stand with his mouth full, the feathers or the white kid knob protruding from under one of his lips. His head was square and the jaw deep and he was very careful so the bird would be only damp or some of the feathers bent. As soon as you touched the protruding part he'd release it and move back in place for the game to resume.

I touched his mouth a lot, pulled a lot of things from it in the course of the games and I came to recognize and even like the smell of his saliva. It wasn't nice – acidic and fishy and it held on, but its persistence made it valid and it was unique to him. He made no apologies.

In the water we played Frisbee. Clyde and I would stand waist deep, thirty yards apart. Dog would paddle up and back in the middle, treading, waiting for the toss. No one spoke. Blue all around us, tan dog in the centre, Clyde narrowing his blue eyes against the light, his loose torso resting on the lake's surface. Then he'd pull his arm back, elbow parallel to the water and flip the Frisbee just over the dog's head. Dog would push against the lake, now grown solid under his feet, and catch the saucer in his teeth. I'd half swim, half drag my legs through the water to get to him and he'd circle on the spot, tail flicking drops, pleased with himself.

Then we'd have our private game. The best part of it was time. Time stopped. The best part of it was his wet fur smell. The best part of it was pushing my nose against his bridge, his two eyes becoming one, becoming mine while I moved into his head. The best part of it was the way the fine wet hair on his face parted and clumped, young and fresh, and earnest like a chick. I'd put a hand on each side of the Frisbee, rest my mouth on the dog's bridge and rock the saucer gently side to side. His head would angle a little left, then right and he'd close his teeth harder on the plastic.

Clyde's voice would be small, petulant, far. 'C'mon, take it from him.' The dog and I would rock, private in the lake. Clyde would only play for so long and then he'd leave if there wasn't going to be more action so I'd slip one hand up between the Frisbee and the dog's palate and he'd let it go and I'd toss it to Clyde and we'd go again.

The game had a rhythm, like everything. And Clyde and the dog had a sense of theatre, an understanding of building to a climax, of pacing, of audience tolerance, because there always was an audience and they stood on shore and watched. As the game progressed the Frisbee was tossed higher. When the game ended it was a spectacle. At the end we had the dog clearing the lake by a good three feet, his four feet all clearing the lake at once. Seal-slick, water falling from his hair, arcing in mathematical perfection, he'd hold the space, domed sky over, flat water under, dog suspended. Then *thwock*, he'd close his mouth around the plastic and drop back into the lake. So pleased, he'd shark around in circles and this time we'd let him keep the Frisbee. The people on shore would move on. We'd wade in, go up to the yard and I'd make us a sandwich.

Clyde worked hard at his job, worked for his family. It was a successful business but they were starting him at the bottom. In the winter he'd get up in the dark, pull on thermal underwear, heavy wool socks, grey with white toes and red bands at the cuff, two pairs, boots with felt inner boots, plaid flannel shirt, a pullover and a green parka. I washed those socks. Dragged them over wire stocking stretchers while they turned to felt and thickened under my fingers. The socks came out of the washer warm. You had to get them still warm or they wouldn't pull over the stretchers and they smelled like feet. Warm and wet and fetid, close around my hand. This, I thought to myself with distaste at least three mornings a week, this is something every person should take care of himself. This is just too personal, too close. This involves love. Or hate.

Clyde needed the socks and all the layers because the work was in heavy construction and all of one winter he tramped over hills of gravel in stock yards and gravel pits, measuring, assessing. Still, his body resisted muscle, was smooth and undefined.

We started showing the dog. He won silver spoons. I had the bowls of the spoons engraved with his name and the date and I used them for serving jam and sugar. We drove across the border to compete internationally. He won more spoons.

[84]

Then I tired of the shows and we stopped going. I sewed a plaid coat for the dog. Red and black plaid blanket wool with straps and buckles that did up under his belly. He was good-natured about it, didn't mind that we laughed, had enough confidence not to be offended even when Clyde said he looked like Sherlock Holmes.

Once, just for fun, I put one of Clyde's cardigan sweaters on the dog and buttoned it up. We took a picture and even in the picture you can read the dog's response – half pleased because he looked so nice, half embarrassed because it fitted him so well.

As he got older his black chops turned grey. 'Now,' we joked, 'he looks like Cary Grant.' Nothing else about him changed. He still cared as much. He still tried as hard. His strength remained formidable and for me the velvety chops were a place to go where time stopped. When he lay out on his side in the sun on the rug or outside on the shaded grass I'd put my cheek against his chops and everything else disappeared. There were no sounds, no people, no other place I had to be.

For Clyde and me, the dog was an important male presence in our household, masculine like in the old Westerns – silent, strong, reliable, unwavering. But we never knew for sure what we were to him. When he was out, the house was empty. We waited for him to come back. We gave up worrying about fencing him in and trusted that his sense of decency would govern his conduct when he went out alone.

Occasionally Clyde and I would be driving in the car and we'd come upon him hurrying somewhere on his own, reminding me a little of the White Rabbit in *Alice*, with appointments to keep. After the red and black plaid blanket coat I never tried dressing him again. All he wore was a choke collar, the biggest size made and from it hung his identification and veterinary tags. They rested on his broad chest like medallions on a concert promoter's neck and sometimes it struck me that he might be something of an operator.

He lived a long time, longer than the books on dog breeds said he would. I needed him, didn't want him to go. Years before, when we'd searched him out, planned the purchase, raised him, trained him, showed him, Clyde needed him too. Finally though, Clyde didn't need Dog or me. The muscle required to define a shape continued to elude him and even need required more rigour than he had.

I left him, took the dog and moved out. One night in early spring, out on his nightly walk, snuffling in a neighbour's back garden, the dog's heart stopped. I worried when he didn't return and in the morning called all the radio stations and newspapers with missing dog notices, stalked up and down the streets and back lanes whistling our whistle, calling his name, pulled on rubber boots and slid along the river bank calling. Two days later a neighbour phoned. 'I think your dog is in my garden' she said. 'I'm studying for my nursing exams. Come and see if it's yours.'

'See if it's mine?' I screamed inside my head. 'No, this six-foot, nearly-two-hundred-pound tan dog with black pricked ears and a grey muzzle isn't mine. Close but not mine.'

He was mine. I brushed his chops with the back of my hand and sat in the wet grass beside him waiting for the men from the crematorium to pick him up. My vet arranged for it all. They really weren't very long and after they'd loaded Dog into their truck one of them walked back and stood beside me, still sitting in the wet grass where Dog had been. 'You'll want this,' he said and handed me the choke collar.

That night my father came over to pay his respects. He'd known the dog well, had, over the years, watched him from the shore, had even joined the game himself. He brought me a five-pound bag of frozen jumbo shrimp, something exotic and special and unrelated to my grief. Sometimes my father's gestures were absolutely right.

It's not the sort of thing you tell anyone, but later, sitting alone on my bed I slipped the dog's collar over my head and let it rest heavy on my chest, cold against my skin, a few tufts of hair still caught in its loops.

Animal Thoughts

There are times, my daughter tells me, when I frighten her, when I begin to transform and am, for the moment, more animal than human. I know when it happens. It's not involuntary like a seizure or a fit. I'm not over-taken by something outside me. My transformations are voluntary.

Most often I become a dog. Sometimes, a horse. Again, it's not random. I become my *own* dog, my *own* horse. It's simply a matter of close observation coupled with a willingness to extend myself. I've always had bright beautiful dogs, females, and there have been men who, from time to time, temporarily dazzled by love, have said, 'You're beautiful, like a race horse, quick and hot and sleek, I love you,' so the transformation is easy. Why not slip into something more comfortable?

Say the dog I've got is an Irish Wolfhound. Mine was particularly hairy and her coat remained puppy soft. Brushed, she looked like an enormous angora rabbit or like Doris Day in her later films, soft and hazy, filmed through a Vaseline-smeared lens. Most people responded to her as though her appearance were the whole dog but that isn't the way she was. She was serious, thoughtful, and she worried a lot. There were things she tried to understand and when comprehension eluded her she was troubled. She'd sit up, set her ears high on her head and pull her brows together. A furrow would crease her forehead and you would sense her concern.

Not understanding is a terrible thing. I worried for my animals and my children, troubled, when they were babies, by

[89]

their muteness, anxious for their inarticulate worries, always wanting to make them understand the world around them. Little person, little beings, small blind creatures. I'll see for you, my fingertips will read the world like braille, I'll be your shield – and I'd imagine the bones in my chest a breast plate – the hard, thin bones in my body, Alhambra grille-work between them and everything.

So it would be with me and my wolfhound. Telling my daughter about a small incident in the dog's day, both of us interested, speaking to each other all the time, sometimes about the dog – and she'd listen. To explain how it had been for the dog I'd stop, sit up straight and arrange myself to be like her. My daughter would say 'That's it, that's exactly her,' and then, 'That's creepy. How do you do that?'

The trip back to the Garden needn't be so long. It isn't always necessary to struggle with what happened after the Fall. I recommend giving it over, going back, joining hand to paw in a ring, letting your fingers slip into the soft, webbed, furred spaces between the toes on each foot, stroking the fur in the direction it grows, or sliding with the scales along the wet green length. So joining in or changing up and back always seemed perfectly natural to me and I was not surprised by the fact that I had a grown cousin my mother's age who smelled like a leopard.

Families are a given. We know that. The place you hold in your family can't be changed. We know that too. But you can like some people better than others, observe them more closely, store up their voices, recall a particular jacket, a silk blouse, replay certain events in which they starred, respond to a scent – eau de cologne, pipe tobacco, remember small gestures, habits, patterns. You gather up these bits, the leaves and layers of your observations. You make, as a child, a slightly damp, musty compost of these fragments and thereafter recognize, by these scented packets, each cousin, aunt, or great-uncle who was noteworthy. The material is received, apprehended, observed because that's what you do when you're little – you observe. No one consults you. You are, mostly, a passive chronicler.

This cousin of my mother interested me and I watched her. Her name was Flora. Her mother had intended a flower. She'd conjured pale skin like her own, someone who wouldn't care for hot sun, a girl with thin ankles and a reedy voice. It was expected that on occasion her body temperature would be just measurably below normal. There ought to be about her an elusive quality – something in the carriage of the shoulders – an immanent shiver, a girl without enthusiasms who was never heard to laugh in a full and vulgar way. No one was to see the inside of her mouth. No utterances needed to be that large.

But Flora was otherwise. She was very dark, with brown skin, and entirely unlike anyone in the family. Her hair was black, black with the opacity of coal-oil soot on a glass chimney. She had a round face with high, flat cheek bones and slightly extended eyes, black as her hair but shiny, a flat round chin which folded in on her neck and a sweet large mouth like a compressed valentine. Too many teeth were crowded there and they pushed her lips out, top and bottom, from the inside, but they were very white like a young dog's.

Her voice was round, high and loud. She talked without stopping, the breathing as much a part of her conversation as the other sounds. Slightly asthmatic, it was a wind instrument, the exotic flute people bring back as a souvenir from South America. There was a foreignness in her style too, in the way she dressed. She wore a white sharkskin fabric skirt and a white linen hat with the brim turned back and I felt she must have arrived by steamer. But where do kids get ideas; she lived no more than six or eight streets over from us in a prairie city.

It was summer and I remember her in our back yard. It could have been any one of six or eight summers when we lived in that house. A high, white fence around the garden, a lower one separating the vegetables from the grassy area, flowers and striped canvas sling chairs. Flora's skin would grow oily under the sun. Her flat forehead shone in the heat. My mother, red hair, pale skin with freckles, pulled back from the sun, back a little from her cousin whose voice filled the garden. Striped chairs aside, we always seemed to be standing when she visited. Something about the noise and her smell made you feel you needed to face her.

Fat around lamb chops smoking under the broiler, after dinner, the lamb fat congealed white on the broiler pan, at the edges of the dinner plates – that was the smell of Flora's hair in the heat, in the afternoon, in the garden, under the sun.

Like her brown skin, no one in my family had hair like hers either. It was understood that any feature that was so insistent was perhaps in bad taste. Too black, too coarse, too curly. The rest of us had fine hair. My mother's poker straight, always curled, her one real vanity. She wore it short but talked about it as if it were long, a part of her more daring than she felt she could ever be. She would turn her head to the side and look over her shoulder and the hair she imagined would drag heavy across her back, lustrous, generous. My hair was light brown, naturally curly, but soft and fine. She kept it short, envied the curl and would play with it, winding strands around her forefinger.

When Flora was born her father was wealthy. He was a furrier in a city at the civilized edge of the north where all the fur was thick and heavy and all the animals quick. He was tall. I remember black eyes, a thick moustache, a big chest, a weighty voice you couldn't avoid, and cigars. Their smell hung about him even when he wasn't smoking.

I was a great-niece, a grandchild he didn't yet have and he would visit me on Sunday mornings in the winter. He'd fill the doorway carrying the cold with him on his good grey alpaca coat. He wore a wedge-shaped beaver hat, thick and lustrous, the long outer hairs catching the light and both of these things he'd hand down to me, his small hostess. They were cold and heavy and heavy with the scent of his cigars. Everything he wore was scented with it, wrapped in that silky brown fragrance. Even today I associate that smell with authority and size. Often since then I've smelled a cigar, say in a hotel lobby, sought it out, turning to follow the scent, disappointed to find only a small soft man standing under the smoke.

Each layer of Uncle smelled the same – coat, suit-coat, vest and, in the summer, his shirts. Like those rolled papery leaves, those aromatic cylinders, he too was uniformly aromatic.

He never stayed long. I don't remember what we said. I was just a little girl but whatever it was we were both content. I'd hug him, sniff him, feel his rough moustache on my face. I loved him. He had authority by virtue of having read books written in other countries and he had something else too. He had a large bold picture of a tiger stitched in highly coloured silk embroidery floss framed and hung in the front hall of his house. I believed that silk piece to be a portrait of my great-uncle. I wouldn't have been surprised on visiting his house one day to find a blank white silk square hanging in the hall. Man into tiger – Uncle and his alternate would just be out on a call. He shouted politics, slammed doors, pinched my cheeks and gave me nickels and I adored the certainty of him.

Great-Auntie was thin, almost transparent. Rumoured to have been a great beauty, now she was without colour or sound. She spoke only to caution against disease and drank hot water from a Royal Chelsea tea cup. With the exception of the silk tiger there was no colour in the house. No plants or cut flowers, no paisley shawls draped over chair backs, no jewel-bright Persian rugs, no crystal prisms scattering rainbows, no pot-pourri to scent the rooms, no peacock opals at her throat. She wore brown, grey, beige, and had tiny feet which she flattered with thick-heeled black English leather oxfords. I had to wear them too but mine were flat and I was told it was necessary to support my arches and ankles which were thin. If I wore them now, then later I would have elegant feet and could wear high-heeled pumps and dance. But Auntie's 'later' had already passed and still she wore those shoes. I began to suspect mine.

Every afternoon she rested. All the blinds were lowered, the heavy drapes drawn together. The house became a brown-light place of rest and the rooms took on the colour of nicotine stains. She cooked without salt. All the meat was boiled. Dessert was tapioca. Having a meal there was like almost recovering from an illness. The only candy I remember being offered were powdery bits of Turkish delight, suspiciously gelatinous – what's it made from, Mommy? – which I loathe to this day.

Unlike all of that, Flora had colour – black hair, red and yellow sweaters, brown skin, a loud voice and that odour. As a child I sniffed Flora out for special attention because then and now it's smell I respond to first.

The infallibility of smell. Think. When a horse lowers its head and presses its nose to the spoor of another animal it can't even see what's there with its eyes set up on its head and off to either side. The day is green and fine. The mare moves easily across the ground, stepping out, ears pricked. Her owner is on her left leading her loosely in hand. They move on quietly, shoulder to shoulder. The mare pauses, lowers her neck and prods a mound of turds left by another horse –

smooth, shiny, egg-glazed wheat rolls stacked symmetrically in a pyramid. '*Croquembouche*,' the woman thinks. The horse thinks, 'Nipper or Jack.' They move on. The day warms and the horse's skin slides over her muscled frame. They stop and look around, both smelling clover. The mare crops the sweet grass. The woman moves against the horse, pushing her nose into its belly, pressing until both nostrils are full and she breathes in. She hears the mare's teeth grinding the clover. She feels the chewing with her face. She smells sweat and heat, she tastes salt and sweet grass. After a while she's full and they move on.

Or, mornings, first thing, or coming home from work at the end of the day, I am greeted by my dog, nose first. We're both pleased, 'Glad you're here,' and she sniffs my face. Equally interested, I sniff hers. When I was ten I had a budgie. Say budgie and I think first not of the acid-green breast feathers, the obsidian bead eyes, the black dots on either side of the face, the cracked yellow beak, or even of the cold grey-pink feet. I remember first the sweet bread-mould smell its feathers always carried.

As a kid I couldn't have used my nose to find my parents but finding Flora was easy. Shiny, hot and thick, redolent like tar, as spreading and uncontainable as the black petroleum amoebas you find on white beaches after an oil spill; persistent, messy, damaging. Nonetheless she risked that white pleated skirt, the white linen hat and I don't recall ever seeing a smudge there.

I learned something else about Flora. A favourite great-aunt of mine died a few years ago. A lovely, lovely maiden aunt. She'd taught school and over the years had been given cards and notes by her children. She'd kept them and being a keeper, she kept family photos too. A short time ago my mother gave me a small carton filled with them. Flora was there. Young Flora, maybe twenty. A sweet, girl figure, a knitted bathing suit, that valentine smile, trim shape, her legs pressed tight to each other. Ankle socks and small, high-heeled pumps. Beside her a blond-haired young man, thin but well shaped, in black trunks, squinting against the sun. Flora had a beau. Flora had a valentine.

When Flora was born – two boys and then finally a flower – Auntie had a nurse live in. The story we're all told about where babies come from had been true all along. Babies come from seeds. Seeds, if properly sown, produce flowers. Flora had her nurse and a high-wheeled English pram and a small white rabbit fur carriage throw to cover her.

In February, in this northern prairie city, we're given days which test our weakness. After reluctant, shallow sunrises and early, quick sunsets, after months of air so cold it fills the throat and nose like fine-milled flour, after months of dark where nothing asks you to lift your head, tip it back and offer your neck to light and heat, after that time we're given some days in February. Days when the air begins to slow, when it turns on itself and nickers its own flank. Days when you can smell water, when leaf stumps seem to thicken, when maybe everything won't always be cold and flour-white and chimney-soot-black. On these days we take risks and in the daring, sometimes lose. Influenza, whooping cough, scarlet fever, measles, pneumonia, death.

The nurse had been looking for an opportunity to put out the pram, to set Flora in it and cover her with the rabbit-fur blanket. The first day when the sun had dried the front walk she did it. She set the dark flower on the lace-edged pillow and tucked the white fur up to her chin. The slightly rounded black eyes were big with the sky – more blue, more colour than she'd ever seen. I expect she was very quiet. So good and so quiet that she was given two hours of that testing kind of February day. She was cold when they brought her in and soon after she was very warm. She developed a fever and came down with something. That part was only half told. It was before penicillin. Medicine wasn't modern yet. She didn't die but later, many months later when she was ready to walk, something seemed to be wrong with her legs. The story is, her bones were soft and that I had better drink my orange juice.

Instead of tapering limbs, long toes, slender fingers and fine ankles everything was stubby, rounded. Not so misshapen that she couldn't walk or even so that it was easily noticed. Only that Great-Auntie had such fine ankles, such reticent, fluttery fingers, and Flora's would never entertain at piano, would never embroider edging on lingerie, might be hard to slip a ring onto.

When I knew her she was full grown, an adult cousin. Being little I spent a lot of time on the floor at close range to her feet and ankles, looked often at the legs that were the same girth knees to shoes, all the way down. She always wore high-heeled pumps, sometimes with ankle straps. Remembering the situation caused by the nurse and probably aggravated by not finishing her orange juice, I figured she could wear whatever shoes she liked. I looked with interest at the puffy feet stuffed into round-toed shoes and I thought of elephants in drawings where their toes are painted in scallops of colour. They must have been expensive. My mother had talked about alligator. Sometimes they were red, one time, a green pair, and I coveted them painfully. My mother had shoes in black and brown, one pair of navy, and brown-and-white spectator pumps. Flora was indulged, my mother told me, the family still trying to recover that February day.

Her mouth was like the shoes – a space too small for all it contained and she rarely closed her lips over her teeth. She had bracelets of soft skin at her wrists and fleshy upper arms.

I never saw prominent collar bones or fine shoulders like my mother's. She was smooth and brown and her oily skin filled all the places where points or shadows might otherwise have been.

Once, in the winter, she came to our house by taxi. She was wearing a leopard fur coat. I had seen enough Saturday afternoon movies to know that that was the most glamorous, showiest, most immodest fur a person could wear. It said things about you. It suggested a past, something foreign, smoke-rings, cocktails, unaccounted-for gaps in a woman's history, travel by train at night, red lipstick.

I didn't know there were yellow and black leopards in the north. Where would my great-uncle have found that fur? He'd traded it. Traded it for foxes and mink and had it made for his flower and she wore it over a red wool dress the day she came to our house in a taxi. The blond man with the squint wasn't at her side.

'You have to kiss your cousin Flora,' she shouted at me. Not anger or reproach, just noise. She pulled me up against her and my nose was full of grilled lamb grease. Now I was under the fat part of the globe, had slipped around the equator and was in Africa. The light turned green and the air was heavy and wet. Fur forelegs and soft paws buffeted me, menacing me gently. Hot meat breath pushed at my face. Like Jonah I was intimate with a large animal – inside out. A leopard smells like lamb fat. I'll know it anywhere now.

She let me go.

My mother took Flora's coat and hung it in the hall closet. They sat in the living room. I paced up and back in front of the coat certain it was animate and wary of approaching it alone. Then chocolates drew me into the living room and I left the coat by itself. Looking back, I regret that. I never should have let the leopard be.

She wore that coat for years. We saw her infrequently. I grew up. The coat became worn, shabby. Flora gained weight and the fur pulled across her chest, rode up on her hips. It ceased being an animal and looked more like upholstery.

I married. Now I could have a fur coat of my own. Not leopard. I'm too young for a past and I don't care for the way it smells. The furrier raised his eyebrows. 'Smells? Leopard has no odour. Look here. Here's a Hudson seal with a leopard collar. There's no particular smell to it.'

And it all came back. I sat down in one of the tufted chairs in the show room and let it all come. The heat, the garden, the white linen hat. Flora's dark skin, expensive shoes, red sweaters, all those teeth. Her coarse black hair, the slightly protruding, glittering dark eyes, the hugs, the odour, her skin, her scalp, her own scent. Flora was the leopard. The mutton smell was her assertion, her particular band of colour, her aliveness. Nothing at all inexcusable. I liked it now, in memory. Naturally, I still couldn't wear leopard. The association, the rareness of the species. Out of the question.

Things didn't go well for Flora. She never married, didn't work. On a day in the winter, climbing onto a city bus she slipped under the front wheels. One leg was crushed. This had nothing to do with February. Just bad luck. There was nothing that could be done to repair the damage and the leg was amputated below the knee.

The small shoes in pairs, the sweaters in vivid colours, the brimmed hats, the visits where she stood slightly toeing in, smiling, waiting to be greeted – none of that could be recovered. Her life as she'd known it was over. She died, still in hospital.

Trapped, caught by one leg, wild but maybe not wild enough, she didn't struggle at the end. It hadn't occurred to me that maybe she'd been, in her particular way, unyielding all along. Children don't think about things that way. She'd probably twisted and pulled and fallen back exhausted and damp with the effort. Early on she'd known about traps, maybe learned about them that February day when she'd lain, arms tucked firmly to her sides, under the rabbit fur carriage cover, sensed danger, felt panic. Her slightly rounded black eyes had grown big with fear. It's possible that everything since then had been a struggle to break free of traps. Too loud, too dark, too hot and scented, too much, she'd always been told.

And now, at the end, tired but no longer grounded by her two stumpy legs, she'd simply drifted up, transcendent, an exotic, highly coloured bird, all that plumage and fluttering finally all right.

I was a child when I knew Flora. I can only imagine what the fit inside her skin had really been. It may have been a struggle, maybe not. But for me, if the metal closed cold and mean on my flesh, I'd gnaw the leg and leave it.

A Love Story

H is first real memory of his mother would have been her smell, the way she smelled when he pushed his small nose up against her belly, would have had to be her smell and not how she looked because early on his eyes were just two seams in his soft flat face. He would think of her smell and also of her warmth, how safe and perfect the world was when it was no broader than the space defined by her fore and hind legs, how crawling or wriggling or being pushed by her broad nose to find his place at her belly, that it was a wide enough world. Always the clear memory of her smell surprised him and made him stop in mid-trot and forget for a fraction of time where he'd been going, who had whistled for him and what it was he was meant to do.

Then he would have to say that he remembered too, the sweet taste of her milk, could never get quite enough, that the four pups who shared her warm fur belly would climb over and around him and that their tiny nails and blunt faces and small, unshaped heavy bodies would squeeze him from his place and to this day he could never get his fill of warm milk. The way his nose would lead him now to his mother's side if she were still alive, that same nose had led him more than once to a swift boot and a kick out of the way when he'd prod the pail of fresh cow's milk or moon around the cows after they'd calved or always want to be in the big kitchen where there was milk and warmth and the women who said *Blackie, away now*! or *git*! but never kicked him. As he thought about it he'd always preferred women, the big ones or the girls, who didn't have the sharp, man's odour and who, while they didn't smell of milk, smelled of something warm that made him think of the fur on his mother's belly and of the pink skin where the fur was sparse and how, even though it was in a close space her belly smelled clear and open like the air over a field after rain. And when he was almost grown, was nearly a year and there was no milk left and he was bigger than his mother, how, if he'd find her lying out on her side in the sun by the barn, he'd lie beside her and rest his chin on her flank or belly or even across her legs just for her smell and how the closeness brought into his young head the sense of a safe and protected, knowable world like the one only as big as the space between her lying-down fore and hind legs.

It wasn't for protection that he sought her out or for the near-to-swooning joy of breathing her deep, although he surely liked the way that deep breath filled his head with her and emptied it of everything else; it was that understanding the space squared off by her fore and hind legs was the last fully understandable space he occupied.

He had grown into an attractive dog with a broad chest, substantial feet, a strong back, a good square head with wide-set, dark brown eyes and full chops. His snout was rectangular, not pointy or wolfish and he had solid white teeth with an even bite and big silky triangular ears that folded nicely to his head. Coarse whiskers sprouted from his muzzle. His nose was big and black, without a blemish – cold and damp. His neck was thick and he carried his long tail, which he was always willing to wag, in a graceful arc over his back when he strode on. His fur was black, glossy, thick. He had one pink toenail, one white one and a narrow patch of soft white fur set deep on his chest like the blaze on a horse's nose. It showed as a wink when he approached at a lope or when he rolled out on his back and flailed his legs for a scratch.

Nothing about him wasn't good-natured. Nothing about

him was flashy or quick; he was big and warm and square and solid. As a result he wasn't good with the sheep. He missed agility in his turns and was always trotting up late. His corners were too wide and he failed to get the hang of the inside, hind leg pivot. He wasn't cut out to be a foxer either; his sleep was as deep as his velvety black chops and with his thick-furred ears folded over like ear muffs he never once picked out a nocturnal red footfall in the henhouse. His blunt nose and thick feet excluded him as a ratter; under his surveillance gophers mined the yards. The little digging he did would only be a perfunctory and shallow grave for a spent soup bone. He was better with the cows but he didn't have much heart for the bullying that was required or the head for the organization the farmer expected. He was happy enough to trot out alongside them as they were taken from the barn and across the road to the pasture every morning. But he forgot to stay to the outside and he'd mingle, sniffing and snuffling with the warm cows and the lickedy calves and he'd grow sleepy and slow in there with them and heady with the smell of milk and pink skin and he'd rock slowly on his feet drunk with remembering or he'd fold his limbs and let the grass make his belly damp and it would be warm and he couldn't have said if the ground had been warm from the sun when he lay down or if he had warmed it through his skin from settling there. None of this interested or pleased the farmer who cared only that the sun nourish his crops, dry his hay and make his cows productive but not that it delight this big healthy young dog who seemed reluctant to earn his keep.

The young dog, who probably was more Labrador than any other kind of dog, never fully understood what was expected. It seemed he came in late when things were being explained and always missed the important part. Or he'd try to listen but he'd find his thoughts drifting to where the cows were or when he tried he fell short and got it wrong and never could say why. One thing – he never bit or growled or was churlish. What he knew was that the farmer and lately the bigger boys on the farm too were angry with him, were harsh in their tone, jerked out with a quick hard boot or a mean jab with a garden rake that never broke the skin except for once and only grazed his head or whistled past his ears. He'd go low on his legs and hurry out of the way looking over his shoulder to maybe see what exactly it was that he'd done wrong or had forgotten to do or had only half done. It made his skin flick in surprise when someone did pat him nice and he found the harshness made his heart pound. It took some of the lustre from his fur. Sometimes his eyes would be less clear. Those times when fear would cloud his eyes he'd look in, not out, and looking in he'd see the safe measurable space that had been his early, first-furred enclosure and he'd wish to be again inside the frame of his mother' s limbs.

The farmer was often heard to say to anyone near that there was no room on a farm for pets, that every living thing earned its keep, man and beast alike, that softness invited the wolves. There'd be no wolves on his doorstep, not while he had breath to fill his lungs and warn them all against it. No sir, you earned your keep or out you went, once you were old enough to stand on your own feet, which that damned useless dog was.

He said it to his sturdy wife, to his big sons broad and brown from labour in the fields, to his young daughters barely big enough to see over the kitchen table but already big enough to scatter feed for the chickens, to his wife's mother who lived with them now and baked their bread and shelled peas and helped with the canning, to the mirror over the sink when he shaved his cheeks and thick jaw on Sunday mornings, to the hard blue sky when he needed rain, to the wind when it blew dust dervishes in the dry fields, to the snow when it lingered too long or came too late.

You earn your keep
You make your way
You bend your back
And far away the wolves will stay.

Everyone on the farm knew the verse and worked to its unavoidable metre. 'That dog, that lazy, big black thing goes,' he said finally and everyone knowing the verse knew there was nothing to say in answer.

Blackie jumped willingly enough into the back of the half-ton and the farmer banged the gate in place behind him. The ribbed metal bed of the truck was warm with having been parked in the yard. There was straw loosed from an untidy bale in one corner and a big wooden tool box bolted in place against the cab. He made a tour of his new quarters, snuffing the straw, the floor, the wooden box. The smells, with the exception of the straw, were new more than foreign and Blackie was at ease. His farmer had gone into the house. He settled himself and enjoyed the sun on his back.

'He'll be fine. He'll be happier,' he heard his farmer say and the screen door to the kitchen banged, bounced open and finally closed. He remembered how he was always skittering through the door on the second bounce, hurrying to be out of the way but not before someone would shout at him. The truck shifted and his farmer was standing on the running board leaning over the truck. Blackie was glad to see him and still wanting to get things right, got to his feet, waggled over and licked the coarse underside of the jaw hovering over his head. 'Pete's sake' the man said, and the head pulled back. The door of the truck shut hard so that Blackie felt it through the floor.

Standing square he looked back out over the gate as the farm and its yard pulled smaller and smaller and began to disappear behind a dust curtain. He wavered on his legs with the truck jerking over the road but found he could hold his balance if he swayed with it. He had no information about where he was going or what was happening but it seemed okay. Okay except he was maybe a little queasy. Maybe it was that everything was rolling away from him fast and faster and there were things he knew he'd never be able to catch or herd together or round up to bring home. He'd look for his farmer, is what he'd do and he staggered a little, turning around on the hopping metal floor, but he did keep his feet and facing this way he was moving toward things instead of having them pull away from him. He lifted his forelegs onto the wooden box. Through the small window at the back of the cab he could see the rough neck, the close spiky brown hair and the dark cap of his farmer. If he leaned to the left his head was almost at the window where his farmer's elbow rested. The wind pushed at his face, even his tongue was whipped to the side of his mouth but it felt good and the queasiness passed. He was strong and excited and he liked standing on his hind legs, liked to feel the muscles tensing in his flanks as he adjusted to the sway of the truck, liked his forelegs on the wooden box, liked being up. He was ready.

The truck travelled all the way to the city and into its centre and Blackie, amazed by all of it, moved from one side to the other, stretching his thick neck to get a picture that wasn't split by the cab in front of him. They pulled into a back lane that ran along one side of a building and parked against a brick wall. His farmer got out, told him stay put and disappeared through a wide opening in the wall. Blackie moved to the gate and looked out. Here there was no dirt, no grass, no fences or cows or any other animals. The only growing things he saw were big trees in a row that stretched on and on along the road. People walked by, moving quickly in both directions. None carried pails or garden forks or bunches of beets and carrots with their greens still on. He heard his farmer say,

'I'll trade for some of the engine parts. I've got no eggs this time but I've brought a dog. Good for the city – young, quiet with a good temperament. I'd keep him myself but he's one dog too many on the farm,' and the gate on the truck was dropped.

His farmer slipped a rope around his neck, the first time Blackie had felt such a thing, but it didn't hurt him and he walked with the farmer, leaning against his pant leg as they went. The road was hard and hot under his feet. Then they were through the big opening and now it was cool and dark.

'You've got kids?' said his farmer to a man standing in the building. 'Every kid wants a dog, ought to have a dog. Here's this one, house-broke and steady, nice coat, looks like a pure-bred. What do you say.'

Blackie looks at the man. He looks okay and Blackie moves away from his farmer's pant leg and gently noses the man at the back of his knee. The man smells fine, not the sharp sour smell of the farm men, a different smell, and the man laughs. His voice is light and in the laugh and in the words, 'Hey, boy,' he doesn't hear the growl of displeasure he hears so often on the farm.

'I've got a daughter,' says the man, 'but she's not really a kid. She'll be grown and leaving in a bit. Fact is, she may well be going away to school this fall and what will we do with a dog then?' But he scratches Blackie behind the ear and then he squats and says to Blackie, 'You a good dog?'

Blackie's farmer says, 'Then it's a deal,' and Blackie can feel the rope around his neck shift as it's passed from the farmer's hand to the man's hand.

'You be good now,' says his farmer and walks through the big doors into the square of light. Blackie hears his farmer grunt and something heavy scrape on the ridged floor of the truck. He hears the gate locked into place, the truck door open, bang shut, hears the motor, a little screech as the truck

[107]

pulls away, hears its sounds get smaller and then nothing. He and the man stand in the cool dark and the man still holds the rope.

'Well, boy, Blackie, you're not four dozen eggs, for sure,' and Blackie is taken to the back office of the repair shop whose owner is now his owner. They walk into a room which has one window only, which looks out on the place where cars and trucks are fixed. The man closes the door and slips the rope off Blackie's neck and Blackie moves carefully around the small room, his head down, his nose working to note what the room holds and he finds that the smells are pleasant to his nose, that he likes the mix of oil, the damp concrete floor, traces of cigarette tobacco, the heavy wool of a jacket thrown over the seat of a chair, the sharp hot smell of welded metal, car paint and the forest green smell of turpentine. It's not the farm. Here are no animal smells, not his lovely cows or the rancid chickens and not the straw or the perfumed alfalfa bales. It's not the kitchen smells either, not the dough-warm smell of the women's legs, not the milk-cheese secrets, the yellow soap or the fruit-simmering scents of the place he was sometimes allowed to enter but not so often once he grew big.

Now he hears the man's voice and he's speaking on the telephone and he's saying, 'I've got you a surprise. You were always asking for a dog and now I've got you one. I'll be home for supper and you'll see.'

The man walks out of the office and closes the door behind him. Blackie walks once around the room, settles on the concrete floor and dozes, wakes and dozes. Once, he gets to his feet and moves around the small office thinking he might find water. At the same time he feels pressure in his bladder and would like to take a pee. He settles again on the floor. He doesn't feel happy but he's not afraid either. He's just quiet, and, at the very edge of the deep place where sleep comes from, there's a small thing he can't quite remember. He sleeps again.

[108]

When the man opens the door he's quick to his feet, his thick tail waving. He feels the rope slipped over his head and its light pressure on his neck. He walks out of the office beside the man and through the bright open space in the wall. The man pulls a big door down behind them, locks it and they walk down the lane toward the back of the building. Here Blackie stops and lifts his leg and the long stream of pee splashes against the building and runs in streaks on the pavement. 'Okay, boy,' says the man and when he's done they move on again, walking behind the building to a gravel lot and the man's car. The man opens a back door and with the rope urges the dog inside. It's close and hot and the dog draws in a quick breath. The man sits in front, starts the motor, then rolls down the windows in front and one in back, half-way. Blackie climbs onto the seat, moving toward the half-open window and the man says nothing. The air is as hot as his own breath. None of the quick things he sees as they drive is familiar. He feels queasy and turns his head away from the movement. His stomach heaves and heaves again and his mouth is full of the bitter contents of his stomach. He lowers his head to the floor and vomits. The man hears him and without turning in his seat utters, 'Christ, dog,' and in the angry tone something is finally familiar.

They pull up behind a house and through the open window Blackie sees that it's only a little smaller than the one he knew on the farm but this house has almost no yard around it and other houses very close by. The man opens his door, leaves it open and leaves the dog inside. Blackie hears him shouting in a voice that's lost its lightness, 'Ev, get a pail of water and some rags, your damn dog has been sick all over the car.' A door slams and it's quiet and Blackie lies on the seat, his head near the mess he's just made. His tongue has grown thick and it hangs long from his mouth. In the heat he can feel where it pulls at the base of his throat. He'd like water. He hears the man's voice but not what he's saying and he hears another voice, a girl's. A door bangs again and the voices are nearer. He hears the man saying 'mess' and 'dumb mistake' and he hears the girl saying 'Okay, okay.' Then the back door of the car opens and he smells her before he sees her and then he feels her and both the smell and what he feels are cool. 'Oh,' she says to him or to the car. And to the man whose almost-adult daughter she is, says nothing special, nothing remarkable; she says to her father, 'What's the big deal, no big deal, stop shouting' and the dog rises from the seat as though an invitation had been offered, as though he'd had a long drink and he moves out of the car to stand next to the girl whose side he knows he will never leave.

Her body is cool from being inside the house and she smells maybe like the small white bell-shaped flowers that grew around the house on the farm in the early summer but he's not sure and the hand she rests on his head feels green and soft like the best cow pasture. Now she's leaning into the car and wiping his mess and he can't see all of her but her legs are narrow white stalks. He moves his dry nose near but can't detect a butter or milk smell, only the white bell flowers and he's not sure he even smells that. He pulls his head back. She won't need the rope, he'll be beside her, always.

He walks beside her into the house and is surprised to find the kitchen small and only one woman in it – the girl's mother who looks at him and at the girl and says, 'I really have no time for a dog, keep him off the rugs, he'll be your responsibility.'

She gives the girl a plastic mixing bowl for his water and a tin pie plate for food. 'Put paper under them,' she tells her.

He can see the whole girl now. He thinks she might be too thin and wonders if she can do heavy work but he likes the way her clothes move around her frame as though a small breeze was pulling at them. He thinks maybe they're a little alike, himself and the girl, because her big eyes are also brown and set wide on her face. Her lips are shiny and dark. After he's been with her for a while he realizes she puts colour on them and he likes the smell of her mouth with or without the waxy stain she rubs on. Most days she takes him into the room she calls the den, which has no carpets on the floor and she reads or sometimes listens to music and he lies out at her feet on the polished wood. She talks to him all the time. He listens closely and she's pleased. Often she'll interrupt what she's saying to him over the top of her book and she'll put it down and kneel on the floor beside him and take his head in her lap and lower her face to his and her dark hair will close like a curtain around them. Inside that dark, silk-lined room he can smell only her and then he's sure her scent is the small white bells from the gardens around the farm house or maybe nothing else has ever smelled this way, only the girl.

She likes the way he smells too and would describe it as a mix of cold air, wool and wood smoke. She thinks he's a handsome dog, very solid and square and manly and when she tells this to her boyfriend he laughs but he never pats the dog, doesn't want to take him when they go for a walk or for a day trip to the lake.

'You're sure close with him,' he'd say to her and her mother would say, 'You'd think you'd raised him from a pup,' and her father would say, 'You can smell him the minute you walk in the house.'

He said it one day when he came home from work and he said it again several more times and then he told her the dog would spend the days outside. He'd have to be tied up since they didn't have a fenced yard and he knew farm dogs always strayed back home if they weren't tied. The girl knew this wasn't true, knew he'd never leave, but her father said otherwise. So they put him out one morning and they tied him to the big birch tree for shade and they put out his water bowl and his food dish and they left for the day.

He'd never been tied, the day was long, the sun kept sliding and he shifted with it, looking for shade. Moving around under the tree he knocked over his water dish; flies beaded the food they'd left for him. There was less and less rope as he wound round the tree. When the girl returned home at the end of the day she found the dog panting in the heat, unable to move. His tongue lolled, the pads of his feet felt baked, his nose was dry and his eyes were wild. She took him inside and tended to him and when her parents came home she told them they couldn't do this again. 'It's inhumane,' she said.

'He'll stay outside,' shouted her father.

'You're cruel,' she shouted back.

'You're out of line, Evelyn,' he answered but the dog stayed in.

The dog never thought of her as Evelyn; he liked when they called her Eve or by her baby name Eve'n. For him she was all of these things. Without knowing, he sensed she was first woman Eve, and the twilit quiet of evening, and an island, Eve'n, steady and calm and safe. She protected him, he'd do the same for her.

They'd planned a picnic, dog and girl, one afternoon so he could run free, dog around, as she put it. She'd rolled down all the car windows in preparation, put him in the back seat and told him to lean out into the wind. For a while he'd felt fine but then the heaving began and once again his yellow bile and the undigested remains of breakfast pooled on the floor. Eve did what she could with the napkins she packed with lunch but enough remained so that by the time they returned home in the late afternoon and even with her careful application of dish detergent and as much water as she could use without soaking the car rug, some sharp bile smell remained. She left the windows down and when her father parked his car next to her mother's, which was the one she was allowed

to drive, he came directly into the house and called to her, telling her, 'That dog has been puking again.' The dog heard
him in the den where he lay on the floor by the sofa and he
lifted his head anxiously to the girl.

'Leave her alone,' sounded inside his head. 'He'll leave you
alone,' she said to him. 'He'll just yell for a bit, we're okay.'

So long as she said 'we' they were okay. He also hoped she
wouldn't insist he ride in the car any more. If they could go on
foot, if he could trot along beside her, they could circle the
globe together, he could go without stopping and he'd never
be ill. It was being inside a small rolling place and the turns
and stops and the shifting – a dog was meant to stand on the
ground. That's why he had solid, even legs, leather pads,
thick opaque nails and bushy tufts between his toes. These
were the furnishings of a ground traveller – but he'd try again
if she really wanted him to.

There was talk in the house about a weekend at their cottage.
'You'll love the lake,' she told him. But how do we get there, he
wondered and felt in his stomach that it must be by car.

There was other talk. About not taking the dog, about
leaving him tied outside.

'If he's as smart as you say,' said her father, 'this time he
won't wind himself around the tree or spill his water.'

'You can't mean that,' his Eve had said. 'You can't be serious.' And while he probably wasn't really thinking of doing
this, once he'd said it her father stuck with it.

Blackie heard her father shout something about 'my car.'
Eve answered with 'my dog.' Her father countered with 'my
house' and the door slammed leaving the dog inside with the
father and the mother. He told himself she'd come back,
always come back. She did always come back and she'd take
his big head in her lap and make that secret room for them
and draw the perfumed curtain of her hair around them. 'I
love you,' she'd say.

One day when they were this way her mother walked to the door of the den and she said to the girl, 'You know that's not healthy, what you're doing,' and the girl lifted her head from his and she said, 'You don't get germs from dogs. There's dog germs and there's people germs and they don't transfer.'

'Well, they do,' said her mother, 'but I didn't mean germs. You're not being fair to the dog, holding him and patting him and being so close. You're exciting him and remember, he's only a dog.'

The girl felt her face get hot. Then she felt tight in her stomach. Then she felt a kind of rage that was new for her. This one wasn't loud and sudden and accompanied by a flash. This one was slow and deep and would never leave, she knew.

With shame that she would be saying it to her mother and with horrible shame that her mother would have thought and said such a thing she clipped off the words, 'You're sick,' and hid her face in the dog's neck.

'Well, I don't think so, young lady. Just look.'

She was pointing to the dog's groin, to the place between his thick-furred flanks, to a place the girl never considered and there, emerging from its fur sheath was the pink tip of the dog's sex.

The girl looked, and she looked at the dog's square head in her lap and the anxious look in his dark eyes and she said, 'It's only the way he's sitting,' and sensing that the dog was in danger, that they both were, she added, now cool and rational, 'In biology we're studying animals and there's no cross-species attraction. Come on, Blackie, let's have a walk.'

One Friday evening when the girl came home she found the house clicking with activity. Her mother was in the kitchen boxing groceries, her father was moving from the house to the car with bags, was pulling the curtains closed, lowering blinds.

'Throw some things in a suitcase, we're off for the week-end,' he instructed her. 'And hurry, we want to get there before dark.'

'Who's going?' she said, feeling the ground sliding. 'I think I'll stay here. I'd rather stay here,' she said, frightened for the dog.

'Out of the question, miss,' said her mother. 'We're all going and your father has it fixed up for the dog.'

'Yes,' he said. 'He'll ride in the trunk. We'll tie it shut and leave a slit open at the bottom, for air.'

'You're kidding,' the girl said.

'Not kidding. I've got a plastic sheet in the trunk and if he gets sick that's that. Let's move, the car's loaded.'

The girl walked past the father, looked in at the den where the dog sat tense and still, walked on to her bedroom, grabbed a few pieces of clothing, her hairbrush, her toothbrush, pushed them into her beachbag, walked back to the den. The dog got to his feet. They passed through the kitchen and she slid the keys off the counter and into her bag. They walked out the side door and to the back of the house and the packed car. She opened the back door and the dog got inside. She opened his window, locked his door for safety, opened the door on the driver's side, slid behind the wheel, started the car, backed away from the house and headed in the direction of the lake. It was the first time she'd travelled to the cottage alone.

She didn't turn on the car radio. She didn't talk to the dog; her head couldn't hold another sound. Her forehead was stretched with a black rage and her stomach was taut with fear. Her father was a cruel stranger, capable of anything, anything. Driving on the dark highway along which she could recognize no familiar signs, setting out on her own with the dog on the seat behind her she knew she wouldn't be Eve'n anymore, that she'd grown up now, that this small trip of barely more than an hour was a journey as significant as any she'd take. Knowing she was grown she'd act responsibly.

The trip took longer than she expected. They'll be worried, she thought, but they'll have realized by now that you can't put a living thing in the trunk of a car. They'll come out in the other car tonight or in the morning. I'll call as soon as I get there to tell them we're okay. They'll be proud, I bet, proud that I stuck up for the dog and that I made my first highway trip okay.

The dog was quiet in the back seat. If anytime he could not have done it, the dog wished more than anything that this could be it but the tension and the dark and the girl's tight silence made his stomach feel worse and he heaved and vomited on the floor of the car. The only thing she said on the trip out was, 'It's okay, you can't help it.'

When they arrived she placed a collect call from the phone booth at the end of the road on which their cottage sat. She heard her mother's voice say 'Yes, we'll accept the charges' and then, when she said 'We're here, we're okay,' her mother said only, 'Evelyn, have you gone out of your mind? That will be it for you with the car, miss,' and she hung up.

The girl parked the car by the cottage, unlocked it, turned on some lights inside and then they went down to the lake. The cold sand felt good under their feet and using a plastic pail and shovel from when she was a kid, brought sand back to the car. She spread it on the dog's mess, scooped it out and wiped the rest away. The night was very quiet but they weren't afraid and the next morning, when her parents arrived, the quiet was maintained. There was no more discussion about taking the dog back to the city in the trunk. She drove home with her mother and Blackie sat in back. She cleaned his mess and for the next long days they all moved around each other on the steel tracks of their tension. The dog thought he couldn't bear it, not for him and certainly not for her, but now something else was added.

As the summer drew to a close there was conversation about when she was leaving; what she would take with her and he learned she would be going away to school, that it was a plan made long ago, before him. She was not taking him. He'd look into her face, trying to hold her with his eyes, to stop the busy movement in the house. The girl and her father barely spoke; the girl and her mother spoke about skirts and sweaters and new shoes and dental appointments, dormitories, roommates and airline schedules. No one spoke about him. Then they all did. They sat in the den at a meeting convened by the girl.

'You have to promise me you'll take good care of Blackie, walk him, feed him, pat him and not ever get angry with him because I love him more, well, I love him and he's ours, all of ours.'

'He'll be fine,' said her mother.

Later, sitting with his head in her lap she told him that first term was short and she'd be home once before Christmas and then at Christmas and when, in three years, she was done with school they would live together on their own and it would be perfect.

He breathed deeply, preferring the way her skin and hair and mouth smelled to any smell in the world and he felt a longing that even lying inside the space created by his mother's fore and hind legs, which space he remembered with less clarity than he would have wished, couldn't answer, couldn't satisfy.

She did what she promised and came home for a weekend in late fall. Her mother was tense, the dog was thinner. Alone in the den, on the floor with his head in her lap she told him, 'I've missed you, the guys are all jerks, my classes are good, I love the way you smell, I'll see you again at Christmas and it will be for longer,' and then, it seemed, she was gone.

At Christmas break her father was alone at the airport to meet her.

'Hi, where's Mom?' she said, their winter coats making their hug stiffer.

'In the kitchen watching something on the stove,' he answered. 'He's gone, Ev. We couldn't manage him on our own.'

'Gone? Is he dead? Where is he – gone? I just saw him six weeks ago. How could he be gone?' and the thought in her head and the feeling in her chest was – I can't make it.

'He stopped eating, Ev. He just lay around and his fur got patchy. He was your dog and he was sick with missing you, I guess.'

'Where is he?' she said with control.

'When we realized there was nothing we could do we gave him to a man who comes into my shop from time to time. He lives in the country and he's got young kids. There's always one or two hanging on him when he comes in so I asked him, did he want a big dog with a nice temperament and his kids said can we, so we figured, your mother and I, that that would be the ideal thing for the dog. When the fellow came back to pick up some parts I said he could have the dog and we went and got Blackie right then.'

'Without calling me, without even asking or discussing it with me you gave him away like he was a thing, like he was something you'd leave on the curb to be picked up?'

'You're making this worse than it was. The city was no place for that dog. He came from a farm and that's where he belongs and let's have an end to this.'

For the time she was home she left her room only to check the den looking for him, trying to locate his scent. She thought of his bulk, the bear-like thickness of his coat, his wide-set eyes, his quiet. No girth would have been sufficient to fill the space in her arms or up against her chest. If she could contact him, maybe visit him, explain it – but her father said he couldn't remember where the man lived, just out in the country somewhere.

She wouldn't visit with the family, didn't take the phone when friends called. She lay on her bed, she walked to the den, she returned to her room and passed the holidays in half light, refusing to lift the blinds or open the curtains. She wouldn't come to the table and the already spare flesh on her body fell away. She looked brittle and her colour darkened like an unhealthy stalk.

Her mother would knock briskly at her door, carrying a tray and she'd list the contents as if they were the words to a song, willing a return of the brightness she could see leaching away. She'd be thanked for her trouble and asked to set it on the bed and her mother would stand there with her hands hanging empty at her sides and she'd smile and nod to the tray and then, 'Eat up while it's hot,' and she'd leave. Later the full tray would be on the floor outside the closed door.

Her parents came into her room a few days before she was to return to school. They sat down on her bed and her father said, 'We'll make every effort to get in touch with the man who has Blackie. Maybe we can get him back, we had no idea he meant so much to you, he was only a dog. We didn't know.'

It wouldn't happen, she knew. She was uncomfortable with their promises and happy enough to return to school.

They phoned her often. They'd call Wednesdays and Sundays in the evening, asking how she was feeling, how were her classes, any interesting young men and casually, how was her weight and one Sunday, three weeks after she'd returned, they mentioned that Blackie had come home.

'You called and got him back?' she asked, her voice showing brightness for the first time since Christmas.

'No, we didn't have much success there,' said her father.

'He just turned up one night, thin and mangy. We almost didn't know him. His eyes were all crusty and he had ice packed up between his toes. He was sort of limping. We brought him in and gave him food and put out a rug in the back hall. You can bet we were happy to see him. At first he wouldn't eat, but your Mom, figuring he was suffering with the cold, heated him up a big bowl of milk. I think he finished off more than a quart. He walked all through the house when he first came in and he did it again after he had his milk. He sniffed your room up and down like he was vacuuming it, the den too. All his old haunts, I guess. Then he lay down on his rug and slept through till morning. We let him out to do his business when he got up, figuring if he'd come this far on his own looking for you he wasn't going to be wandering off again. He didn't come back, Ev. Sorry.'

Killing Time

There were four of them, two couples – and there was the lake. They'd been spending their summers at the lake for years. The blessed lake, gentle, quiet, sand-bottomed, soft-bottomed lake. Thin, shallow waves slapping the shore, children at its edges, ankle deep, squatting to fill plastic cups or pails, any vessel, to scoop the healing lake and carry it in soft hands on unsteady dimpled legs up the barely-there rise of sand to sit suddenly down and spread the water where they'd stopped in the sand.

Or hard and glittering, the top of an enamelled casque, sun diamonds jewelling its surface, so smart and quick under a little wind, a sight to square your shoulders and make you vigorous in your walk along the broad curve that held the town where these four people spent their summer every year.

At night if the wind picked up it would be grey, a fish soup smell stirred to the surface and carried by the waves that rode in and clattered on the sand rim and slipped back and rode forward and made timpani of the night. But the next day would be fresh and sweet and the lake, tired, would rest.

If it happened that the next day was Sunday the sand beach would spread to carry picnicking families out for the day and they'd walk with city feet on the still damp, packed edges and gather the gifts the lake had brought forward. If the picnickers had been at a surprise party made for them they couldn't have been more delighted, more astonished at what was given. Or if someone hadn't heard the chop and chorus the previous night and had come down early to the lake's edge they'd be just as surprised to find: log bits, some fish net, a float, pieces of rubbed beach glass, holey stones, a bruised gull, oh my God a fish, one sandal, drink cans, a child's shovel – beak yellow, shells – wholes and halves – all of it still wet and fresh and bright, clean from its bath in the broad, blessed lake.

And to come here year after year, and see it unchanged no matter how much they and everyone around them did – they all knew it was their River Jordan and they would be renewed; they needed no other body of water, they'd need nothing else if they could come, as they did every summer, to this lake.

At five o'clock, if the couples came together there would be gin and tonics, the quinine perfect, settling inside just right, tasting the way skin smelled after a day in the sun, near the water. The way skin would get – a little pink and tight and warm. And they'd stretch and taste lime on their lips and look at each other with genuine love, loving about themselves and each other that they lived each summer beside this wonderful lake.

So slow, it was. So limpid and slow. Dinners together or after days spent separately, each couple with work to do, or families, other friends, maybe business in the city. And later the treat of dinner together, just them or with invited friends. People called to come out from the city, from the cinnamon summer heat to dip feet at the water's edge, to join them in cool drinks, for the pleasure and benediction of the lake and friendship, to be restored and freshened, here by its shores. They'd come sallow-skinned from the city to turn rosy on the deck or by the lake, to dip and rinse, to lower themselves into the soft water, to eat and laugh and be joyful in this splendid place with gentle friends.

Voices were never raised here. They understood, these four people, that the lake's tone was sonorous, that their voices were lightened by the bass of the lake or kept from being shrill by the small licking sound it made when it was almost still.

One perfect night they'd come together for a meal. Quietly they'd praised each other for the food they'd taken such care to prepare, one couple always bringing something to the other – to share the work, to offer a gift of nourishment, to please each other with something new.

This night, after the meal, they sat by the open windows. The screens were black against the trees, just beyond was the lake, whispering and muttering along the shore. They were just four – and the lake and the dark night drew them close. To each other this night they offered their voices and their stories.

'When I was a kid,' she began, 'we had a bird, a budgie. I was maybe twelve or eleven. Maybe just ten, around there, still interested in hacking around on a bike and keen on small things the way girls that age are.'

Reaching across the space that separated them he slipped his bare foot between the seat of her chair and her thigh. He wiggled his toes against her skin. 'Hey you,' he said. 'Are you going to tell your bird story? Every year around this time or once every summer, anyway, I hear about that bird,' he told them.

'Well,' she said, speaking now just to him, 'you're right. I know I do that. You're right. I do. And you know why, too.' She turned to their very dear friends.

'I'm not very big. I'm not what you'd call powerful. When I listen to the news on the radio or read the paper and terrible things are happening I know I can't make changes. I can't fix it. I send money. I sign my name to petitions. I always vote. I put my loose change in the jars they put beside cash registers. And when I was a kid I was never sure so I didn't step on cracks, I never teased cats, I don't think I ever pinched anyone in my life, I made paper covers for all my school books. I did what a kid could do. I do, in a small way, what an adult can do.' She pushed her fingers through her hair, lifting it off her neck for a moment and she stared off in the direction of the lake.

'Look,' the husband of her friend said in his deep, slow voice. 'You seem disturbed. There's no need for that. Not here at our lake and after such a lovely meal,' and he poured brandy into the four small glasses she'd brought from the table when they'd settled near the windows. She liked to tell stories and they'd always listen. Now they were going to hear something new. But it seemed possible this one might not close with a joke or some whimsy. The lake had taught them tempo and rhythm, the importance of pace. She spoke quickly, but low, moving for now, in counterpoint to the small waves they could hear through the screens.

'I'm okay. If you'll listen I'd like to tell my story. He's right. I need to tell this story once each summer. Because even though it's a small story and I never felt very big when I was a kid something happened and I should have been just big enough to change it.

'Like I said, we had a budgie. Blue. We'd had him for a couple of years. Long enough to teach him to talk. I knew he wasn't a pet like a dog. There's only so much a bird can do but he did what he could. He realized his potential,' she said, and in the half light and even though she was looking through the dark screens when she spoke, she knew they were smiling.

'He said three or four phrases and my name. You couldn't expect more. You know that? You wouldn't say he could have done more.' Now she could feel their concern.

'I trained him to sit on my index finger, little cold pink and grey feet, and on my shoulder. Sometimes I cleaned his cage. Sometimes my mother did. It was never an issue but *I* taught him to talk. When we bought him with a cage and a chrome floor stand we also bought a book on budgies. You know the kind. They still sell them. Pet stores have them on all kinds of pets – you know – *Tropical Fish, Your Turtle, Get to Know Your Cat* and then individual ones on each breed of dog. Well, we got one on budgies and it had instructions on teaching them to talk. *Spend twenty minutes each day with your budgie*, and so on. You know, that was one of the most gratifying things I ever did because that bird did talk. He had maybe three phrases and he'd whistle and chirp and then out would come identifiable language. Even other people could recognize it. He was really good and I really liked him. You know how it is when you're a kid. It's your pet, you love it.'

She could feel his big hand on her shoulder, pressing to ease the pain he knew she always felt with remembering.

'I'll tell the short version tonight,' she said to him. 'I'm okay, really. Well, the story is, I was a kid goofing around on a bike out here at the lake and I was out of the house more than I was in and I didn't pay the bird a whole lot of attention. It wasn't up to me in any organized way to feed him and I guess my mother was involved in other things and one day for some reason we both looked into his cage.

'His little plastic dish was full of seeds. It looked that way. But I put my finger into his dish and the stuff in there was just shells. I can still remember the soft, light feeling of the shells and pushing my finger through them to the bottom and going into the kitchen for seed and the box was empty and I think my mother said hurry and I peddled hard on my bike into town and bought a box of seed and peddled back hard to make my chest hurt because I think I knew it was too late and I filled his dish with seed and I can't remember exactly what happened next but I'm sure I heard him fall dead off his perch onto the floor of his cage. Some thing, some creature, this blue bird who said the words I pressed into his brain track, a thing living in the house with me, starved to death. And it made me sick and when I think of it it makes me sick and over and over like the ending of *Zabriskie Point*, where, in the movie they blow the house up over and over and over again, that bird falls off his perch dead and I hear it every time.

'Of all the things in the world you can't fix that wasn't one of them and it happened anyway. Every summer I tell this story and every time it makes my stomach hurt. I'm sorry if I've upset you.'

She was quiet. And now she was a little embarrassed. No one spoke and she'd made them uncomfortable, had introduced pain as a party to their small group. It had no place here, just now. But they were friends, congregants gathering here at this healing lake.

'I have a story about a rabbit,' her good friend said quickly. His voice was deep and he always spoke with authority. They waited.

'I have a story about a rabbit,' he began again. 'It's no cheerier, I should warn you.'

He sat with his back to the window. He had a big head and he wore his thick, white hair full around it and long. He had a beard, too, and moustache, and his broad, intelligent, sun-pinkened face emerged benignly from this circle of white.

This particular night he was wearing a dark blue shirt and against the screen his head seemed disembodied, a lovely, close moon. Whenever he told stories his voice assumed a Nordic kind of rising and falling off and tonight in the low light they leaned to him when he began.

'You've met my brother Mike,' he said. 'He's four years younger than me. He's the teacher. The one with the two small sons. Well, he was always a sensitive boy. He loved animals. But remember, we grew up out here and people from around this lake all hunted. There was nothing wrong with adding the occasional rabbit or deer or goose to the table. So my dad taught us all to use a gun when we were old enough. Mike was never keen on the animals' being dead, or on the preparation that came after. In a good-natured kind of way he was teased about his fussiness.

'I guess he figured he'd work himself out of it and to show us, he decided to set a trap and catch a rabbit to bring home. He did this on his own. He must have been ten which would have made me fourteen.

'Out in the bush about a mile from our house he'd set this thing up and I guess he knew better than he thought because he caught a rabbit. I'd just come home and I was fiddling with my bike in the yard. It was early in the summer and still light and he came running to me out of the bush crying, his face wet and he grabbed my arm with both his hands and started pulling me into the bush saying I had to come and help. I couldn't figure out what he was saying, pulling me toward the bush and crying about some animal screaming. I made him understand that I wasn't going anywhere until I knew what it was he wanted and he pulled himself up, his skinny little body all shaky and he said, "The rabbit. It's caught. One of its legs is caught and it's crying. Help me get it out. We've got to get it out."

' "Okay," I said to him and we walked or ran the mile into the bush. I could hear this crying long before we saw anything. It sounded like a little child and there it was. A rabbit, still in its white coat. It was caught by one leg and the other one was twitching and it was sobbing like it understood grief. Mike was frantic. He kept saying "Do something, make him stop, help him." '

Turning his big white head toward her he said, 'Remember you told us you never felt very strong as a kid or as an adult. Well fourteen-year-old boys have a stupid idea that in fact they *are* strong and tough. I wasn't happy about the rabbit, especially with it crying like that and I didn't know what to do with Mike who was crying again himself. I mean, he brought me out there to fix it. I didn't know what to do any more than he did but I was bigger.

'The rabbit and the trap were at the base of a tree. I picked up the rabbit. I remember I held the trap in one hand and the leg just above the trap in the other and I swung both hands at the tree. I smacked the rabbit against the tree until it stopped crying. Mike didn't say anything. He just stood there. It was worse than his crying. I'm tough, remember. Fourteen, I said to him, "Don't worry about it. It was just a goddamn rabbit."'

He stopped and they said nothing, each of them picturing the rabbit, feeling its white soft weight, its terror, its interrupted quickness, each imagining the inevitability of the next step and denying it and then seeing the rabbit's glazed still eye and being appalled, each of them having had some experience with small animals, with the shift of weight from living to dead. Each in their heads knew all this and they nodded, recognizing their individual knowledge.

'Brandy?' he asked, finally.

Outside, small bugs clicked against the screen. Inside, they drank the amber liquid and felt the pain their friends felt.

'I know what you mean,' he said after they'd all been quiet for some time. They looked at him sitting back in his chair, his dark hair cut close to his head, his green eyes round. She always used to tease him, saying he looked like an otter, but tonight the story he'd started to tell was about gophers.

He told them he'd moved to the small western city when he was four or five years old and after they'd lived there a few years his dad designed a house and had it built in a new development on the flat prairie. The kids around were really farm kids but they all went to the same new school in this raw subdivision.

'I was probably nine at the time. I guess I was a big kid but I had no sense of my size and never thought of myself as one of the strong guys. I wasn't a fighter and whatever athletic skills I developed later certainly hadn't shown themselves at that point.

'One of the kids from around there suggested we go hunting gophers. He explained it to me like it was a standard game with rules and all, and the prize was a nickel a tail. It's funny how you can hear words and know what they mean and still not understand any of it.

'So they gave me a piece of two-by-four board and they each took one. There were lots around because new houses were starting to go up. We'd filled a couple of pails with water from home because they said we needed water. They told me we had to find gopher holes and pour water down them and keep doing it until the gophers came up for air. Then we were supposed to plough them with the board. So I did that. I poured water into the hole, emptied the whole pail. We waited and then this little gopher pulled himself to the rim, totally soaked. He looked kind of cute and it didn't occur to me that he'd come out because he was suffocating. Anyway, one of the bigger boys was standing there and he yells, "Bean him, hit him with the board," and I did that. I pulled back and whacked it. What I did was crush it. It actually split and suddenly there was this horrible smell. Guts and shit. There I was, this stupid, big kid not smart enough to figure out much but I sure recognized what death smelled like.

'I stood there for a moment dumb with the absolute bewilderment of death and killing. The kid standing next to me said, "Good-o. You killed him. Take his tail for the nickel."

'I just looked at him and I went home and was sick. Even now I remember the colour of the insides.'

As though they were passengers in an aeroplane accelerating for take-off they pushed back in their chairs. 'That was

the last thing that died at my hand,' he added. 'Hell, I even
carry spiders outside, I can't crush a damn bug.'

'Jesus,' their friend's husband muttered and turning to his
wife he said, 'There surely can't be a story like that in your
gentle life.'

They all looked at her and knew there wasn't. Serene and
soft-spoken she had about her a modesty that made every
word she spoke seem temperate.

'Well, actually there was something' she said after a time.
'I was twelve I guess, around there, and we had this lovely
little dog. Brown and white. A sort of spaniel. He was
everybody's dog in the family but he used to follow me
around most of the time.

'It was summer and we were at the lake we used to go to.
There was some discussion about going for a walk or to visit
someone. We were outside and I can remember the place
exactly. There were lots of trees along both sides of a road. It
was sort of a dirt road and we were all standing together. It
was sunny and there were leaf patterns on our arms and
shoulders. I still love that kind of dapple even though it makes
me think of this story I'm telling you.

'I think I wanted to take the dog with me and my mother
said I shouldn't. I can't remember why. There was a sort of
argument, well, you'd call it a discussion, really. We never
argued right out in my family but I was twelve and you know
how girls that age get – quickly emotional and weepy at nothing. I don't remember exactly but I stomped off on my own
across the road and then to show my mother, I called the dog.
I turned and a car was coming and the dog was crossing to
me. It was like a sequence in a dream, things moving slowly,
some danger you had to escape but couldn't. I'm sure my
mouth was open in a scream but there was no sound. The car
hit him. It was my fault. He was killed. We all felt terrible. We

had a funeral and buried him and my mom tried to make me believe it wasn't my fault. But it was.'

They sat there, close in the dark. Outside, quick shallow waves touched the sand almost without a sound. A moth pulled itself across the window, deaf to their stories, drawn instead by the dim light inside. Someone sighed. One of them shifted in a wicker chair. A glass was refilled and in the half light they looked at each other with love.

Summer Stories
1. Stella Gorenko,
A Tribute from the Folks Who Knew Her

THE SETTING: A small town on the prairies by a large sand-bottomed lake. The terrain is flat right to the edges of the water which is shallow, that is, no more than twenty feet at its deepest. Along the lake and for three streets in, the houses belong almost exclusively to summer people. Cottages, most built between the wars, are modest. The occupants of these cottages appear in town at the end of June; by September most have closed and shuttered their small properties and the population, which grows by 3,000 during this time, returns to its steady 1,500. The two communities, summer people and townspeople, are separate but equable. Between them lies no common ground but the actual, somewhat spare ground over which they move in the months of July and August. Some of the summer people have recently winterized their cottages. Some few have built new ones which accommodate year-round use. Their extended presence has not changed the way the two communities relate. No bridges have been built, not to suggest gulfs or chasms. There is no real interest in changing this on the part of either group; things are fine as they are.

Some pine trees, maples, a few cottonwoods, mountain ash planted for their red leaves in fall and their berries for the migrating robins, clusters of willow near water and along ditches, also aspen or poplar. These make up scrub forests where farmers haven't turned the soil. In some places north of town, a few paper birch amongst the scrub. Near the edges — chokecherry, plum, pincherry, and lower to the ground, raspberries and currents. In the ditches and beside the railway tracks – wild strawberries.

To the north, the west and south of the town are small farms. The land is stony and thin, better for cattle than grain but some is grown. In recent years farmers have planted canola, for the oil. For a time, midsummer, when the canola is in flower, the fields are a glorious pollen yellow and some farmers – rivalling the post-impressionists – have planted, beside these yellow fields, other fields of sky-blue, mauve-blue flax. To the east of town is the lake.

The town is orderly. But for the crescent of its one perimeter which follows the shore, it is laid out in perpendiculars and the streets are sensibly named by numbers. Twenty years ago, or more, the streets were covered in asphalt. The two intersecting streets on which business is conducted have sidewalks. On the others, walkers make their way along the gritty shoulders which are flanked on both sides by shallow ditches. Town people and summer people alike have planted grass in these ditches and they're kept as clipped and tidy as the lawns. Only here is there a roll to the land and on weekends residents push power mowers to the edges of their property and then dip down into the shallow grassy troughs and up and down. Some houses and cottages have flag poles; some have elaborate, multi-storied birdhouses. Increasingly, cedar bird feeders swing from the branches of trees planted within sight of kitchen windows. Gardens show marigolds, petunias, geraniums and gladioli. Polychromed, cast concrete ducks, geese, calves, rabbits and deer are frozen in their march across many of the watered lawns. At night multi-coloured patio lights reflect rainbows on the hard smooth skins of these static menageries.

There are children on bicycles, mothers and babies, half-ton trucks, station wagons, the occasional large four-door hauling an inboard behind it. It's a nice town.

THE CHARACTERS: First, two men talking together. One of them, always referred to by a single name which, it turns out, is his surname, owns the town's only hardware store. He is maybe five foot ten and thin and he hunches toward whomever he faces giving the impression of being a taller man stooping to listen. He has sallow skin and dark pigment appears to have sifted into the hollows under his eyes, the creases that follow from either side of his nose to his jaw and the lines on his cheeks which might have been dimples when he was younger and fuller-faced. His hair covers his head but it's fine and without lustre, the colour of a dirt road. He wears it short and parted on one side, partially covering his forehead. His eyes are dark and worried and his speech and gestures are slow and spare.

His companion is a short man. He owns a car dealership, has for years. Now it's run by his two sons, and he's prepared, at any time, to visit. He has a smooth head with a close-cut fringe of hair which runs neatly in a half-circle from one ear to the other in a band, like a headset that has slipped back. His face is round and plump and his stocky body carries extra weight. He has a broad smile which displays short, widely-spaced strong-looking teeth. The gaps make his grin mildly sinister. On his face are several moles, like small round beach pebbles held under the surface by his unlined, opaque skin. He has been a successful businessman and can be serious or discreet as the situation requires.

Then, Stella Gorenko, who wouldn't have been more than five two. Her body was solid and undifferentiated, that is, a body seemingly without the dip of a waist or a curved hip. As a girl she may have been different. Her legs no one could comment on; she always wore a loose old pair of her husband's trousers. The skin on her fleshy arms was pink and mottled. She had an oblong face with a square jaw which was, nonetheless, not unfeminine, plain brown eyes set close together like a small brown bear, a broken front tooth, a missing front tooth and an unselfconscious smile. Her hair was an even mix of brown and grey. Once a year she gave herself a strong permanent wave and she held the tightly curled hair off her face with two hairpins, one for each side. The barber who cut her husband's hair trimmed hers three times each year. She and her husband would drive into town together, a little shy, like kids, on those occasions.

Also, Magda Gorenko, who was Stella Gorenko's only child. She grew taller than her mother by one inch and was thin enough so that the tendons and bones and veins that ran the length of her inner arms were visible like fine stretched ropes. She had small nervous hands with painted nails, which was possible because she had work in an office in the city. The skin on her face was pink and her hair was the yellow colour of a canola field in flower. She wore narrow black skirts or black slacks with a wide belt. Her eyes were small and dark and she came to her mother's garden farm just outside town as infrequently as she could manage.

BACKGROUND: When the Gorenkos moved to town, Mr. Gorenko was already suffering shortness of breath and he often had pain in one leg when he stood too long. The doctors told him it was his heart and that he'd best take it easy. They bought three acres along the highway that ran west of town. On the property was a small low house with three rooms, a slanted roof and no basement. Also two small outbuildings. At the time, there was a pump but no indoor plumbing.

The Gorenkos put their place in shape, insulating the low-ceilinged house, putting down new, patterned linoleum throughout with plans to introduce plumbing as soon as they were able, which plan they implemented four years after moving in. All the work they did themselves as Mr. Gorenko was handy and skilled in rough work if not in fine finishing.

He did similar work around town to supplement a pension.

Stella Gorenko turned a garden which she expanded each year. Along with vegetables she put in raspberry canes. She cleaned for the summer people and let it be known that she had vegetables and raspberries for sale. Mr. Gorenko drove her to each job and when asked, she would bring with her first peas, wax beans, then carrots and later in the season tomatoes and corn. By mid-July she had raspberries.

When Mr. Gorenko died the car was sold and she stopped cleaning. Summer people could still buy her vegetables and raspberries. It was necessary to bring your own containers. Occasionally Magda would be there, stepping from the kitchen, the screen door banging behind her, a patchy dog at her feet. She was always dressed in city clothes.

DIALOGUE: 'Didya know Mrs. Gorenko, Stella Gorenko?'
'Sure.'
'Didn't see her so much these past years. You knew her?'
'Sure. Came in from time to time with her husband. Bought linoleum off me some years back.'
'Didya hear she died last week? Passed on.'
'Oh yah? Sick, eh?'
'Not that I heard.'
'Oh? What then?'
'I figure tired. Always worked hard and these last years on her own. Only the one kid, that thin girl, lived in the city. She was alone out there in that little house for years. No grandchildren, neither.'
'The girl never married?'
'Oh, she was married, all right. Some slick guy from the city, with a fancy car. No kids, though. Too thin, I figure. Came to buy a car this one time. Came to my lot. Figured we were country, wouldn't know the price of things. Looked and talked and bargained. Didn't buy nothing, though. Hot and

cold he was with his talk. Big guy with a big ring on his pinky. No digging in the garden for him. Poor lady.'

'His wife?'

'Naw. Stella Gorenko. Bet Fancy liked her peas and corn just fine. Bet he never dug a potato in his life. Not with a ring on his pinky and her alone there for years. You gonna have pie with that? Lemon's good here. Geez, I'm glad for my boys. No grandchildren, this one thin daughter always looking unhappy. Who's to remember Stella? Who's gonna think of her now?'

'It's like that, I guess.'

'Worked all those years in that garden. What good times did they ever have? Never saw her come into town dressed up. Never saw their yard full of cars for a party. Who's gonna speak for her now? Who's gonna say she was ever even here, I tell you. She came and worked and went, dust to dust. A pity. No one'll even remember five, ten years from now. Just who is there to speak for her, I ask you?'

'Me.'

'What?'

'Me. I'd say I was there the odd time to drop off things she'd order. Even once or twice in winter. In her front room she had a plant hanging from a hook in the ceiling near the window by the TV. Never saw it, it wasn't blooming. Covered in flowers. Blue flowers. Blue like before rain. Deep blue with white centres. The petals like blue stars. I asked her, what's it called? She told me Star of Bethlehem. Never seen another one. Never seen it not blooming. Never seen a plant like that, flowers trailing almost to the floor. I'm gonna remember that. How she could grow a plant I never seen anywheres else. I'm gonna remember that.'

2. Laurence, Whatever Happened to Him

THE SETTING: Same small prairie town. The business street by which most people enter from the highway runs past the hardware, the bakery, the dairy where it was possible to also get ice cream in a cone, the furniture store, the hotel, the small new supermarket, the real estate office with the denturist in the back, a clothing store – men's, ladies' and children's – and the post office. Follow the street to its end and you find your car nosing the dock. To the left and right are buildings relating to the business of fish. There's a large brick-red, high-roofed structure – a plant for filleting and packing the fish to be shipped to buyers in the city. Women in heavy red long-sleeved cover-alls and black rubber boots, their hair covered by white kerchiefs, work in this building, its wet concrete floor and proximity to the lake keeping it cool even in August.

The dock is built of heavy timber, thick boards tarred against water damage. The lips of the pier running its full length on both sides, two hundred feet out into the lake and angling back to shore by 30 degrees to form a harbour, are thick as railway ties. It's on these that casual fishermen casting lines rest or tie their tackle, it's against this sun-warmed edge they press their backs when they pause for lunch, or kids in knots settle, tough and unmindful, their bony adolescent legs stretched on the slivery boards. Boats, the open ones commercial fishermen use for setting and collecting nets and the larger ones with spare upright wooden cabins and holds for fish storage, tie up in the harbour along its protected arm or beside the fish plant's loading wharf.

Most of the casual fishing is done along the outer length of the pier or at its very farthest end, the conviction among fishermen being two things – no point fishing in the harbour because: one, the boats moving in and out of the harbour disturb the fish so they don't gather there, and two, minnows flick in silver schools and the fish which may swim there in spite of the boats have sufficient to eat and wouldn't nibble your salted dead bait minnow anyway.

THE CHARACTERS: All the people, mostly men, who are old enough to have worked at a job for at least fifteen years who fish on the outside length of this pier, and specifically two who are near retirement, one of whom was born in this prairie fish town, and a third man, who is younger and has never worked.

Two men are standing on the pier. Since they can remember coming to fish each has found the other and by agreement has chosen a spot midway down the outside edge facing north. It's early in the season and the sun is consistent, reliable. They can just feel the warm planks through the soles of their shoes. The heat raises a scent of tar and fish caught and laid briefly down for securing on a stringer. The occasional translucent scale, lost in the flash of a tail, glints silver on the boards like tiny flecks of mica, more mineral than animal. Salt crystals from the minnows packed in cardboard cups show white. Otherwise the surface of the dock is pure and certified clean by the relentless wash of the bleaching sun.

The younger of the two likes a rod and reel, likes the whiz of casting out, the click when the string has run as far as it was set, the soft twang the pale green fibreglass rod makes when it bows and the weights hit the water, the handy chrome reel that winds the line and never tangles and the way it feels resting against his shoulder when he heads for home.

The older man wasn't born in the town but came as a young man looking for work on a farm. He prefers to keep things simple. He has three set-ups all of his own design and all the same. A length of wood maybe an inch thick, an inch and a half across and eight or nine inches long, painted and smoothed, the colour hand-rubbed through use to the subtleness of a fourteenth-century fresco, muted green, a true blue like the Player's cigarette tin and white like whole milk. Wound around each and humping in the middle are green cotton test fishing line, torpedo-shaped lead weights, dark and cold and heavy, three on each line spaced out, and two silver hooks between. To watch him throw his lines is to see Greek men dance. He gauges how far down the fish are swimming; he unwinds that much string. It pools in orderly circles at his feet; he tucks the remaining line on the stick under his shoe. He steps back on the other foot. He holds his arms away from his body and to one side. One hand pinches the line just above the highest lead weight. The other is four feet along the string and shoulder height. He rocks forward on the foot securing his set and back on the other, knees flexed, forward and back, his arms rocking too, the bait and weights swinging, the string between his two hands looped and easy, and when the rocking has wound his own personal gears sufficient to get the line where it needs to go, he lets it out over the lake. Then it descends slowly enough into the sand-opaque water for him to watch it disappear under the surface. Or using a one-handed technique and only when the dock is free of walkers, he'll swing five feet of line with hooks and sinkers in a circle over his head, his other hand on one hip and then the line is a lariat and he is a fisherman cowboy before he lets it go.

The third man is much younger. It's difficult to say his age from looking. His hair is straight and dark and he uses a hair tonic so it always looks wet. He wears it longer in back than the rest of the men in town. He combs it straight back from his forehead and maybe it has receded a little but you couldn't tell his age from that or from his face which is puffy and therefore unlined. Nor from his physique because, while of average height and weight the tone is slack; he has a soft girth around the middle like flesh slid off his chest and shoulders and settled, caught in his trousers. Unusual for the time and unmindful of the season, he always wears a black shirt.

Sometimes, when you looked at his head it seemed just the smallest bit unusual, not so noticeable that you could say right off, but maybe from the forehead down it was a little flat and maybe the back wasn't quite rounded enough. His eyes were brown but if you went to describe them you found yourself thinking the colour of liver. His skin was light.

His father owned the drugstore and was the pharmacist too and this set him apart because other than the doctor you couldn't think who else had graduated from university and being the only druggist in the area he was assumed to be well off. The primary indicator of this was his car – a big white four-door sedan with a red leather interior. On the street its boat-like width occupied more than its one lane. It was the only one like it in town and was as easily identifiable as a portrait photograph. Laurence drove the car which belonged to his father. Maybe he had a driver's licence, maybe he didn't. No one knew for sure. He didn't drive the car often.

While no one commented on it and no one could really even put words to it, it was like Laurence smelled of pee. That is; out of line as this sounds, he seemed to have an odour about him which no one ever really smelled but which drew the young kids in town to follow him in a pack like he was a gamy head dog. It was always the younger kids and he liked them and was nice enough to them if they didn't pester him and there was nothing off or odd about it except that he was never seen with anyone else, had no friends his own age, whatever that might be.

DIALOGUE: 'Seen Laurence lately?'

'Nope.'

'Been a while he's turned up with his rig and his questions. Where'd he be I wonder? That boy's a pest for sure, always borrowing. Borrowing – he never returned none of what he borrowed. Never meant to, not that he was trying to take advantage – he just needed something he didn't have, you had it, he'd ask. There were days when he'd drive me off the pier with his noise. I come here for some quiet and to do a little thinking and there he'd be. "Sir, could I borrow a minnow, sir? Sir, do you have an extra one of them lead sinkers, sir. Sir, can I borrow a knife to cut my line, it's all tangled, sir. Can I borrow a coupla hooks off you sir so's I can set up again. Whaddya catch sir, whaddya get? Hey, lookat your stringer, eh, lookat all them fish, sir." He'd go on talking and yapping and standing practically right up against you to do it. Couldn't overlook him, for sure. His folks worked hard teaching him manners but they couldn't teach him sense. Kid never caught a fish I saw, always jerking his line in and out of the water, casting and winding and casting and winding and he wasn't no fly fisherman looking for trout, not here in this lake. No. He just couldn't stay still. How many times we gave him fish off our stringers to take home and him pleased like he caught them himself. Jeez, what a thing though. Doctors found some growth on his brain when he was just a little tyke, wasn't even talking yet. Don't know what made his folks think there could be something wrong with his head. Maybe he was late walking. This was just afters I got here and I only heard talk. Opened up his flat head – maybe wasn't flat before they did it. Opened up his head like it was some musk melon. Did something in there, who knows. So he's just this big kid now but looks like a grown man more or less. I mean, you look at him and his face is awful soft for a man and kind of dishy and flat, scooped-out, kind of. I don't know; there's something, but like I said, his folks have done a good job. He's no trouble, he has his manners, taught him to dress himself properly and all and even to drive a car so long as he stays off the highway. He makes his way okay in this town. Wouldn't do half so well in some bigger place but then this is his home and we all know him, kind of look out for him.

'Haven't seen him for some time now, as I think of it. Wonder what he's up to?'

'They sent him away two weeks back it was, I guess.'

'What do you mean, sent him away? Who did, where?'

'His folks. Couldn't take no chances with his father being the druggist and on town council, maybe even thinking of running for mayor. Sent him away.'

'But why?'

'I've been thinking about it. Laurence in his dad's big car, his elbow out the open window, driving with one hand. Him in his black shirt and his slick black hair long in back like some of them rock n' roll singers. That big white car all red and fancy inside and Laurence with the windows down and the radio up and dark glasses covering those liver eyes, him cruising up the street slow and loud.

'One of the three girls, sisters – their family has the small place with all them old cars in the yard on the west side of town – wouldn't call her the prettiest girl around, anyways she gets into the big white car early one evening. Everybody saw her, was right downtown just up the street here. She's walking near the post office is what I heard. He slows down, pulls over, leaning on his elbow out the window; she stands there on the curb not three feet from the car. He leans out, she looks inside, sees the red leather interior, hears the rock n' roll, goes round to the passenger's side, opens that big heavy door, gets in, slams it behind her and they drive off, straight down the street right to the end and turn onto the highway heading north. That's what I heard.'

'So what then?'

'I didn't hear no more. For all's I know maybe she wasn't even late getting home. Coupla days later I heard they sent him off to an uncle. Somewhere's in Saskatchewan. Guess that'll be it for his fishing.'

3. Sisters

THE SETTING: The prairie town by the flat-bottomed lake. The general store on the main street which runs parallel to the lake. The store is located on the east side of the street facing the lake and occupies a large corner lot. Anyone standing in front of the store by its northeast wall can see the lake when it's high and can hear it without difficulty when it's wild. The store is in fact two stores and was built that way at the outset. The common wall has a doorway from which the door has been removed. The exterior is finished in grey asphalt shingles and each store has its own centrally placed set of doors, that is, a wooden door with a square window at the top and a full, wood-frame screen door. The doors and the trim around the large display windows flanking each set of doors had once been painted dark green. On each screen door, at the mid-point where the metal handle is, painted tin advertising plaques had been nailed in place; one supplied by Coca-Cola, the other indicating Export A tobacco was available inside.

The stores are built in the length and with the only windows being those at the front, the interiors are always cool and dark. Inside, both are finished the same, having oiled wooden floors and pressed tin ceilings. The store nearest the corner sells dry goods: clothing, shoes and boots, fabric by the yard, buttons, zippers, shoelaces, coarse woollen socks. Also pots, kettles, fly swatters, sieves and strainers, metal hoops with cloth bags for making jelly, sealers for preserves, coffee, crackers, boxes of tea, flour, sugar, porridge in cardboard cylinders and boxed cereal.

The adjacent store has a counter which runs half the length of one side. In front of the counter on a raised platform are red leatherette-covered stools which spin 360 degrees. Behind the counter is a mirror. In front of the mirror are the ice cream coolers. On a ledge behind the coolers are ice cream scoopers soaking upside down in glasses of water, machines with tall metal cups for preparing milkshakes, flavoured syrups and thick-stemmed glasses in different sizes for floats, sodas and milkshakes. From the beginning of July to the last days of August and as late as Labour Day, if the weather holds, all the stools are occupied and an extra girl is hired part time.

The syrups, the various essences for flavouring the sodas and the ice creams themselves, make the air sweet. The soft wood floor and all the cardboard signs that cover the walls, the paper goods stored in boxes behind the counter and the extras stored at the back of the store, all absorb the vanilla and chocolate and cherry, and even in the fall and all through the winter until the next summer the store is perfumed by promised treats and rewards.

Beyond the counter are four booths which are rarely used. There's a low wooden counter on the other side. Behind it is a large upright cooler for bottles of milk, cream, sour cream, butter and cottage cheese. On the counter in boxes are seasonal fruit. Long heavy bunches of bananas hang from iron hooks in the window. A knife like a small scimitar rests beneath them. Behind the bananas hangs a metal scale with a large brass pan. In the mornings the best fruit, still in the shipping boxes, is propped in the window by way of advertising. The screen door bangs all day. The store on the other side counts the summer months slow.

THE CHARACTERS: There are four, all women. Two are

sisters, two are women with husbands and children. All live in the town. The sisters are unmarried. One, the older, is a teacher. The younger is a dressmaker but more, in that she designs, as well as sews, clothes. The older sister, whose name is Clare, took her teacher's training at the normal school in the city. Nan, the younger sister, learned her craft at home from her mother and by closely following the fashion magazines Clare would send from the city. By the time they were adult women both had acquired skills by which they could support themselves if necessary.

They were small rather than short, with light-coloured hair, somewhere between brown and something lighter. Their faces were pleasant, well-shaped and regular, neither big nor small, not plain or pretty. Both had learned to use make-up in a flattering and modest manner; a little powder, a very little rouge and some lipstick in a shade of pink. They wore their hair curled, both with side parts and cut to show off their slender necks which they recognized were attractive features. They looked like sisters.

One of the married women is the same age as the sisters, in her late thirties or perhaps a little older, and was in school with them. She is fortunate to have three children, a home of which she is very proud and to which she is devoted and a husband with a good business in which there appears to be room for growth. This woman recognizes her community obligations and plays an active role in church, school and recreational projects. Her baking is much sought after for teas and sales and she is known to be generous with her time and advice if people are in difficulty.

The second married woman who lives in the small quiet town is very like the first; decent, helpful and happy.

BACKGROUND: The sisters had both lived in the city at one time. Both had returned; Clare, when she recognized that her career as a teacher could be pursued as successfully in the lake town as in the city and because the size and tempo of an urban environment didn't correspond to her own pace and scale. Nan's return to the town had been unexpected and was assumed by everyone to be temporary.

DIALOGUE: I'm phoning to tell you this because I can rely on you. I have no fondness for gossip, as you know, but before I knew it there I was hearing it all. I'd gone into the store for a float and to get out of the heat before I went home to start dinner. I'd settled myself down on the end stool as deep into the cool of the place as I could get without taking one of the booths which I've never liked anyway. I've placed my order and in front of me I've got this lovely tall glass with the cold beading into drops on the outside and the ice cream bobbing in the fizzy orange soda. Anyway, I'm about to dig in and really enjoy it when I hear voices coming from one of the booths. They're soft and it takes me a minute to recognize them, but it's the sisters, Clare and Nan. They have those cool city voices where everything is spoken very clearly, all the words with tidy endings, and like it or not, I can pick out every word. You won't tell a soul about our conversation which is why I can tell you, because neither would I.

There I sit and I'm dying to get at my float which is melting in front of me but I can't use the spoon for fear it'll knock against the glass like a bell. They're into their conversation, sure no one can hear a word and here am I hearing it all. Not that there was so much said nor so terrible either.

Nan's been back in town for a year now, more than that maybe. Went off with everyone's good wishes to open her small shop where she would sew dresses for city women with the pocket-books to pay for them. She's clever with her hands, for sure, always just so in outfits of her own design. Little enough demand for that here so good luck to her, I said.

Now she's back and the two sisters, always close, are having a heart-to-heart in one of the booths.

Clare, who was always a sensible, stalwart girl, is talking to Nan and she's urging her to leave, to go back to the city. She's telling her, working behind the soda fountain is no place for her, that there's nothing here. She tells her that in order to carry on – to wake each morning and wash and dress, to toss your head and feel your hair swing with the gesture, to fasten the buttons on your dress, to pick up your purse and gloves and move smartly out with the kind of smile that tells people, My life is just fine, thank you – to do that you have to be making choices. She tells her sister she has to move in a direction like she's on a road and she's got her compass with her in her purse, that she can't drift and waver and find herself someplace because she stumbled into it.

Now, here I am. I've ordered this orange float and the girl behind the counter who served it to me is looking at me funny because I haven't touched it. She's up at the front near the window so she can see the boys pass by and she can't hear what I'm hearing for which I have to say thank the lord. I can't use the straw because it could slurp and I'd die if they looked around the edge of the booth and saw me there, knowing I'd have heard every word they said, not that so much was actually said. It was more the tone.

Clare was really pressing Nan and I could hear Nan like a stubborn child near to tears but not letting it go. It sounded like a decision had to be taken now and she was pressing Nan to do it. What it was I don't know. She kept saying to Nan that she couldn't stay, had to go back, had to set her course, something about sighting a goal where the sky meets the edge of the prairie and heading for it in a straight line.

There's Nan in her small voice saying, What's wrong with here? and, to myself, I'm asking the same question, although you and I are unusually blessed. And she points out, quite

right, that after all Clare has come back and there's Clare saying it's different, she has her career at the school and she's
come to terms with what's possible. She tells Nan there's no
shame to changing your mind, nor any shame if someone else
does.

I hear Nan say this is different, very different, that there's
no way to explain it away, that she's too tired now to pick a
point and aim for the horizon, that she'll just stay where she
is, that it's fine. And I hear Clare saying no and the no pushes
out like it's squeezed and wouldn't you know it – along comes
this stupid, moony-eyed girl from behind the counter, pulling
herself away from her window and she picks now to come
over to me and say loudly, louder than is necessary – 'Is there
something wrong with the float, ma'am?'

The conversation in the booth stops. There's not a sound
in the place. It was like the overhead fan stopped circling, like
the screen door stopped banging and no one is ringing up
change at the register. It's the kind of silence where you're
running in a race at school on field day, you're running full
out, one leg buckles under you and you land flat on your
belly; everything goes solid black and heavy for a minute till
you can get to your knees and you know you're going to be
sick right there in front of everyone. It's suddenly quiet, like
that.

What did I do? I picked up my purse, left some silver on
the counter and got out.

4. M. Kazmariuk, Dog Catcher

THE SETTING: The prairie town by the lake. Two women in the IGA supermarket. It's an overcast day; there's no hurry to be outside. They stand in the aisle with the sugar and the Certo, the boxes of pickling spices and the rubber sealing rings. Their painted toenails show through their sandal straps and they stand at ease on the green and beige tile floor toeing the squares and sliding their fine shoes in slow geometric patterns while they talk. They're summer people.

Summer people and town people see the weather differently. For the town people dry sunny days are for gardening, farm work, reshingling, painting the fence and carpentry. For the summer people the hot clear days are idle and chores like putting up jam or trips to the laundromat or grocery shopping are saved for grey wet weather. Even an overcast day will fill the aisles of the IGA or bring people to the bakery.

THE CHARACTERS: Two women from the city who are spending the summer in the town by the lake. Both are in their mid-thirties. One has been coming to this melodic, shallow, changeable lake every summer since she was a child. She stays in the same cottage her father built, where she was a reed-thin little girl with sun-warmed brown arms and legs covered in the finest little gold hairs, where she was a bold girl with a new waist and rounding flanks that stretched the legs of the shorts she left in the dresser drawer over the winter and wore every summer but now suddenly couldn't, where she was a young woman who had regained the innocence and clarity of the very little girl she'd been and where she was now a young mother and wife and knew the town with authority and moved through its few streets with the comfort full knowledge brings.

The other woman was an acquaintance from the city. This was her first summer in the town and she was renting a cottage with which she was not entirely pleased, since its location two streets in from the lake meant that on good days she was obliged to carry one child in her arms and pull the second in the chipped red wagon that came with the cottage, packed with a beach blanket, cookies, juice, sand toys and the paperback book which she never got to read and which also came with the cottage.

Their children attended the same nursery school in the city, which was how they'd become acquainted, but their presence in the lake town was a surprise to them both when they'd met one cool day at the IGA. Since that day early in the summer they'd become close beach friends, spending most sunny days on the sand, their children all jammy and pink and warm together, spending most weekend evenings together with their husbands all pressed and cool and dressed in smart cottons, their lovely intelligent tanned thin legs showing bare and confident, one leg each the women tucked under them on the worn cottage sofas, the other swinging as free as they were.

One man who had also been a child in this prairie town but not only in the summer and who had, for at least some of his childhood and maybe for all of it, the same innocence as the young summer girl with the golden down on her brown limbs, if not her clarity, who lived now all the time at the edge of the town, summer and winter, who was also in his mid–thirties but had no children, not in nursery school or anywhere and not a wife either. Not a farm, not a business, not a boat for fishing and not a car to slick the streets.

He had an old pickup truck closed in back with a canvas curtain and a chain across the gate. He had a place where he lived with an acre or so of land. On it grew wild raspberries and nettles, purple thistle, goldenrod and willow. He would have been five foot ten or eleven. He had good thick black hair which he rarely washed, brown skin, a small straight nose, a little wide, a little small, almost no upper lip but a fuller lower lip and blue-grey eyes like Cary Grant only crazy. There was something about his carriage or maybe it was that his gait was lower behind like a jackal dog or hyena and when he moved it was unevenly in an unbalanced lope, although his legs were sound.

He wore heavy dark green cotton trousers like mechanics wear and they were as oily as if he'd worked in a garage. The legs of his trousers were unhemmed and therefore frayed and dragging. His shirt was like his trousers. He wore a belt of thick leather. A wallet stuck up from his back pocket and was secured to one belt loop by a chain which swayed and rang with his uneven movements.

BACKGROUND: The town needed someone to keep dogs off the beach; mothers were complaining, children were frightened and whining. People wearing only bathing suits and moving at their leisure along the shore barefoot were made uneasy by unaccompanied dogs.

Mike Kazmariuk didn't have a job, didn't like dogs much, had a piece of property where he could hammer together some kind of a shelter with a chain-link fence around it. The job was his. M. Kazmariuk, Dog Catcher.

DIALOGUE: 'I can't keep green grapes in the house. The kids go through them as soon as I put them out.'

'Isn't it true. But I like the children eating fruit. I encourage it.'

'Oh, I couldn't agree more. The habits you establish early stay with them for life. By the way, dinner on Saturday was lovely. I meant to call but my family came out for the day on Sunday and then yesterday was just too weird. It was the kind of day where nothing went right and I thought to myself, now why hadn't you pursued a career where you'd be cool and competent and have time for your hair and intelligent conversation with no one spilling grape juice in your lap and no one pulling at your blouse with sandy hands and not another peanut butter sandwich but of course I don't mean any of that and then there was the really perfectly creepy incident on the beach.'

'What happened? What was it? Tell me.'

'I've got jam on the stove. I'm doing strawberry now. I'll be quick because the babysitter's watching the pot for me.'

'I'm dying to know; what really weird thing could have happened out in the sun on a Monday at this lake?'

'Well, I'll tell you. I had settled the kids down at the beach after lunch. Yesterday, as you said, was a perfect day – where were you, by the way? I was wearing my red-and-white polka-dot bathing suit which I usually wear only on weekends when I've got help with the kids because the top isn't as fixed and solid as the brown one I wear all week but it was hanging on the line and I didn't bother to bring it in. I put on the red and white one and the way it fits, which of course my husband just loves, makes me feel – I don't know – a little less sure, vulnerable if I had to run. But it was a perfect day and mostly it was just me and the kids on the beach and I brought the dog, too. I hate leaving him alone in the cottage and I'm afraid to leave him tied up in the yard. The dog catcher, who I think may not be all there, has it in for him. Twice I've caught him standing at the fence looking at Sandy and Sandy who loves everybody wags his tail and smiles his dumb spaniel smile and of course, since he's a dog, he barks. The guy just looks and then he drives off in that old truck. Have you ever seen where he lives, by the way?'

'No. Have you?'

'Well, yes. I know everything about this place. I was practically raised here, remember. It's just south of town near the sewage lagoon. I think he squats there but who's going to move him off? I mean, after all, it's not exactly prime real estate. I guess he's got heating there because he doesn't move out in the winter but certainly no plumbing. I think there was an old shed on the land that he tar-papered and maybe added to. There's an over-grown gravel track that leads off the highway, some rusted stuff, cars or trucks or maybe farm equipment in his yard. I think for a while he had a sort of junkyard where he sold scrap. The area is low and swampy; I guess that's why the sewage lagoon is near there and nothing good grows, just nettles and weeds and the low willows we have everywhere. That's where he lives. And he's built this horrible little compound for the dogs he picks up. Actually I think he kidnaps or maybe it's dognaps the animals to claim the fines.'

'Have you ever been in there? Like, on his property?'

'Well, I have, actually. He got Sandy once. I had to call all over town before I found out where he was – the mayor, the Mounties. I didn't know we even had a dog catcher here. I figured the guy was still selling scrap. It was the middle of the week and I was alone with the kids. I couldn't leave Sandy there until the weekend; he could have beaten or starved him. I had no choice. I packed the kids in the car – the baby was only five months at the time, and off we went. We pull into this guy's yard – his name is Mike, you know – and he comes out hitching his trousers. Sandy is in the pen, spots us and starts yelping and jumping up and down. The guy looks at me, one kid on my hip, the other hanging onto my skirt and stupidly I'm wearing sandals and I'm picking my way over the weeds and scrub and he just looks. What did he think I was doing there, anyway? Finally he says to me, like he doesn't know – "That your dog, lady? You got proof? Got papers?"

'The kids are both crying now. The dog is hysterical on the other side of the wire pen. I said to him, and I was shaking – scared and mad – and I said to him, who the f (pardon me) travels with dog papers, give me my dog or you'll be in real trouble. Where I got the nerve I don't know. I guess we were both shocked. He opened the pen and poor Sandy ran at me. I had to pay a fine – thank God I'd remembered to bring my purse because I sure didn't want him coming to the cottage. The whole time he kept looking at me and smiling. Yuck.'

'Poor you, but what happened yesterday?'

'I'm down at the beach with the kids. We were practically the only ones there. It was lovely and quiet. The kids were playing nicely in the sand beside the blanket. Even Sandy was quiet. He'd dug himself a cool trough in the sand and he was dozing. I must have closed my eyes for a second too but I opened them with that start you get when someone's there even though you haven't heard them and there's the dog catcher in that greasy outfit he always wears – even in the heat – and he's got his hand on Sandy's collar and he says to me, "You've got no licence to have a dog on the beach, ma'am!" He says *ma'am* like that makes it official. I said to him – licence to have a dog on the beach, what are you talking about – there's no such thing. Meanwhile I'm holding up my bathing suit with one hand. The kids are frightened and they're leaning on me and he's starting to drag poor Sandy away and Sandy's yawling. Somehow I got to my feet. I said to him, one hand on that stupid suit – actually I was shouting but I felt calm – I said to him – you let go of that dog right now, immediately, you let him go or I'll kill you.

'I felt calm but I must have been crazy. What did I mean –
I would kill him? With what, a plastic sand pail or maybe the
strainer. But he did let go of the dog and he started to back
away. Then he turned and with that odd walk he has, just sort
of loped off a hundred feet or so. We watched him go and now
I was shaking. I started to pack up the kids. I wanted to be
home. Suddenly he turns around. He limps or whatever, back
to us. He stands there right at the edge of the blanket with his
wild eyes. I know he doesn't drool but he sort of looks like he
might. I mean, he's not exactly all there.

'Do you know what he said to me standing there uneven on
the edge of our beach blanket. I still can't believe it. Do you
know what he said? He said, clear as could be, "Would you
marry me. Please marry me." I couldn't believe it. I guess I
was shaking my head in disbelief without knowing I was
doing it. He looked at me. I guess he figured he'd gotten his
answer. He says, "OK, sorry," and then he just turned and
walked away, back to his truck and not another word.'

Perfect Skin

You can't always anticipate the end of something. You can't know exactly when it will stop, if it does. How can you until it does? and by then it's over. And if someone asks you much later, When did it happen? – you can't always say.

So it's been a number of years now since I've been divorced and it came to me only yesterday that two things marked the end. And the two things that marked the end – well, one was something that happened over time and the other was a single event that started and finished one day and the evening of that same day.

When I met him Simon was juicy. I'd describe him as juicy. He was in his mid-twenties. I never thought of him as short but he was, I guess. I didn't think of him as short because he was narrow and that made his proportions right. But he wasn't little either. He had good hands – clumsy, blunt-ended fingers a decent size across the knuckles. And his feet weren't tiny or narrow. 'Effete feet,' I'd say in my head, hearing a canary speaking privately to me. 'Effete feet,' I'd smile to myself and I was never drawn to men who looked as if they were wearing kid slippers even when they left for work – he wasn't one of those.

Simon's proportions were manly enough. His voice, though, was a problem. Even at its very deepest and when he had it most under control and spoke with measure, it could only be described as a tenor. Often it was a good range higher than that. When I loved him, which I certainly did, and for a very long time, I heard it velvety. I loved its ripple – and its tendency to petulance I saw as nerves, passion, intensity, commitment.

Another thing about Simon. He had perfect skin. Fine-textured, unmarked. The kind that tanned easily but always held a little rosiness. He never tanned sallow. And his skin had a slight sheen, as though he'd just come in from walking through a cloud, I loved him that much.

In the early years he had a full mouth, no disappointment there. You know yucca or maybe aloe plants – how you can snap the leaves to get a soothing balm from them and before you snap the leaf, just before it breaks you feel the juice filling the skin, pushing it smooth. His mouth was like that early on. Juicy.

Huge square teeth too. Thick. Almost not like teeth. Small spades maybe. Like those shovels you buy at Army Navy with the folding handle, for emergencies in your car. Like that but of course not green.

And his hair was very soft. Beaver under-fur with an auburn cast. Soft hair, not really like an adult's and curling on his neck at the back, like Pan, I thought. And not like an adult man's. No hair at all on his neck at the back. Just this beaver fur curling against this perfect skin on his neck.

A funny chin. Pointed but weak at the same time. Never mind. And his nose – big, long, hooked but narrow. Fine, I called it. His nose is fine not coarse and across its narrow bony ridge was stretched this unbelievable skin.

When we first met his eyes were young or maybe I was thinking of a picture I'd seen of him, when his eyes were young. Never mind.

His brow was beautiful. Clear. A well-shaped head, good forehead, that skin, and beautiful eyebrows. 'Brows,' I'd say. 'I love your beautiful eyebrows,' and I'd draw my thumbs across them.

When he spoke his mouth was juicy. Fascinated, I'd watch his teeth and his lips and listen for him to swallow. He never spat or dribbled or anything. But he was juicy. And he perspired a lot. I guess you'd say sweat but it was so specific, so localized it really was perspiration – armpits only. Never his hands or his back – just his armpits and of course I loved that too. His smell. What in all my growing-up years my mother had described as something people need instructing on, or maybe as typically 'foreign' – what she'd always guarded against – body odour – he had it. I loved it.

So you see, he *was* juicy, wasn't he? And full of ideas too, convictions, right thoughts. Like his skin which was perfect, there was no room for improvement, no need for change.

Did you know that vellum is the skin of unborn lambs? Those beautiful medieval illuminated manuscripts, those ecstatic renderings, monks alone with their own fires, drawing in ink stains, violet dye from ground mollusks, Murex, colour of kings. Gold leaf applied – touch your thumb to your brow and the sweat and oil will dampen it. Touch the thumb to the beaten, papery gold and it adheres. Press your thumb to the page and it clings. Did you know that holy records, heavenly utterings, wisdom of ages is pressed on the soft, unmarked skin of foetal lambs? Or maybe that was just for the very special volumes. Maybe finely prepared lambskin, kidskin, calfskin was the ground for that labour, was the focus for all that passion, was the surface for so much saved knowledge. Anyway, you can see that even here, in our earliest libraries, the skin is crucial.

What happened over time was that Simon wasn't so juicy any more. He had, over a period of years, slowly, gradually begun to dry up. And there were fewer ideas. The convictions, those that remained – locked fast and rusted shut and the right thoughts – I pictured it this way: in school we learned about tropisms and I understood that a plant grew toward light or water. With Simon going dry the thoughts turned away and leaned to a better climate.

That perfect skin, that rosy, brown, glistening skin – if you closed your eyes and rubbed your wrist lightly across a vole's belly, that kind of soft, smooth, unmarked skin – became powdery. Moth wing dust, smudges of white chalk where he'd been sitting. Simon went dry.

I'd had an afternoon meeting away from my office and had taken my car. Late as I always was, I'd parked at a meter on the street, stuffed it full of change and run inside. Inside I forgot about outside and when I stepped out into the five o'clock light my car was gone. Towed. 'Damn,' and I suddenly felt like crying. This is stupid. I'll flag a cab, get home just as quickly, still prepare dinner and when he gets home I'll tell Simon. He'll laugh because he likes to see me caught in small problems. He has a good sense of timing – no rhythm, a dreadful dancer, but a good sense of pace, a feel for the moment, a man who likes to apprehend the immanent. What he likes to do before he helps you out is wait for that fraction of time, just long enough to allow anxiety to begin to ball in your chest. Then he takes care of it all – usually with money. He pays the fine, the late fee, antes up for the repair bill, buys a new expensive thing, makes a generous donation – some solution, some cure, which always needs money.

While I fussed with dinner he called around to find out which lot the car had been towed to. I'm funny about my car. I was like that about my bicycle too. It was something Simon couldn't understand but I was never interested in replacing a car I'd driven for a while. For me it was like a pet or more like a colleague – someone with whom I had a good working relationship. Mutual respect was exchanged and interestingly my cars never had mechanical problems. I'd take them in to the mechanic's spring and fall for whatever tests and treatments were necessary. I never inquired. It seemed invasive and other than that we dealt with each other professionally. *Quid pro quo.*

From the kitchen I could hear Simon noting the location. His voice was high. He was cowed by anyone in a uniform and he had called a district police station for information.

'Shit,' he said, coming into the kitchen. 'It's way out in the north end. Why do they do that?'

'Look,' I said. 'We'll eat quickly. Supper's ready and then we can whip out there. We'll be back in less than an hour. I'll do the dishes when we get back.'

I thought of my car, my ideally suburban, wood-grain panelled station wagon hoisted on a winch, hooked through the lip like a big fish, the dirt-covered under-workings exposed and I felt shame.

In the time it had taken to eat supper the weather had changed. It was cold and what had looked like mist or fine drizzle was an icy slush now. The few yellow leaves that had held to the branches were worked off by the wind. Like sharp flakes of yellow vinyl, they slapped at my face as I squeezed between Simon's car and the fence.

'Close the door. It's wet,' he said. There was a thin sheet of black ice on the windshield and we sat with the car idling waiting for the defroster to work. Every so often Simon would flick the wipers across the glass and a small piece of ice would slide off. Each time, he would touch the roof of his mouth with his tongue making a short, irritated click. Finally enough of the window had cleared on his side and he backed quickly out of the driveway.

There had been a time when being alone in a dark car, removed from children, the phone, work, other people, was an opportunity we'd relish. I remember the giddy feeling, like we'd put one over on someone, escaping alone. God, we'd enjoyed our own company. Tell me some thoughts, Simon, I'd say, and he'd talk about holes in the system where people weren't being properly cared for and he'd fill those holes and I was so proud. *And tell me some more. What else are you doing that's good, special, brave.* He would tell me and I'd watch his mouth and sometimes touch his hair, stroke his head from the crown to the smooth, hairless nape, noting his perfect skin, checking on it, monitoring its colour and gloss as a measure of his health. His custodian, his minder.

It's hard to know when it was that I recognized the stories he told weren't about himself. It wasn't that they weren't true. I couldn't fault him there. It's just that *he* wasn't doing those things. It was other people who were being brave and good and right or if it wasn't other people – well – it wasn't him either.

Simon drove fast through the centre of the city, turning off into an area I didn't know. Small houses sitting close to the street, little squares of garden between them and the side-walk, few lights, no foot traffic. Then warehouses, garages, cinder lots with two or three trucks sitting on them.

We crossed some tracks and for a second the rubber tires on wooden planking sounded soft and intimate. I don't know why, but I thought, There's still time to turn around. Let's not go through with this. We don't have to do this. And there was panic in my throat. I remembered the feeling from before. The first time I'd left my newborn with a baby-sitter I knew God would strike me down, the house would burn, the sitter would kidnap the baby, run off. We'd come home to find an empty crib, a window thrown open, the curtains blowing.

'Simon? Is this okay?'

'What. Is what okay? What are you talking about?'

'We're going to pick up my car. You'll pay the fine and then we're going home, right?'

'Of course,' he said. 'What do you think?'

I don't know what I was thinking.

He pulled left into a driveway and stopped. There was a small, two-storey building, a factory or something. It was dark but I had a sense of smoke stacks and unused mechanical parts. A dog barked. Behind the building was a lot with smashed cars and whole cars and trucks jumbled all over and behind the lot was a river or a lake or a swamp or a chasm. This was land's end where the earth dropped off. This was no place. There were no lights, no signs either.

We honked. No one came out.

'Can you see your car?' Simon asked.

'No. It's not here.'

'Of course it's here,' he said irritably. 'This is where they said. We'll drive through.'

Then, 'There it is,' and pleasure rushed through me. We'd found it. It was all right and I'd come for it.

'What do we do now, Simon? Is this where we pay?'

'Get in it. There's no one here.'

'But don't we have to pay?' I could tell Simon thought I was whining. 'Isn't there a fine? They must have the licence number. We can't just drive off,' and I had that sense of curtains blowing at an open window.

'Look,' he said slowly, as if he were speaking to someone who was simple or uncooperative, 'you can't be accused of stealing what's already yours. Get in. Let's go.'

Maybe he was right. I had the keys. I'd paid the insurance. My licence was current. Sure, he was right.

The car had been in the lot since late afternoon. The ice on the windshield was thick. 'Simon, I can't see. I have to scrape this off.'

'No,' and I thought I heard him stamp his foot. 'We can't wait here. I'll drive first. You can follow me. You'll see my tail lights. There's no traffic. Come on,' and he drove out of the lot and onto the street.

I could follow or I could stay. It occurred to me that since we'd been married this was probably the first time I'd had to make a choice of any kind.

For his mouth which had been full and luscious, for the soft beaver fur hair, for the memory of that perfect dewy skin I pulled in behind him. Blind. I'm blind. I'm blind inside the space between me and the glass and blind I drove slowly forward.

We couldn't have driven more than a block when a truck with a winch and orange flashing lights pulled tight up behind me, honking. Then a voice on a speaker said, 'Pull over. We've called the police.'

Simon kept driving. *Can't he see?* I couldn't see in front, only behind. Simon had picked up speed. *I can't see.* The truck pulled out and came up beside me. 'Pull over. We've called the police.'

'Simon!' and I leaned on my horn. 'Simon!'

The tow truck wedged me against the curb. I couldn't move. A big man leaned across my hood. Another one stood at the door on my side.

Simon finally stopped, backed up to where we were, left his car idling and got out. He paid no attention to the two men. He walked over to me and stood there for a second in his leather windbreaker. His neck, I noticed, was very thin and I hadn't remembered its being so long. It looked bare. I thought to myself, 'In the winter his fur will come in, he'll get his winter coat.' He stood there and he was mad. He was angry with me.

'Why did you stop?' he said.

'Simon, I couldn't see and these men have a big truck and I can't move my car. They've called the police.'

One of the men reached into my car and pulled the keys out of the ignition. He told me to get into his truck and handed my keys over to the other man.

'He'll drive your car back to the lot. You,' he said to Simon, 'you follow us.'

Simon paid the fine. The police didn't come. They gave me back my keys and I got into my car. The windshield had cleared and I drove home on my own.

I'd said earlier – there was something that had happened over time and something that happened one day and the evening of that same day. I saw it as the end.

Turtles Scupping Toward the Sea
with Grace

'**M**asticate. Do you know the word? Do you know what it means? It means to chew, to grind up your food, to chew it up. I love words. You know that? I love to use words, a new one every day, a word I haven't used before.'

She lay on a chaise on the terracotta patio in the room above the voice that defined, in relished detail, the meaning and use of the new word for his silent listener and for her, who had become an eavesdropper and an unwilling party to self-congratulatory instruction on improving and expanding a vocabulary one word at a time, one day at a time.

She waited. The other party, the listener, so far silent, would say ... There was a gap, then a voice, a female voice in a soft whine of sound but nothing she could distinguish, and then silence. Beat – beat – beat she thrummed on the towel draped over the chaise. Now it's his turn. She could hear his voice with its distinctive hoarseness, like he'd been shouting encouragement and instructions from the sidelines but he must have stepped to the back of the patio because she couldn't pick out any words.

She had fruit and coffee the next morning on her terracotta patio. Deep pink hibiscus the colour of a yawn, some in peach, the same colour as the underside of her stretched-out foot, a pelican slanting across her square of blue on updraft, downdraft, the thunder and rustle of waves breaking and sucking back, then the heavy slide of the doors on a patio and below her again, his voice.

Today's lesson. She waited. By what word would her world grow today? How could she better understand the immediate, or the future, how could she better deal with pain or disappointment, what lustre could she apply to the surfaces around her, with what new tools could she measure pleasure? Please. Today's word. Silence. Now just the sea and its song, small birds and their personal discussions, potted palm frond rustle on the patio, speechless pelicans in their stately sail.

She and Sebastian lay out on chaises, covered in sunscreen, covered by the thatch of the beach palapa. Honeymooners shrilled in the surf, the white-suited waiters whispered, Something from the bar signor?, the dry thatch chafed itself in the light wind. Sebastian read to her that Brassai wrote what Henry Miller said about being broke in Paris, so broke that he'd wait all day at La Coupole on a café-crème and a thin sandwich for someone he knew to come along and pick up his tab and they both said imagine and then she heard the dry gravel voice say, 'Put it on my tab,' and she sat up. 'Bastion,' she said (she called him her Bastion of everything), 'Bastion, follow that voice. That's the one, the man with the vocabulary, my linguist, my patio etymologist.'

They looked around them at all the unremarkable people who had managed the fare for a holiday in this beautiful resort; the people who came on packages, the people who jetted in from Mexico City for the weekend, the couples just married or almost married or would-be married, the unmatched couples put together from other couples – old guy, young mate – the guys with scars down their middle like zippers who said not me, never again, I'm gonna live now, and their wives who would never be easy again and plain couples who'd promised themselves a trip to remember and brought their own towels not knowing what to expect and the occasional couple from Europe, Germany, maybe France who'd come such a very long way for the exotic and new to the New World with their solid good sandals and soft upper arms, but they couldn't find him, the man with the words, her virtual literal man.

'I'm all eyes,' she said.

'Use your ears,' he said and she looked around her, listening.

Next morning she could barely eat her fresh fruit and yoghurt. Come on, she urged, let's have it, give us another and through the tropical bird clack and the breathy sound of the hibiscus opening around her, discernible through the brush of the bougainvillaea petals pushed by the wind across the unglazed tiles of the patio, she heard him.

'Gustatory. I bet you think it has to do with wind, gusts of wind.'

The murmured response drifted up, high and thin and scattered before it reached her ears.

'It's nothing to do with wind at all, it's about food and eating with pleasure like I'm going to do with every damn thing I eat for the rest of my life, every peach, every whole wheat cracker, each cup of coffee, the chicken, the fish, all the lean cuisine a guy like me should eat.'

'Murmur, murmur,' came the reply from below, and no more.

'We have a clue to his identity,' she said when she joined Sebastian on the beach. 'He's eating lean, watching his diet.'

'Okay,' Sebastian answered. 'That'll help. It means he's either fat or thin or he's achieved his ideal weight and he's neither fat nor thin. Or, further to your theory that this piece of information could help in any way identify your word lister, we could hang around the snack bar and listen in on lunch orders. The guy who orders the burger, hold-the-mayo, or scoops the guacamole with a spoon, eschewing (there's a good one) the fried taco chips or any one of the guys ordering his shrimps grilled instead of breaded – he's it. Or, maybe he sent his wife to order so we listen at the bar for an inaudible murmur or maybe she's emboldened (there's another dandy) as soon as she's out of his sphere and she speaks a firm and clipped loud tongue and she's ordering extra mayo to do him in so she doesn't ever have to learn another polysyllabic, no–longer–in–use–by–contemporary–speakers–of–English word ever again. We'll need a new clue, something that narrows things just a little.'

'Okay,' she said, undaunted, and, on a holiday, otherwise unengaged. 'This beats crosswords. Why would he be eating lean and savouring every peach, this guy's not Prufrock, he's resolute. Remember he said he was going to savour every-thing he ate for the rest of his life? Listen here, Watson, there's more going on than a guy making a declarative super-lative. He put "life" in there, put in "for the rest of my life", because he's had to consider that his could just be finite. Now why would a guy with a voice powerful and abrasive enough to plane raw cedar boards even think, in a luscious and costly location like this, that he has to consider anything as unpleas-ant and insulting as his own death?' She waited.

'Bastion, you with me?'

'Right,' he said, lifting briefly out of the tropical torpor they'd come for. 'My turn. I'm following. I'm with you, just a little behind. Okay, why?'

'Because he's faced death and since he's still here, still alive, he's faced it down, made it back off, but he knows it's out there, way out, a tiny speck on his horizon, a fly speck, a dot like the cucaracha poop we find on the patio every morn-ing, a little black dot of shit. It's out there – his death.'

'Love, that's morbid. You're really embracing all this Day of the Dead stuff, aren't you. Any poop on my horizon? Wait, forget I asked.'

'Bastion, who are we seeing here other than honeymooners, local jet-setters and folks like us? We're seeing a lot of grey-haired guys with tanned slopy bodies sucking in their gut and pounding the shore up and back on their thin legs, one end of the beach to the other, either alone or with a young partner for fresh blood, or with worried wives with loose legs – poor souls, time's so mean to women – marching for their lives. At least sixty percent of these guys have scars down their front. Note – the scars come in a variety of configurations from under the ear, across to the space between the collar bones, down the chest to the shorts, the trail disappears here but picks up at the leg of the shorts and carries on down the inside of the thigh, up over the hump of the fleshy part of the inside of the knee and down to the calf. Or, there's the seam that's just from the breastbone to the gut with scars in pairs on either side that look like clips or staples, the kind Elsa Lanchester held dear, she of the first frizzed coif, or....'

'Stop, stop,' said Sebastian weakly, his voice muffled and filtered through the thick towel against which his ruddy firm cheek lay. 'I've got the picture. Open heart surgery.'

'Precisely, Watson. You're learning. The guy has faced death and with the help of a team of the best heart surgeons, the health insurance he was clever enough and rich enough to buy, and his own indomitable will and courage and the support of his family, colleagues and friends, he's here today to tell you he's got it licked. Henceforth, and after having drifted out of the anesthetic to see his surgeon give him the thumbs up, he's going to live, really live, I'll tell you, every sweet moment pendulous with promise, with meaning – which makes perfect sense of his obsession with definitions.' She lay back against her chaise, exhausted.

'Holmes, you've done it again. Secured your place in the firmament of genius. You're right. The field narrows. The man we're seeking has: a) a loud, irritating or irritated voice,

b) a notable scar, c) a female companion of undetermined or indeterminate age with either a tiny voice or a cowed demeanour when in his company. We're closing in.'

'The thing is,' she said, 'the wives don't get a second chance, a new or refurbished heart, a little machine to keep them rhythmic. They never see the flare of white light that beckons and from which they're pulled back just before the embrace. Their patient domestic souls aren't washed with the equivalent of a celestial Visine to open anew their eyes to the light and clear day, the true meaning. While their husbands have had their chainmail seared down the middle with an acetylene torch, have laid down their lance and sword, have pastured their steed and gone forth with the ultimate courage, ungirded and alone, the wife wrings her hands in the hospital's airless waiting room reserved for close family, green and sallow under the thin light, mouth like ashes, sleepless, frightened, considering for probably the first time whether the mortgage is secured, is there insurance, how will she live, and furtive with these thoughts which show her to be faithless and unworthy. He, for his part, lies bathed in a blaze of light and millions of dollars of training and technology and years of research and practice have conjoined to focus on his pale chest, pale noble lion. He'll pull through with this entire team cheering on his side. She, for her part, will have dragged through on her own steam and will later bring, for his favoured glance and anointing approval: his specs, newly minted magazines, a Dixie cup of vanilla ice cream, his own preferred freshly laundered and pressed shorty pyjamas. God, it's the women who are really chewed and beaten. Shit. It's always the women.'

'Well, I'll bear your sympathetic position in mind when I next consider eating the fat around the lamb chop and I'll go instead, for poached tuna on a bed of lightly toasted poplar shavings.'

'Oh, Bastion, that would never happen to either of us, especially if lamb chop remains a term of endearment and not a menu item. Now we look and listen – scars and a voice like stones in a barrel.'

She closed her eyes, he kissed her lips and rubbed sunscreen on her legs and feet, especially the soft white between her toes and she dozed and drifted in air as warm as a bath. Waves and their far-off breaking, rush and soap-foam receding were a murmur in the theatre of her mind where Miss Thomas, her sewing teacher, bent over her chair, took the square of fabric from her hands and with a straight pin picked out the stitches she'd knotted to mimic a buttonhole. A loop and then through and pull it in place, a loop and then through and pull it in place, a loop and then through. They joined hands, she with Miss Thomas, and they moved in the aisles between the tables gathering girls as they went and each girl straightened and ceased squinting and left behind her grimy square of sewing and they dipped like swallows to the vixen song, a loop and then through and pull it in place, their young voices soft and high with the verse. Oh, murmur, murmur.

She sat up. Not his voice. Hers, soft and slow and teary like a child past her nap on a very hot day. She saw no one before her uttering those sounds. She swivelled on her chaise and there, six or seven feet beyond was the retreating, pale and rounded back of a woman. Over her shoulders like a trail of luminous soap bubbles breaking in the air were the sounds she'd been tracking. 'Murmur, murmur.'

'It's them. Did you see them? Bastion, we've found them, almost. It's them, or her, over there. I'm sure of it.'

By the time Sebastian had lifted his hat from his face and raised himself to sitting, the woman had rounded the hump of rock that shielded the stone steps to the hotel and had disappeared.

'If he was with her I didn't see him because I didn't see her

[175]

until she was some distance from me and I heard her with my eyes closed so I didn't see her until she was almost gone.'

'Too bad. With a statement like that it appears you could have used his facility with language.'

'Not at all. I'm still gathering information which will most assuredly lead us to him. I now know she's about five feet, three inches tall. She has that sugary hair, she —'

'She has what?'

'Sugary hair. You know – brown with a dusting of grey like a sugar-milk glaze on sweet rolls.'

'Right.'

'If you add almond extract it's really quite nice. She has slender legs, she's a little thick through the middle and understandably her shoulders are rounded. She was not moving with alacrity (there's one for you).'

'We're understanding that her shoulders were rounded? Is this because of the worry and pain she's suffered as a result of her husband's sighting death on the horizon?'

'Good for you, Watson. Precisely.'

'Stentorian. Today's word is stentorian. Again you could be misled. It has nothing to do with secretarial work, it means an authoritative, loud and firm voice ideal for delivering edicts and speeches.'

On her patio above him she hummed with pleasure and put down her bowl of yoghurt. For no reason at all she tiptoed across the terracotta tiles through the room and to the open door of the bathroom.

'Bastion,' she whispered behind his ear as he leaned to the mirror with a razor in his hand. 'Our word today is stentorian.'

'The next word he gives us should start with a vowel and be one that's been spoken sometime in the last seventy-five years.'

'I admire his choices,' she answered. 'He's not being dragged unwillingly into the twenty-first century; there are no sci-fi techno terms. If he saw God or someone in a blaze of light he isn't choosing spiritual words nor has he embraced science. On the other hand there's no profanity, scatology or pornography. He's a straight-ahead kind of guy and I like his turn-of-the-century track. I bet he'd like Dickens. Let's lower Dickens on a rope over the side, to his patio.'

On the small private beach with a curved shoreline no more than a quarter of a mile long, marked out and protected by nature from interlopers, with dark volcanic tumbles and hummocks of rock at either end and secured in the fine deep pink sand, stood four steel frame and vinyl mesh bins. She and Sebastian had noted them on the walk they'd taken in the early evening just after they'd arrived. She'd looked at them and thought, with their plain unfinished surfaces, how unlike anything else they seemed. At this lovely resort everything was either fresh and white, or newly-stuccoed terracotta, or enhanced with vegetation, each planting chosen for its colour or shape or height in relation to the other, the whole a carefully constructed and deceptively casual lush garden minus the serpent. If the bins were for refuse that was inconsistent. A battalion of well-shaped men in impeccable white shorts and safari jackets took orders for the bar and snacks, collected empty bottles, glasses, plates. Not so much as a plastic drinking straw fell to the sand without its being scooped and disappeared. Anyway, the bins had no bottoms. If they were for rubbish they weren't functional. They must be for damp towels. There were sufficient white towels at this beach – bath sheets, really – for Christo to have wrapped the Reichstag if he'd chosen cotton terry instead of the slick white synthetic fabric he'd used. No. Even though she did see towels draped over the side of the bins almost every day and even though there'd been the occasional crumpled Frito bag, cigarette butts and empty Evian containers and once one of those baseball caps women wear for fashion, its peak bent like a Toucan who'd suffered misfortune, the bins weren't for towels either. Towels were to be returned to the tiled station midway up the steps to the hotel, where you received a receipt indicating you'd returned the number you'd taken, which could be as many as you wanted.

When she'd sat on her chaise and looked up from her book and around at the people rigorous in their daily regimen on the wet packed sand or at the others indolent like she was and lazy or just reading or dozing or looking, she'd see those bins and be, for the moment and only very briefly, puzzled by their presence and apparent lack of utility. There was a sign on each, something haphazard and unofficial, hanging crooked and therefore inviting disregard.

At the end of maybe their third day, slowed by the heat, she'd stopped in her walk across the beach to return the towels and bent at the bin nearest the steps and straightened the sign and read:

Attention!!!

El area acordonada es un nedo con huevos de tortuga.
Favor deno tirar basura o cualquier otro objecto. Gracias.
Attention!!!
The enclosed area is a turtle nesting ground.
Please do not throw trash or any other object inside. Thank you.

Turtles nest here. It was a stunning piece of information. It was a stunning fact. On this smallish private beach which is emptied of people only between eight o'clock at night and half-past seven the next morning, over which, in a year if you added it all up, hundreds of thousands of heavy white chaises are pulled and dragged, across which thousands and thousands of pairs of feet, pedicured and polished, callused, halting, young and pudgy, old and sclerotic, brown and attentive, brown and relaxing, all kinds, all colours, all sizes, all moving at different paces, all pulled to the water, the ceaselessly moving blue and green water. And pulled there too for as long – no, much longer – the turtles, to lay their eggs, to see them hatch, to see the hatchlings pull to the water.

She thought – if the beach were raked at dusk, then if I came down at first light, if they dragged their slow heavy bodies up from the water, over the sand and located those bins and dug underneath them and settled themselves, scupping the sand with their flippers until they got it just right and quickly deposited their eggs, then covered them over and dug their way out and dragged themselves back and caught the first wave and paddled away, then I'd see the tracks.

She never made it down to the beach at first light and as fastidious as they were at the resort they didn't rake the sand every evening. Without wanting to appear that she had an unseemly interest in what most took to be containers for towels or trash, she did carefully circle each of the bins and peer in as though she'd been careless with something, but there were no signs of turtles or eggs or their ever having been there. In fact the only natural tracks she found on the beach were the three-part chevron pattern of a small sand crab taking residence in an empty shell which he hauled around with speed and grace.

'That's the ticket, Bastion,' she said to him as they sat up on the chaises looking out at the blue pearl sea. 'Grace under pressure. This guy here has it right. You shoulder your load and carry on like it's nothing. See that little crab there. He's found himself a covering someone else abandoned and while it's not a fit moulded to every nub and knot and contour of his body, not fine-cured Spanish leather riding boots made to measure so the boot becomes a second skin, he's managing just fine and is even moving at a pretty creditable clip. Admire him.'

'Well, Aesop-by-the-sea, we'll take him as the model. Sand crab's the man,' and he lay back and closed his eyes.

She continued sitting up watching the shore where people took their exercise on the hard damp sand. Each is heroic in their own way, she thought. Each of us carries a weight – well, many do, and some of us are luckier, blessed, really. The holiday had given her time to count her very good fortune. And grace is something we must, each of us, keep in mind. I admire that quality. I'll try to achieve it. But humility is also required. I'll seek after both. Maybe you can't do that. It's not, after all, like shopping for something and picking it up or studying for a degree. Also, those probably aren't qualities you identify in yourself. They're a state you somehow achieve, something you come to and others recognize.

Near one of the arms of rock that sheltered the hotel's beach stood a man with a full head of closely cut white hair and a deeply tanned body. His back was to the water and he looked up to the *palapos* set in front of the stone rise on which the hotel was built. One hand shielded his eyes as he scanned the shaded spaces. Then he must have spotted the person he was seeking and with his other arm he beckoned in quick short gestures.

She leaned forward on her chaise and turned to see who he was signalling. People moved toward the water but none, it seemed, in response to his waving. Then a woman appeared, not old but not young either. In silhouette, against the sunlight, detail was obscured but her shoulders were low, her brown hair a haze and she seemed to be moving in the sand with difficulty. At first it looked like a mannered gait, like children playing – curling the foot so the instep touched down first, then dragging it forward until the toes brushed the sand, left, right and incredibly slow and this is what the woman was doing. But she wasn't playing because the man toward whom she was moving was indicating speed and he wasn't playing.

Waiting, he'd turn his upper body and look out at the water and then turn back to see how far she'd come and little by little she was coming.

She touched his arm when she got there, he shouldered her bag and took her sandals. With her hand on his brown forearm they walked slowly along on the hard wet sand and there she moved with more ease. They were speaking to each other as they went.

The woman rose easily from her chaise and walked to the edge of the water certain that this was her couple, one patio down. She recognized his voice first, saying, '... tonight, for dinner, we'll have ...' and they passed directly in front of her. The wind threw back her soft voice, '... that will be nice.'

Now they left the hard sand and headed across the beach to the stone steps that led up to the hotel. Once again, the slow drag, so deliberate and laboured she left two shallow troughs where she'd walked. The tanned man watched her begin her ascent then he returned to the shore.

'Excuse me,' she said to him. He stopped and faced her and she could see the taut shiny seam from his neck to his chest, down his belly to his shorts.

'Excuse me,' she said. 'I think I recognize your voice. We're neighbours here, sort of. We're on the patio above you and sometimes I hear your voice. Not whole conversations,' she added hurriedly. 'This is a wonderful place for privacy. Not conversations. But you have a distinctive voice. It's lovely here, isn't it? A perfect place for a rest. So restoring. I don't mean to pry, but is your wife feeling better? I mean, is she recovering her health here?'

'It'll be a while they tell me. It's going to take some time but she'll come back. Took it hard.' He cleared his throat.

'I'm sorry. Did she have a stroke?' she asked him.

'No. Her heart's good. I'm the one with the bad heart. See this scar. A triple they did on me. Just made it. No. Her heart's good. What they say she's got is clinical depression following my near death. Happens sometimes, they tell me. Couple's close, together a long time, one of them gets sick, falters, you know, the other takes it hard. She's medicated, can hardly walk around. But that's what they say she needs.

'Quite a place here, all the birds,' he went on. 'Those pelicans, and at night we see small bats on the patio and little lizards, and on the way into town people standing by the road holding up those iguanas when you drive by. Plenty of wild life.'

'This is a turtle nesting ground too,' she wanted him to know.

He looked at her.

'Yes,' she went on. 'Those bins on the beach are for hatchling turtles.' He turned his head to follow where she was pointing.

'There's none there now. I've looked. I haven't seen them here but I've seen films on the Galápagos Islands and other films, too. I love the giant turtles. Forgive me, but when your wife was walking through the soft sand – she must be very courageous – when she was walking so slowly she was making troughs in the sand and I thought of those giant turtles dragging themselves from the sea to lay eggs in the warm sand and then pulling themselves back to the water.'

'Well,' he said. 'She won't be laying any eggs. That I can tell you,' and he hoisted his shorts and walked off along the shore with vigour.

Going Down

Just near freezing is what it is at night here in Las Vegas and being February it gets dark pretty early too. It's nice, though, the dark. Sets off the lights on all the hotels and shops and casinos and the lights make the air seem warmer. Course, the cool suits most of the women who wear fur, not that I haven't seen mink in July. Fur isn't so much a question of keeping warm out here, as how you look.

Now, if you're lonesome, which from time to time I might be, there's nothing like being out with all those lights on and jumping like they do. And also, how lonely can you be sitting in the lobby of a swank hotel with crowds of people moving in and out and some settling down where you are to rest and everyone dressed, I'll tell you. I've seen some women with more sparkle on their fingers and ears and necks than you find on a billboard out front here. And the hair curled and put up and sprayed stiff and it glittering too. High-heeled shoes in silver and the heels so thin and high and their little feet scrunched down to the toes of those things. Men like the sway women have when they teeter on those high points. Makes the stride short and the women seem busy without actually getting anywhere. I'm going to try them one day just to see.

The necklines interest me too, although not in the same way a man would be interested. It's like a contest, I figure, to see how much chest can balance on the edge of a piece of taffeta or satin or chiffon with sequins before you're over the line and into the soup. Now with the short stride and the hurrying, there's a fair bit of movement and that's putting a lot of tension on some awfully thin shoulder straps. So far, I've seen no damage. In the old days you had a fellow buying you an orchid; there's no way you could attach a flower at any location from the shoulder to the hip now. I guess corsages aren't a Las Vegas kind of gift. I like a corsage and with it, if you're asking, I'll have the transatlantic cruise, the stateroom with a fruit basket and while I don't drink it, I'd take the champagne for the look of the bottle with the foil collar and I see me in a small hat with a short veil and that coloured paper tape caught in the fox at my neck. I know classy when I see it and I have some ideas on that subject; Las Vegas – I don't see too much of it.

On those nights when I feel I could use a little company, I'll come down to one of the nice hotels. I like the ones with a good-sized lobby and arrangements of big chairs with a low table in front, set up like a living-room grouping. Some, you can order coffee or a cocktail right there in the lobby. A waiter brings it to you nice on a tray with a little napkin. Some places, you come at five and there'll be a bowl of nuts on each table. It's friendly, a nice homey touch and so long as you order a couple of drinks and you're dressed neat you can sit there the whole evening. Cheap entertainment I say, getting out to sit in a nice posh place, a drink, those nuts and all the people to watch.

Flights land all hours at the Vegas airport but it gets really heavy after six. I like to settle in to my lobby of choice around seven – makes for a nice night. It's just dark, the lights are on and showing, there's some kind of excitement at the start. The night is young, as they say.

Hotel buses, taxis, limos bring people in from the airport with their bags. The regulars, people who come all the time for the gambling, have a sleek fox-groomed look about them. They're in a hurry. They're nervous. They don't come for the shows much. They want their rooms ready and then they

[184]

want to get to the tables. Some of them leave their bag with the desk and go straight in. They almost drop their coats behind them on the carpet like big kids with one sleeve turned inside-out caught on the wrist, they're in such a hurry to play.

First-timers you can tell right away. They come in all ages. I like the honeymooners. They're the easiest to spot. First off, they're young. Their clothes are new and there's something about the way the shoulders of their coats sit, awkward and stiff, still carrying the shape of hangers or the box they were packed in, like the kids don't own them yet. Then there's the way they stand at the desk, some part always against each other, pressing hips, touching legs while they check in and sort of sneaky about it, getting away with something and not yet used to wanting each other and being able to – though today there's probably less of that. Still, there's where you'll see a corsage. Carnations or roses and some net with sparkles and him with a flower on his lapel, green wrap tape and a pin with a pearl on the end of it. Kids from the midwest.

There's the convention set. Older, wider, louder. No touching. Mother has her hair curled and it looks nice. She checks her handbag, opens it, looks inside, clicks it shut. Opens it, takes out gloves. Clicks it shut. Opens it again puts the gloves back in, clicks it shut, smiles and tucks her hand up under her husband's arm then steps back to let him take care of business at the check-in. He pats his breast pocket, pulls his shirt cuffs, shifts his tie at the knot and looks around for his wife.

These people will go to the shows and play the slots. I see them at different hotels and they're happy. They like the lights as much as I do; I could talk to them. They could sit with me for a bit and enjoy the complimentary nuts in the little dishes. But they're in a hurry, only here two days, three nights and they're not missing anything.

[185]

Some couples come alone like this young one, at least they checked in alone. They might have been here for some convention. Sometimes I know which one because it's posted on those black easel boards by the door – 'Welcome Home-Suppliers, Northern Region' or 'Midwest Trucking and Affiliates, Main Ballroom'. Then I try to figure out who came for what. This couple, it was hard to tell. They weren't honeymooners because they weren't touching. I figured they must travel some because she lets him go up to the desk and she just stands there quiet, by the bags, looking out like there's water and she's watching the sun set over it.

He's a fairly big man. Six feet, not heavy, not slim. Wearing a good suit. Short hair, light brown, must have been blond when he was a kid. He isn't one of those who pats his breast pocket or works at his tie. He knows what he put on and he's comfortable enough in it.

I'm watching this pair because they don't look like anyone else in the lobby just now and not probably yesterday or tomorrow either. He's wearing good shoes. I know shoes because my dad always owned good ones. Two pairs, brown and black. Kept them polished, pushed those wooden cones into them, said shoes told the story about the man – scuffed and down at the heel – unreliable, maybe even untrustworthy; polished and solid – well, you could say the same about the fellow wearing them. He might not have been right with that but it's made me always look at the shoes.

I can hear this fellow's voice but not what he's saying and I bet he gets what he wants when he asks. Not rude, just sure and not much room for discussion either.

She's younger and dressed like she thought they would be landing some other place. She's medium height and slim. She's got on one of those sets, ensembles they call them in the magazines. It's a coat and a dress, the same. They're a dark green wool. Looks soft. The coat's open and the dress has no collar. It's one of those loose styles that skims the hips if you're thin enough. This one stops just short of her knees. The coat has small gold buttons, which I like. She's wearing black stockings and little black pumps, almost flat. These make her look very young, also her hair-do. Well, given the curls and the spray and all the different colours you see in this town, hair-do isn't what she's got. She's just pulled her hair, which is the kind mothers would say 'brush one hundred strokes before bed', into a tail behind one ear and tied it with a wide black ribbon, but not just black. Here's this kid and I'd bet you dollars-to-doughnuts she's the only woman or girl wearing a polka-dot ribbon in Las Vegas, ever. However, I'd say it looks very nice and her hair is shiny and dark, as are her eyes.

She's got her gloves in one hand and I see a plain gold band, no sparkles. He finishes at the desk and comes up behind her, takes her elbow firmly, like a pinch and she comes off the sunset on the water with a little jump and moves forward with him toward the elevator. I haven't heard her voice.

I'd be curious to know who they are and why they're here. Like I said, they checked in alone but this being a nicer hotel, real posh, maybe the convention's somewhere else and that's where the others are.

Well, it's been a nice evening, lots to look at and this young couple has me wondering, food for thought, as they say. Time to go. Tomorrow is another day.

They walk along after the bellman who pushes their bags on a cart. He doesn't touch her now but he's still behind her and they walk like that, single file to the elevator, wait for the doors to open and they ride up in silence, the bellman holding the key, the young woman watching the light above the doors touch the numbers as they rise. Down a quiet, carpeted hall and for the moment she forgets if it's morning or evening, tries to think if she's hungry and if she is then for what, trying a catalogue of food – orange juice, muffins, tuna salad, lamb chops – to see if her response will provide a clue to the hour. Then the bellman pushes open a door and gestures them in, switches on lights, the TV, points out the bathroom, the room service menu, the ice bucket, wishes them good luck and leaves, pocketing folded bills.

She moves to the wall of drapes and can't find where they separate, struggles to part them and finds, under the brocade, a second set in an opaque rubber, thinks of hurricanes and rain falling in sheets, remembers Jamaica, thinks of gales and gusts of wet tropical air and she says to her husband, 'How thoughtful of the hotel to protect us this way. What a good idea, a second set of waterproof curtains.'

'In the desert?' he says to her. 'This is the desert, remember? Those are for the light. They keep out the light.'

And now what she wants is light and she needs to smell the air, wants to smell the night that was still and cold when they got off the plane. It was still and cold and she'd recognized the air had smelled of dust, that the cold air supported the dust and her nostrils had lifted at the corners to identify it. She'd stood at the open door of the plane on the stairs they'd wheeled up and she'd stopped to find her place. The sky beyond the terminal was tinted pink with the reflection of the city lights. In the other direction it was empty and black.

'Las Vegas is a grand place,' she'd said to him over her shoulder.

'You don't know the half of it,' he'd answered and he meant the city and the shows and the sequins and the girls who wore them and she meant the big sky and the cold air and the clean dust. Still they both were happy.

She parted the rubber drapes and pushed each half up against the walls on either side of the big glass rectangle. It was a solid piece.

'But we'll have light in the morning, first thing,' she said mostly to herself when she realized they couldn't have air.

They hung up their things. He urged her to hurry. They could see the lounge act this first night. Down the long quiet hall they went and down the elevator, just the two of them and her green coat with the small gold buttons hung in the closet behind her.

Now she wore only her green wool dress without a collar and in her hair the polka-dot ribbon she'd ironed that morning and with her bare arms and her black stockings and her shiny hair she seemed smaller and younger than anyone else up that late.

When the girls in the sequins began to take off their clothes and the music rose and the people clapped she remembered the cold air with its clean dust smell and she still held that Las Vegas was a grand place. He could have stayed on for the next act but remembered he was here for business and it had been a long day. In their room, before she turned out the lights she confirmed that both the rubber and the brocade drapes were pushed back to the wall so she'd see the light just as soon as the colours began to seep at the edges of the new day.

She knew a lot about construction. She liked the things she knew and she'd been to these conventions a few times before. Let's see; she liked the smell of tar on roads in the country, again, clean dirt; she liked gravel, and knew the different kinds by size; pea gravel – small, smooth round stones like pearl barley, the big jagged large stones which were the most desirable – yellow and damp and smelling like clay – aggregate, the mix. Good concrete, she knew, needed enough aggregate for strength and she knew slump and what that meant for testing strength. She was proud to know the terms men knew and when she said those words she thought of herself as strong and didn't know they made her seem even smaller. And how about the big machinery with children's-book names like a sheep's-foot packer and a wobbly which she could pick out at construction sites. Her husband had taught her before they were married. She'd worn short cotton dresses and bare legs in flat sandals and sometimes, late in the afternoon she'd drive to meet him where the highway met the gravel road. She'd lifted her bare brown legs high up to the step of the mixer he drove in the summers when he was off school and she'd ridden high up on the hot plastic seat with him then and he pretended to work like all the other men but his father owned most of it and after work he'd shower and go golfing.

When they married he didn't drive big trucks any more but now they went to conventions and the big trucks they saw on the convention floors were clean and new and there was no dust at all, just young women in cocktail dresses opening the big doors or leaning across the hoods to show their breasts or pointing one silver-toed, high-heeled shoe up against the big rubber tires that made her think of elephants in circuses, big and being put to the wrong use.

Her husband knew everyone at these conventions, which he sometimes attended alone, and he thought the fancy women improved the trucks and made the consideration of pre-cast or poured concrete a lot pleasanter. She, with her vocabulary knowledge of the business and her attention to such unnecessary aspects as dust and colour and clean smells and firm lines felt they took away from the dignity and seriousness of building things. Here they disagreed.

They'd walk together up and down the aisles looking at the displays and she'd take brochures from the pretty women in each booth and her husband would slap the men on their shoulders and they would do the same with him and they'd move on.

Somehow, important, solid information was being

exchanged. She could sense that and she felt it was good to be there where the things people knew later became buildings and bridges and roads.

'Say, if you like buildings and bridges you'll have to see Boulder Dam,' a man from Chicago had said to her that first morning. 'Take the lady up to see Boulder Dam, son. Rent yourself a car and make a day of it. Once you're here, it'd be a pity to miss it,' and her husband had nodded and shown his even teeth and people knew why they liked him.

And more walking up and down the rows of trucks and booths and as a souvenir someone gave her one of those metal tape measures on a tight spring, which she held in her palm until it became warm and heavy. She received a straw boater with the company's colours on the hatband, a very long pencil calibrated like a yardstick, a plastic shoehorn with a coloured felt tassel and the sales agent's name in gold letters on the spoon end, and a handful of lapel pins.

She wondered what time it was and though she'd eaten a lot of glazed cocktail wieners on toothpicks and had had a Coke and some coffee in a paper cup she was hungry and for now, as serious as she was about gathering more information and expanding her knowledge base, she was very tired and wanted to be outside in the air, whatever time it was. Parties were being arranged, room numbers exchanged, hospitality suites located.

'Make yourself pretty, darlin',' a man in a broad hat had said to her, 'and come party with us,' and she wondered hadn't she been pretty the whole day and she'd touched the crown of her shiny head and run her hand down her smooth hair to be sure.

Okay. What she'd wear was her gold sweater like a man's knitted vest and her black silk skirt and her black silk shoes with the black beads on the toes and she'd wear her hair loose and that was as pretty as she could get. So they returned to their room to wash and dress and they would eat later.

Each hospitality suite they visited, and there were three that night, was filled with the same people; she wondered, had they all moved from one hotel to the next as a unit? The spaces not filled by laughing, calling, happy people were filled with pewtery cigarette smoke so that, like she'd learned in a science class on molecular construction, no space is empty unless it's a vacuum, no space in the hospitality rooms was left unfilled either. Everyone knew everyone and they all seemed to know her too.

One room had a table set up in a corner and on it was a big black old-fashioned soup kettle filled with clam chowder. Beside it was a bowl with little crackers in the shape of fish. A cup of the soup was put in her hand and it did smell good but she was afraid the crowd would jostle her and she'd spill the soup and no one had given her a spoon and she was concerned that should she eat it her breath would smell like fish and how many more rooms did they still have to enter that evening.

She drifted with the crowd in the room, supported by the heat and the noise and the smoke and plans were made for more fun and she didn't need to think of a thing.

They'd cap off the evening at one of the big shows in one of the big hotels where a Follies from Monte Carlo was playing to packed houses. He'd promised her she'd get her dinner there and he'd moved off, back into the crowd again.

Finally it was duck with cherries in an upholstered banquette on a tiered floor, best seats in the place, and she could sit and watch and eat the sweet dark meat and feel the ice from her drink cold against her teeth and look around her with big eyes at the lights with their crystals and the women with their jewels sparking the night.

The lights went down. The tallest women she'd ever seen slid onto the stage from both sides and formed a line that shimmered. They wore brief costumes cut like swimsuits.

The taut fabric was covered in white sequins but where swim-suits would have had a scooped or v-neck there was nothing at all and the sequins, it seemed, were applied directly to the skin. The women glided slowly across the stage, their arms held away from their bodies, palms curled up. On their heads they carried elaborate white feather plumes attached to bon-nets that tied under their chins. Their eyelids glittered, their teeth reflected light. They moved slowly, carefully on very thin, high-heeled, white satin shoes. The music was quick and loud, their movements deliberate and slow, only the changing coloured lights playing over the line of dancers matched the tempo. The women moving against the music seemed to agitate the audience and they began banging the table tops rhythmically. Some men shouted 'yeah, yeah, yeah', then 'more more more' and she wondered, her mouth full of sweet flesh, looking up and around her at the audience, what they wanted more of since there appeared to be little happening on the stage – only the deliberate and steady glid-ing movements of the women, and the fast coloured lights.

Her husband sat quietly, his teeth glittering like the danc-ers'. His head moved slightly from side to side as he followed them. Then the line divided in the middle to show two other women standing still. The music stopped. At the periphery, the lights dimmed, leaving the chorus in half light. The spots, which were steady, were on the women in the middle. They looked directly at the audience. They stood quietly and for what seemed a very long time they looked out and around at the crowd, as though they were scanning for someone in particular, but their glances didn't stop anywhere. When it appeared that they'd looked fully at each face, they looked straight ahead again and the music resumed. From the silence it began like a clap of thunder, loud and quick and anxious. The two women pivoted. Now their backs were to the audi-ence. Again, ignoring the tempo, they removed the pieces of their costumes until they wore only their thin-heeled shoes and their elaborate headdresses. The lights held on their white skin. They were shapely, young. From where she sat their skin looked very smooth. Naked, like that, with the audience behind them and nothing to cover them, with the music very loud and moving faster, with the lines of the chorus dancers filling the wings, there was no exit for the two women.

She put her fork and knife down carefully on the plate, side by side, and she pushed the plate, with the mostly uneaten meat and cherries still on it, just a little away from her.

The audience recognized what was presented for them on the stage, identified the two slender creatures trapped in the lights, and once again they began to slap the table with their open palms. After some time the two lines of dancers moved slowly from the wings toward the centre of the stage and covered the two naked women, whose faces hadn't been seen again, and the curtain dropped.

'Who's for dessert?' her husband asked her as the house lights brightened a little. But she only shook her head. She shook her head and she flicked her shoulders, although no one had touched her.

This room was also filled with cigarette smoke and the smell of alcohol was very strong. Waitresses dressed like drum majorettes moved briskly around the tables carrying trays of glasses.

'I'd like to leave now,' she said to him.

He turned his head fully toward her, looked at her, turned away and said to the waitress, 'No dessert. I'll have a Scotch on the rocks. My wife will have a gin and tonic.'

She drank her gin and tonic and when the glass was emptied another one replaced it. A big band moved onto the stage where the women had been and once or twice, she wasn't sure, a man came out and stood in front of the band and told jokes. Men she'd seen earlier looking at big trucks and earth moving equipment – front-end loaders, she knew – came by their table and said hello. Some sat down, slid their arm behind her along the back of the upholstered banquette, leaned in over the table to her husband and exchanged words she didn't catch. All of this was done in plain fun and good humour she knew, and the men would laugh. She could tell they felt a closeness, like members of a fraternal order, brothers. They'd laugh but they could also be serious, these men who knew their business. Then they'd move off and others would come.

'And are you having a grand time, darlin'?' one of them asked her. 'Isn't this the best yet?'

She remembered nodding, wanting to be agreeable, then feeling dizzy, holding herself very still while the room nodded around her.

'I think I'm not well,' she said to her husband. 'We have to go.'

He smiled at her and returned to his conversation with the man who had called her darlin'.

Outside this nightclub, she told herself, is the same lovely night I stepped into when we arrived. Outside this room the air is dark and cold and holds suspended in it tiny particles of clean clean dust. She could move her arms through them like the women on the stage had done, making graceful arcs, and if the moon were shining, the dust particles would catch the light and glitter too. I could dance, she thought, I could dip and sway and turn, I could spin in the thin glittering air, but instead it was the room that was spinning and again she said 'Please, I feel very ill.'

This time her husband did stop his happy conversation. He turned his face to her. He looked directly at her, only her, and his lips were closed over his friendly teeth. He stood up, then helped her to her feet and held her firmly by the elbow.

'I'll see you guys later,' he said. 'Hold the table. I guess it's too much excitement for her.'

Wanting to give her the support she needed, he guided her very firmly by the elbow, out of the nightclub and into the foyer. Grateful that he'd finally agreed to leave and wanting to help him as much as she could, she held her arm rigid. My arm is a piston and he is the driver moving it along. We are an efficient, well-oiled machine, a team, she thought.

'That'll do for gin for you,' he said to her ear when they stood outside waiting for a taxi.

'I only had two.'

'It was more than that,' he said.

'No, I'm ill. I've caught something. I'm sick, not drunk. I can't drink. You know that.'

'No kidding,' he answered and said no more to her.

She remembered a taxi and riding with her head pressed back against the seat. She remembered the long hall and her husband hurrying her toward their room. She remembered the warm, dark room and falling onto the bed.

'You need to sleep. That's what you need. Sleep it off and don't do this again. I hate scenes. This has been very embarrassing. People were looking at you and I didn't like it.' He said all of this without raising his voice but she heard him very clearly.

'I *am* ill,' she said, trying to be as even as he. 'My chest hurts, I'm dizzy and I think I might vomit. Please call a doctor. I need a doctor.'

'Where will I find a doctor? I don't know doctors here. People come here to party and gamble. You're fine. You're just upset. I'll leave you to sleep. They're holding the table for me. I've got to get back and that's all,' and he closed the issue of conversation. He looked at her lying on the bed in her pretty clothes, her black silk shoes with the black beads on the toes, still on her feet. She looked at him standing at the foot of the bed, his body filling his well-tailored suit, his neat hair evenly clipped on his large, well-shaped head. The room was warm and quiet. If there was a bright moon in the cold, still night, neither of them had seen it.

Then, in a softened tone he said, 'Let's get you into a nightie. I'll tuck you in, baby style, right? And you'll be just fine. There's the girl.'

He helped her out of her clothes. He draped the pieces over the chair near the desk: stockings, bra and panties on top. He pulled her nightie down over her head, helped her slip her arms under the thin straps, even drew her hair back from around her hot face and with both hands stroked it into a tail for her.

'There,' he said. 'There's my good, quiet girl. Aren't you fine now, yes you are. You sleep. I'll just say good night to the guys we left at the nightclub and be back in a wink.'

His hands had been firm but careful when he'd stroked her hair and through the cloak of cigarette smoke his white shirt cuffs had still smelled the good smell of laundry. He could drive a big truck over rough roads, he could make easy conversation with all kinds of men, and he loved her. Still, she felt ill, she was frightened and she wanted a doctor.

'Okay,' he said, again impatient. 'Okay, I'll call the front desk. Maybe they have someone.'

Yes, they did have a doctor who would come to the hotel. He would have to be paid directly. He would be there within the hour. All this he repeated to her.

When she opened her eyes the man standing beside the bed looked more like the person who'd stood in front of the band telling jokes than like the round-faced pudgy man who was her doctor at home. This doctor was slender, with short grey hair and a tanned face. He wore a navy blue blazer with brass buttons and grey flannel trousers. Lying on the bed she

was well positioned to note the sharp crease in his trousers.
He wore a strong, spicy cologne.

She smiled at him and thanked him for coming and started
to explain how she was feeling but her husband began speaking and the doctor turned toward him and listened. Then he
spoke and she heard him tell her husband that this often happened; Las Vegas was exciting, there was too much to do, the
wives often overdid it – the shopping, the night life, the gambling, rich food at odd hours. This was a case of over-
excitement, nothing more. He would give her something to
help her rest and then, moderation was his advice for the rest
of their stay.

'Show me your hip,' he said to her. 'I get compliments on
my needle technique from all the stars and celebrities who
play here.' She'd have to lift her nightie to show him her hip.
She couldn't say no. There would be no more discussion; no
one wanted that. She folded back the edge of the covers into a
neat triangle. She took the hem of her fine cotton nightie in
her fingers, glad she was wearing the white one with the pink
rosebuds set into the smocking on the bodice. The air was
cold on her bare legs. I really like flowers, she'd thought. She
felt only a quick jab and then a numbness in her hip. She
heard him say 'She'll sleep now' and she remembered the
long, carpeted hallway to their room and the cool night and
home and leaving home for the airport with new clothes in
her suitcase and rushing to be ready to go and she also
remembered the television on in the bedroom while she
looked in her closet to choose what she'd bring and a man's
voice on the television urgent and frightened, interrupting,
and she remembered no, saying no, and phoning her husband
at work, to tell him come home, right away, Kennedy has been
shot, come home. Then she slept.

While she slept the drapes stayed closed. Once she woke and

the room was dark. A light showed under the bathroom door and she'd called her husband's name but there had been no one there. She'd stood up beside the bed more dizzy than she'd been in the nightclub, had swayed and staggered to the bathroom supporting herself first against the bed and then along the wall, weaving her way back to the bed where she'd fallen again into a deep sleep. Beside her, the place in the bed remained empty.

When she awoke again the lamp on the desk was on and her husband was stooping beside it, adjusting his tie in the mirror.

'Better?' he asked.

'I think I might be hungry,' she said. 'And I'm very thirsty. The room is warm.'

He picked up the phone, placed an order, instructed the front desk to let themselves into the room and told her, 'Consommé only, for you. Doctor's orders.'

He kissed her head and pushed her back against the pillows. She heard the door click shut behind him.

As they'd been directed, room service sent up a waiter who let himself in.

'Where would you like this, ma'am?' he asked and then looking quickly around the darkened room, answered himself and said, 'Right here's the spot. Eat hearty,' and placed the tray on the bed beside her where her husband would sleep.

She pushed herself up, interested to see what she'd been brought. Under a stainless steel lid was a bowl of clear dark consommé, smelling strongly of beef. Beside it, crackers in cellophane, a small pot of tea, a cup and saucer and on the saucer a wafer biscuit filled with vanilla icing. She drank half the warm, salty soup, ate her cookie and had some of the tea. Then she walked to the window, separated the curtains the width of her body and looked out into the night. She didn't know how long she'd been asleep and there was no one to ask.

She walked back to the bed, moved the tray from the bed to the desk, fixed her pillows and slept again.

'Lazy, lazy,' her husband called. 'Up you get. Two nights and a day in between is enough for you. How do you feel? Good. We're going to eat a big breakfast and then I have plans for us.'

He had a towel wrapped around his middle. She noticed the smallest bulge of flesh at his waist. He had circles under his eyes but his gestures were vigorous as he moved around the room and his voice was jolly and loud.

'Is this morning?' she asked.

'Yes, of course,' he said, and he pulled the curtains to the wall. Not sure of herself, she moved carefully from the bed to the window. She was okay. The sky was blue, Sèvres blue, she thought. The sun cast shadows in the courtyard far below. She knew, if there had been trees nearby and if the windows could have been opened, that she would have heard birds. It was that kind of morning. She was desperately thirsty and maybe hungry. What were his plans?

'We'll eat first. I've rented a car. We'll drive to Boulder Dam. That's where we'll really see a piece of construction. There's a contract I wouldn't have minded getting.'

She showered, picked out the pleated wool skirt and her blazer, like the doctor's, she thought, and in the hotel coffee shop, while they were waiting for their breakfast she asked him what he'd done while she slept.

'Missed you, of course,' he said and he winked and showed his teeth.

She found she couldn't eat much of what she'd ordered and with her coffee realized she had a headache, but she wanted no more of their dark, warm room. Being out under the porcelain sky would help a lot.

It was a nice car and they could keep the windows down. On the outskirts of the city there were gift shops, low buildings like cottages, with awnings advertising fancy jams and dates, dried fruit in baskets that could be mailed to folks back home and crates of grapefruit for shipping. She saw no citrus orchards or date palm trees. The country was flat, like at home, only here was sand instead of dark soil; then it became a little hilly and they drove through an Indian reservation. Signs offered museums and tours of authentic native villages. They drove on. The sky held its china blue. The sun through the windshield was warm. In the mirror, over her visor, she could see the clouds of dust their car turned up as it rolled neatly along. He was a good driver. Big hands. He knew what he was doing. He could drive them anywhere and get them back.

A billboard set back from the road identified the location of the dam, 'Hoover Dam, One of the World's Engineering Wonders.'

'What will there be when we get there?' she asked. 'What will we see? Is there a museum? Maybe they've published a book about the actual building, maybe the book will tell us everything,' because, as it became evident they were nearing the dam, the uniform sand colour, the lack of trees or green, the absence of any domestic activity, like houses or people or schools – all this made her uneasy. Then the asphalt road became a paved concrete street with curbs and boulevards and now on the boulevards there was close-cropped, star-tlingly green grass. Regularly spaced lanes intersected the street along which their shiny car moved. There was almost no traffic and since the road on which they were driving was set low into the ground and the cross streets climbed a slight rise on either side they could see very little around them.

'This is sort of like driving in a tunnel, but without a roof,' she said. 'Did you know I don't like tunnels, or subways?

Have I told you that?' she asked.

'You've mentioned it,' he said, 'about a hundred times.'

'How come the signs said Hoover Dam? I thought it was Boulder Dam for Boulder, Colorado. Where is everyone on such a sunny day?' she asked him.

'It's sunny because this is the desert and the sun always shines. I don't know where everyone is, working probably, and I have no idea about the name.'

He never wondered about the things she wondered about. They never asked the same questions. That's probably good, she thought. We're not the same, which is why we were drawn to each other.

'Isn't it true that they did nuclear testing in Nevada?' she asked. 'Isn't this where all the soldiers and officials watched those hydrogen bombs being set off and they were just a couple of miles from the site and they gave them dark glasses for protection? Wasn't that here?' she continued. 'Could we have made a wrong turn because this looks more like army grounds than a tourist spot? Where's the map?'

'It's fine,' he said. 'We're in the right place. Do you think the Americans would open up a radioactive area to tourists? Relax.'

'Lucky you didn't catch the same flu I had,' she said changing the subject. 'I still feel a little sick. It's good we've got the windows open. The fresh air is what I need.'

'The doctor didn't think it was flu. He said you were over-excited.'

'Well, then, why do I still feel dizzy and my stomach is unsettled. I love to travel, I'm a good traveller, you know that, and this isn't the most exciting or the most interesting place we've been. It's not even foreign, you know,' she said, defending herself.

Hoover Dam, One Mile. They passed a big sign.

'Which Hoover?' she asked.

[202]

'What do you mean, which Hoover?' He looked at her.

'The Hoover from the FBI who frightened all the actors and writers in the States who were liberals. You remember. They had hearings and some people betrayed friendships and others refused to answer and their careers were ruined. They were heroic. They all went to England and lived in exile in those jackets with the broad shoulders and everyone wore hats. My mother used to talk about it a lot. Or is it the Hoover who was President?' she finished.

'We're here,' he said, turning into a paved parking lot.

'This is Lake Mead,' she said to him. 'It's one of the largest man-made bodies of water in the world.'

He looked at her. 'How do you know that?'

'I remember it from school,' she said and she was pleased to have this information, feeling that it belonged in the same category as her growing knowledge of heavy machinery and construction materials.

They moved across the parking lot. A sign indicated an observation deck at the top of a short flight of stairs. *Lake Mead*, the sign read. They stood on the broad concrete expanse and looked out over a metal railing at the motionless water. *Lake Mead, 115 Miles Long, 589 Feet Deep.*

Far below the protective railing the lake lay smooth and translucent, neither green nor black. She imagined it cold to the touch, like obsidian. Nothing moved on its surface, not the flick of a fish, not a wire-legged beetle, no ducks or gulls. She wasn't sure if she heard or felt a low, rhythmic rumbling somewhere beneath her.

'This is awful,' she said. 'No one would ever be found.'

'What?' he asked. 'What did you say?'

'If someone fell in they would fall straight to the bottom like a stone. Nothing could be supported in that water. You'd drop like an elevator snapped from its cables,' she said, looking out over the endless dark pool.

'Then don't lean over,' he said, and meaning to joke, he flicked his fingers against her back.

Guys did this, she knew. Knocked into each other, clapped each other on the back, shoved the next guy playfully, then grabbed to right him if he lost his balance.

'If someone asks me what to see on a trip to Las Vegas,' she said, 'I'd say don't go to see Hoover Dam. It's awful. There's nothing but water and concrete. Nothing.'

'Hey,' he said. 'Don't knock concrete. Let's see what else. This guy told me you could tour the inside of the dam and see the generators.'

'No. I don't like it here,' she answered. 'We'll pick up a brochure and I'll read it to you on the drive back. We should get back before dark. Don't we have tickets for a show?' she asked, hoping to stop him before he made her do something she knew she didn't want to do.

He was moving her along toward a two-storey building, his hand fixed on her shoulder, steering her firmly through the doors with a group of people who had been on the observation deck with them. Others moved in to join them from across the grassy knoll where a few picnic tables sat under the dish-blue sky with its round yellow sun.

'Where are we going?' she asked him, as the group closed around them.

'We'll take the tour. I'm interested. You can't come all this way and not see the place,' he told her.

'I can,' she said. 'Please, let's not do this. I don't like to be underground, remember?'

'Okay. Wait for me outside by the lake,' he offered.

'That's the same. I don't like it there either. I don't like this entire place. We don't need to do this. I can't go underground. I'm frightened. A lot of people have phobias about that kind of thing, or about heights or small places. Don't make me do this, please.' Her voice caught.

'You're being a baby. Work it out. In fact this will be good for you. You have to face it and beat it. I'll be here. Be big,' he said and she wanted to be. She wanted to be big and good.

A young woman in a blue uniform walked over to them where they stood with the others waiting in the reception area of the two-storey building.

'Hi,' she said to the semi-circle of people facing her. 'My name is Wendy and I'm your guide. Shall we move forward? You know that Lake Mead is one of the deepest lakes in the world. Good. Now we'll just move into this elevator here. Okay, everyone. Suck in your tummies and we'll all squeeze in.'

The doors slid shut. Her husband was on one side of her. She could feel something angular pressing into her back, someone's purse, probably. On her other side, shoulder overlapping hers, was a stocky blonde woman. She could smell the woman's face powder. Wendy stood directly in front of her, her back to the elevator doors.

'Cozy, everyone?' she asked and she showed a broad, confident smile which she held for a moment, then bit her lower lip and paused, indicating that what followed was important.

'This is one of the highest dams in the world. It is 726 feet high and 1,244 feet long. The elevator in which you are riding is descending 44 stories into the centre of the dam and do you know – we still are not at its base.'

'Dam right,' a man's voice agreed, from the back of the elevator.

'Oh, you,' a woman's voice answered.

Wendy smiled and continued. 'The concrete base of the dam is 660 feet thick and contains 4,400,000 cubic yards of concrete.'

Here her husband whistled a sustained note to indicate he was impressed and understood. He and Wendy exchanged smiles.

This journey they were all taking to the base of the massive concrete wall, to the underside of the deepest lake in the world – what were they expecting to find? She held her breath against drowning but wasn't sure she could make it back up to the surface. They were still descending. Wendy went on.

'The construction of the dam created Lake Mead, as you know, one of the largest man-made lakes in the world. It can store about ten trillion gallons of water. At the dam's base the water exerts more than 45,000 pounds of pressure per square foot. Here we are, folks. Let's move out,' and the doors slid open. Her husband turned to her. 'Pretty impressive, huh?'

'There's no air. Take me out, please,' she said, taking his hand.

'You'll be fine. You're doing great. Let's hear what else she has to say,' and he pulled her by the hand back to the group listening to Wendy.

'Over there, those are some of the generators which pro-vide the electrical power which serves much of this state and several neighbouring ones. This power plant has a capacity of 1,249,800 kilowatts and power lines lead from right here all the way to Los Angeles.'

The dense concrete above and below and around them absorbed Wendy's voice and she had difficulty hearing what their competent guide was saying. She thought she recog-nized the rumbling she'd heard and felt when they were standing on top of the dam; now they were under it. The machines thrummed in her ears. In her head her own moving blood made an equivalent noise.

'I can't stand this. Get me out of here,' she pleaded.

'So now you can all say you've stood at the bottom of one of the largest man-made lakes in the world and stayed dry as a bone. Follow me please, and we'll take the elevator back up to the top,' and the group moved off after her.

'Look,' he said quietly, 'don't pull a number like you did in the nightclub. Just can it. Now,' and he squeezed her elbow, pushing her toward the elevator. 'You have just about ruined this trip, you know. Grow up.'

In spite of the close air she began to shiver. She told herself about the round yellow sun and how she'd liked the clean dust smell of the air when they'd arrived and how she'd look at the sky soon and she named the pieces of heavy equipment she'd seen on the convention floor days earlier, big machines painted in hard-baked enamel colours – green and sharp yellow and red, and then the doors opened and everyone moved out.

'You've all been just great. I hope you liked the tour and please come see us again when you're in this area. Bye now,' and Wendy walked smartly off.

They said nothing to each other on the ride back. By the time she could see the lights from the city tinting the night sky pink she had stopped shivering.

'You'll hurry and change. We have tickets for a show.'

She picked a black wool dress with long sleeves and she wore pearls. Probably the wrong thing, she thought, but some of the chill had stayed with her even after a hot bath.

She couldn't remember who the star performer at the nightclub was – some singer. If there was more she didn't really notice. She knew she wanted to go home and she thought only about that. She guessed she must have eaten something for dinner. She packed her suitcase when they got back to their room that night, leaving out the green wool dress and the green coat with the small gold buttons. The polka-dot ribbon was somewhere at the bottom of the bag.

In the morning, at breakfast, she drank some orange juice, poured maple syrup on her French toast, cut a small square but left it uneaten on her fork.

'I'll check out. You can sit down in the lobby,' he told her. Once they'd returned to the hotel the previous night his tone had again become pleasant and even. They didn't speak about their visit to Boulder Dam.

She sat on the edge of one of the sofas arranged in the lobby. She held her gloves in one hand. Her coat was over her arm.

'Did you get lucky?' asked a woman who was settled back in the sofa's corner.

She looked up.

'I saw you and your hubby come in a few days back. Recognized your green outfit. Changed your hair-do though. Left off the dotted ribbon.'

She lifted her hand to her neck where she'd used the ribbon to pull her hair into a tail and she looked over to the woman on the sofa opposite her.

'You've seen me before?' she asked. 'Did we meet in one of the hospitality suites?' Had she been introduced to this woman earlier? She remembered no one with tightly curled grey hair, wearing a mauve double-knit pant suit, but she'd met so many people. Mostly they were older than she was but younger than this woman appeared to be. Maybe she'd been wearing something different.

'I've seen you before but we've never met. I was sitting in this exact same spot the night the pair of you checked in. I take note is all. I look and make my observations to myself. Noticed your shiny hair, and that dotted ribbon you were wearing caught my eye. I lean to the unusual myself. What's the point of looking like everyone else, I always say. Course the opportunity to get done up doesn't present itself so often now.

'I said to myself when I saw you come in – there's the only person in this town wearing a polka-dot ribbon. Don't get me wrong – showed a lot of style. Like I said I like the individual touch myself. No need to follow like sheep, every one of us dressing the same.'

'Yes,' she answered. 'I've never been here before or to any place like this,' and looking down at her dress and the coat over her arm she said, 'I seem to have brought the wrong things and I don't expect I'll ever be back but thanks for liking the ribbon. I wasn't sure.'

'Now, you look fine. I like your hair loose too, lovely hair, yours. So shiny. If you weren't leaving just now you could sit for a bit and order a drink. You may not have noticed but in nice places like this they put out dishes of nuts for the cocktail hour. Too early in the day just now. I'm usually not down here myself till later. My days are full but I was in the mood for a little company and I figured my work can wait – dusting, the few dishes I mess on my own, what laundry there is. It can all wait. Nice to sit here in the sun.'

'Yes, the light is nice. I wasn't always sure if it was light or dark outside. I mean, we were working and most places didn't have windows.'

The woman in the mauve pant suit was listening and nodding. 'You'll be going now. There's your bags brought down over next to your hubby. You two do make a handsome couple, as they say.

'Well, sweetie, looks like he's wanting you. I know you've had yourself a lovely, lovely time and that'll bring you back again. I'll watch for you this time next year. Take care now, dear.'

Fairy Tales
1. Chocolate on Her Breath

'It will be great,' he'd said to her, 'just what you need. A complete rest. You won't have to move, not even ever leave the room. I'll take care of everything,' and he'd booked a double room for them in the hotel that was built like a castle with towers and turrets and crenellated walls.

Their room looked onto the fast-moving river that was open all winter. All winter it moved quickly between its high banks and in the cold air a fog rode just above its surface. When the temperature dropped the fog rose higher, obscuring the houses and cars and the people with dogs who moved along the opposite bank. This is what she saw when she stood at the tall double windows and looked out.

She stood at the windows of their peach-coloured room and looked out at the white gardens below her, or she lifted her head and watched the cars move over the bridge. At night the city would be full of lights: the paved walk along the river picked out with its pairs of glass globes marking the path, the houses on the opposite bank, the towers of the university far in the distance outlined in coloured lights for Christmas and just below the window the small skating rink with its little island of trees at the centre, laced with lights. She thought she could hear the blades on the ice when the skaters bent at the waist and pushed off but really she only saw the movement and remembered the sound which she knew she couldn't possibly hear in her room on the sixth floor.

'Read and rest, my dear. You've worked hard and it's what you said you needed. Read and lounge and be lazy,' he'd said.

'Don't even dress if you don't want to. Rest, my darling, in here where it's warm and I'll be back soon.'

The first day they'd eaten breakfast together in their room, sitting at the small table near the window and he'd said, 'I'm going to order up. I don't want you to move,' and it was just what she wanted. She'd pulled on the big white robe that came with the room and waited in bed. When the breakfast had been laid out she'd come to sit, like a child, in the big wing chair beside the window and, with her bare feet tucked under her, had eaten every scrap. She'd looked out at the misty river and then moved, like a very good child, back to the bed where he'd led her. He'd pulled the covers up around her and kissed her and told her to be good and rest, not move and wait for him.

She had been good and the peachy room was warm and she'd slept, all eggy and full of breakfast and it wasn't until nearly two o'clock that she'd wakened and stood and stretched and dropped the fuzzy white robe and showered and finally dressed and left the room.

She'd wandered through the hotel's public rooms, trying the big chairs in the lobby, pressing her nose against the glass in the heavy double doors at the front and imagining the cold from the puffs of white around the cars and near the faces of the people walking outside. She'd crossed her arms in front of her for warmth and was glad she was inside. Then, she'd bought a bag of cream-centred chocolates from the little shop by the elevators, picking six different ones, and taken the candy back up to the room.

'It's so cold, we'll stay in,' he'd said hours later when he'd let himself into their room.

'See, the lights are just coming on now,' she'd answered, standing at the window and he'd moved up behind her, circling her with his arms, bringing the cold on his mouth and beard, bringing the outside into the peach room.

She'd leaned back against him and he'd put his outdoor lips to her warm cheek and then her neck, nosing her mouth, where he smelled chocolate.

'You thing. Where did you get chocolate? Were they the ones that were left on our pillows last night?'

She'd shaken her head, feeling again like a little girl.

'So where did they come from? You have a secret cache somewhere, you wretch. Come on, where are they?'

And when he saw the bag he knew where they'd come from and, hurt, he'd said 'You went out. You left the room, bad girl,' and his tone had changed, darkened for a moment, and then passed.

'You're so bad and I bought you something. If I'd known, I might not have,' and he held up to her a paper shopping bag with coloured tissue tucked in all around the top.

Like the child she sometimes felt she was and like the eager girl he loved, she plucked the paper out of the bag and scattered it around her on the floor. Inside, at the bottom, was a flat cardboard box tied with gold string and inside the box, when she'd pulled the gold string off and draped it around his shoulders – now you're the gift, but save it for my hair – lay something made of pale grey, figured silk.

'What?' she asked him. 'What have I got? Do I guess before I get it or is it mine right now? It should be mine right now.'

'It's something very special and rare,' he told her. 'The only one, in fact, so lucky it was your size. It suits this place and it suits you, captive lady. I knew you'd wear it here, in this warm room.'

Picking up his story, she carried on. 'I know I'll love it and it will fit because whoever made it knew it was for me to wear, here. The lady in the shop knew we'd come and though hundreds tried to buy this gown she would not yield it up until you came. When you opened the door she lifted the gown from its hook and brought it to you draped across her arms.

She held it out, curtsied just a very shallow little bit, wrapped it and gave it to you without uttering a word. And, without hesitation you gave her the correct change, like you always do, and the store lady dipped again and vanished and here you are. It *is* so special and magical,' she'd said, moving to the window and looking out at the mist on the river and the clouded lights from the opposite bank, 'that it can only be worn here because once it's worn here in this room, once the enchanted maiden puts it on, then if it's ever put on in another room it crumbles to a very fine dust, but if you gather up the dust in a piece of tissue paper and sift it over a garden, white roses will grow there. Or something,' and she turned back from the window and looked at him.

'I don't really mean that, you know. I'm just playing,' she'd said. 'It's these old hotels. I guess I'm caught up by dark wood and a certain kind of light. What did you get for me? Let's see it really.'

What she pulled out *was* extraordinary. A long silk gown, cut wide but fitting closely over the bodice, with deep sleeves and two silk braid closures at the throat and breast. In the back, one long pleat ran from the neck to the hem. She put it on over her skirt and sweater. She could feel the weight of it. The gown was cut longer at the back and when she walked the pleat fanned behind her in a train and slowed her. Her movements became deliberate and she picked up and placed each foot with care. When she turned, the train caught for a moment on the wool carpet and the gown opened in front. She could almost step around inside it. She lifted her arms and held them out from her shoulders and the sleeves dropped and swung. At the cuffs, her hands were small.

'You'll wear that at dinner tonight but not with woollens underneath. You look wonderful, just as expected. A lady, in a castle, in a gown, at dinner. Now, what should we eat?' and together they looked at the menu they'd found in the drawer of the big desk.

They'd ordered a splendid dinner with two kinds of wine and brandy and there'd been candles and a rose on the dinner cart as if the hotel too, had known about her fine gown which she'd worn, as he'd instructed, without woollens underneath.

And the next morning – breakfast again by the window and now the cold outside had clouded the lower portions of the glass and to see out she had to rise up on her toes. Again he'd ordered them an egg breakfast.

'We have yellow food in the morning to conjure the sun in this grey place, don't we?' she'd said and she'd pressed her fork into the yolky hollandaise on her plate.

He told her, 'I know you have your work and all that reading to do and the air outside is too thin and bitter for you today. Keep warm inside and if you're perfect I'll bring you another gift when I come back.'

This was the pattern. She found the days passing and she was inside the stone walls of the old hotel with its towers and high double windows and its long halls that angled and bent suddenly to reveal dark alcoves with two leather chairs and a table. She would round a corner and come upon them and she'd sit for a while and swing her legs and watch the pattern on the carpet and then she'd get up and move on.

Some days she'd take coffee in the glass-roofed garden room and from her table by the window she'd look out over the snow-covered lawns of the hotel and watch magpies swoop and lift off with their long forked tails. She meant to hang small mirrors in the bushes near the window or drape the hedge with the gold string from her gift to test the stories she'd heard about the birds being drawn by glittering things. But she never moved outdoors.

The chef who prepared the meals for their room recognized the pattern and saw in it a part he could play, too. Without consulting anyone he began to insert himself into their rhythm, understanding, through the nature of his work, that sometimes a hotel can be a whole world. Their trays would be impeccably prepared; nothing was ever missing. One day, as well as everything they'd ordered, there was a speckled quail's egg, pricked at each end and blown hollow and tied around the middle with a pink ribbon. When they'd settled down to eat he'd said, 'This, of course, is for you,' and he'd handed it to her. They'd eaten their meal and said no more about it. For a while, after he'd gone, she'd held the small egg in her hand to warm it.

One day on the tray with their supper they found violets made from butter icing pressed into the glass bottom of an emptied caviar jar and another time, three goose feathers bound together by a long, unbroken curl of orange peel. Sometimes, one piece of buttered toast would be cut out in the shape of a dove, its feathers drawn in a soft white cheese; a champagne cork had been cut with a very small knife into the shape of a brown squirrel no bigger than a man's thumbnail; one of the linen napkins would be folded into an elaborate chrysanthemum; two perfect, mauve freesia buds had been frozen inside an ice cube and placed in one of the water glasses. The gifts were subtle. Always they were things from the kitchen.

In the hotel she felt so comfortable. What, she wondered, could she ever need outside. And while she could feel herself grow pale, could even see that it was true when she looked in the big mirror near the heavy front doors, she would say she was happy.

Accustomed to seeing her in the hotel, no one objected when she made the empty ballroom her indoor track and jogged around its edges some mornings, watching her profile splinter in the long mirrors as she moved rhythmically past them or measured the distance she'd covered by counting the repeating patterns in the inlaid floor.

On these days she'd return to their room, soak in the tub and then wrap herself in one of the big white robes that were brought fresh each day. Then she would eat fruit, write journal entries and rest.

Sometimes she would sit in the deep brocade chairs in the foyer and watch women wearing big black or brown fur coats come into the hotel. When they left, some time later, their small heads, showing above their fur collars, would be coifed, the hair nicely shaped into thick, even curls or orderly rows of waves and these same women would hold their gloved hands stiffly out in front of them as though they'd been newly made aware of possibilities.

They've just been to a salon, she realized, and they've had their hair and nails done. One day she'd climbed the staircase set to the side of the entry doors and found the beauty salon on the mezzanine level and she'd gone in and asked to have her hair and nails done, too.

Later, she'd sat in their room watching the sun tint the frost on the windows and when he'd walked in she'd turned to face him.

'See,' she'd said holding out her hands, each finger tipped in pink enamel.

'And, see,' she'd said, turning and turning in front of him so he could admire her hair which had been curled and looped and folded and held in place, high off her neck, with tortoiseshell combs. 'Like a princess, I am.'

'Formidable, for sure,' he'd said, touching the stiff mass with his fingertips.

Before dinner, she'd brushed and brushed until all the lacquer had been brushed out and now her hair rested on her shoulders once more but he remained wary all evening, watching her with side glances and looking often at the shiny points in which her fingers now ended.

It happened that the next day was a Sunday and his work was done.

'I can stay here with you all day,' he'd said. 'Two bugs in the broadloom, two eggs in a nest, two trout in a pan, two peas in a pod.'

She could hear him in the shower, taking his time, then drying his hair and the air softened with the moisture from his washing. When he stepped out of the bathroom he too was wearing one of the white robes and he knotted the long belt around his waist.

'We're twins now, in our kimonos. We'll be close as two horses in tandem, or Dancer and Prancer. We're hand in glove, spoons in a drawer, cheek by jowl, thick as thieves,' and he went on in this manner until breakfast arrived.

They sat opposite each other at the small table in front of the window, both in their white bathrobes and they took their time with breakfast. They looked at sections of the Sunday paper and read stories of interest out loud to each other. They stretched in the warm damp air and were comfortable enough to never think of leaving.

'I could stay like this forever,' he'd said. 'I could stay inside this warm place, behind these thick stone walls and never ever move again. If anyone phones for me today, tell them I'm all tied up.'

He'd looked over to her. They'd been together for a long time. That's why they travelled so well. It's what accounted for the quiet spaces between them when they'd spend a day, just the two of them. They knew each other so well.

'How about it?' he'd said from the bed where he'd stretched out. 'I'm yours,' he'd said, holding his wrists together over his head and dangling the belt from his robe in one hand. 'Have your way with me,' he'd urged, feigning bondage. 'The thin light has weakened me, the damp air has diminished my strength. But be kind.'

The bed had a mahogany head-board with tall posts. She'd looked at it with interest, more taken with the logistics of securing such a big man using only the tie from a terry towel bathrobe, than in any sexual games. Even with his cooperation there simply wasn't enough of the belt and what there was was too thick to tie in an effective knot.

With a sure gesture she wrapped one half of the belt around both his wrists, looping the thick stuff into a loose clumsy knot. He lay back with his eyes closed in a hammy swoon.

She continued. She wound the other half of the belt around the brass neck of the very nice lamp that sat on the desk by the bed. She switched on the lamp and the bulb shone through the green glass shade. Then she pushed the lamp to the edge of the desk, half on it, half off. If he moved, the lamp would fall to the floor and shatter.

'Okay,' she said. 'You're all tied up,' and she walked over to the dresser and began opening drawers.

They should be at work on Monday. There were appointments to make. If they phoned right away they could probably get on the early morning flight. She'd call the front desk and order a taxi for the next day and using both hands she swung her heavy suitcase onto the end of the bed, all by herself.

2. As for the Chef

As for the chef, he found himself confronting a full-blown obsession – his own – with a woman whose name he'd only just learned. He hadn't even been sure he wanted to know her name. So what, he'd thought, whatever she's called, so what?

Is this what it is? he'd questioned in the hot kitchen. Is this tight, go-nowhere circle I'm locked into an obsession? Do I know this? Close-up work, deliberate and fine attention to details – he was accustomed to that; it made him good at his job. The flourish, grand gestures, the big sweeps, histrionics, tantrums, extravagances were for movie chefs. Here in the big stainless steel kitchens you didn't shout, you didn't slam copper lids onto bubbling stock pots and you never rapped a whisk against the edge of a copper bowl to flick off excess meringue. The noise bouncing off the tiled walls would make you crazy. You controlled yourself, worked carefully, pacing the day, moving deliberately through the steps, doing each in order, this before this before that.

Then the couple checked in. Eight floors separated them from him, insulated their events from his, he down here in his tiled white and stainless steel kitchen, warm and efficient, with his superbly trained staff moving quickly through their paces, murmuring comments, exchanging necessary information, a team of reliable schooled professionals. The couple was on the sixth floor, six stories above the lobby, eight floors above him in their big carpeted room with its tall windows overlooking the hotel gardens, now snow-covered, and if he remembered, their room had an excellent view of the river. It had been probably two years since he'd toured the whole hotel, just after the renovations had been completed and all the staff had been invited to inspect the building top to bottom; his kitchen had been part of it too. That would be where they were, up there in one of the peach-coloured rooms with the big chairs near the window.

So how, with the soft peach carpeting, eight solid floors and no common business between them, had they come to his attention? Never mind come to his attention, become trapped, like a stringy piece of beef between his teeth, wedged in his consciousness so that his tongue was tender with trying to dislodge them. Not them, her, with trying not to think about her and when, he'd like to know, did they plan to check out?

He wouldn't have noticed them if they'd taken one of the weekend packages – two nights, continental breakfast in your room, all exercise facilities included – Health Club, they call it now. They'd have come and gone like all the others, filling rooms at reduced rates on slow weekends. Or if they'd had the business package – in late Monday, out by Wednesday, quick check-in, fast and courteous check-out, newspaper at your door with the 7:00 a.m. in-room breakfasts.

He didn't know what day this couple arrived; if he thought about it and went to the trouble he could find their room service orders. They'd be the ones with eggs Benedict and two carafes of coffee ordered at five to eleven, just before they stopped serving breakfast to the rooms. He probably didn't notice the first time, it was only when it became a pattern, an inconvenient pattern, that he noted it. He'd no longer be thinking eggs and would have cleaned out the pot with the hollandaise and there it would be – eggs Benedict times two for room 623. And at first he didn't really notice the meals taken in their room at night because all the room service items were on the dining-room menu too and a lot of people ate late.

It was the chambermaid on their floor. She started it. One day at coffee she'd mentioned that the couple in 623 were not the usual kind of hotel guests. At first she'd thought maybe someone was ill because the DO NOT DISTURB sign was out almost the whole day and every day. She told the chef she felt like a stalker pacing the hall in front of their room waiting for the sign to read PLEASE MAKE UP THIS ROOM. She'd leave the floor for a minute maybe to pick up fresh linens or soap and she'd come back; the sign would have been turned and the room would be empty. She said she always knocked any-way before she put her key in the lock, but the room was empty.

'So what, other than that they were layabouts, made them so different from other guests?' he'd asked her, only casually interested.

'Well,' she told him. 'I've been doing this work a long time, as you know. Housekeeping is a professional position just like yours and I have a lot of responsibilities. I'm good because I'm careful, quick, mind my own business, keep my opinions to myself. But I notice things. I use my hands, my back, let me tell you, my eyes and my nose. You once told me you could pick out different cheeses by smell alone. Well, me, I can tell if a guest uses a good perfume the minute I put my foot in the room. This one did. Nice and light and flowery. I expected a messy room, they'd been in it so long. But it wasn't. The beds of course were unmade. For me, I'd stay in a hotel just to not have to make a bed for once. All the wet towels were draped over the tub. There were no clothes lying about, just a pair of silver slippers with little heels, those mules. The top of the dresser in front of the mirror looked like some library in an old movie. There were books lined up and a fancy bottle of brandy with two of those fat snifter glasses. On the TV was a bouquet of pink roses in a glass vase; the table near the window had a few more books and one of those leather-bound notebooks and two pretty nice-looking pens. On the window-sill there were three potted plants, two white and one pink. I thought, that's a lot of stuff to bring in for a couple of days but then they didn't stay for just a couple of days, did they. So after a week like this I was getting curious to see them. Him I did see, leaving one morning. A nice-looking guy, very nicely dressed in a business suit and dark coat. Tall-ish, broad shoulders, short dark hair, trim beard, no glasses, no cologne or after shave. Pretty regular, pretty conservative, moved quickly. She was still inside.

'One day, I guess early in the second week they'd been here, my friend who does the fifth floor says to me, "You know, she jogs in the ballroom, the princess in the tower."

'What do you mean, she jogs in the ballroom, I say to her and she answers, "What I said, she jogs in the ballroom. The management lets her run around in a leotard and track shoes in the ballroom, mornings when it's empty."

'Now's my chance, I figure. I'll get to see her. So after the first early-morning rush, when I'm picking up fresh towels I go down the back stairs to the second floor and I look into the ballroom, the door's ajar, and sure enough there she is just passing me in her leotard. "Good morning," she says to me, out of breath, and she carries on. Didn't want anyone passing her on the inside, I guess.'

'What did she look like?' the chef asked her. 'Is she pretty?'

'I guess, yes. Slim, medium height, taller rather than short, longish darkish hair. I only saw her a minute; she was running.'

So what did he have? Two people who were staying a long time in the hotel. Most mornings they ordered eggs Benedict. Every three or four days they'd have just fruit, 'Please send up all the fruit that's in season,' and always two carafes of coffee. What else? She wore good perfume, flowery, she liked flowers, the room was full of them, she was thinnish, tallish, had long dark hair and silver slippers and she read a lot and maybe she wrote in the leather-covered notebook and she was tidy. So what? What did he care? Why did he think about her at all?

But he did. Why didn't she ever leave the hotel? (His contacts on the floor told him she never went out. Now a whole, very quiet network laced all through the hotel watched her, their room, her partner, their food trays, but always discreetly, always kindly.) They told him she never left the hotel. Was she frail, hiding, desperate, famous, dangerous? Was she free to leave? Was her partner keeping her against her will? Should he help her?

Certainly not. He'd continue to run the best kitchen in town. He'd be efficient, orderly, creative. That's what he'd be. Through his craft, his art, and with the absolutely impeccable discretion with which he'd always conducted himself, he'd allow himself this one involvement. Above reproach, maintaining the highest standards he'd set for himself at the beginning of his career, he'd enter into a relationship with a guest of the hotel. He'd do it or he'd go crazy and he would bang the pot lids, create a cacophony of kettles, thrum the whisks against the copper bowls, whack the freezer doors shut, throw eggs against the white tile walls and howl up the dumb waiter, winding his agony through the hotel.

He'd deal with his obsession, but he wouldn't put at risk his whole carefully wrought career; he'd use the skills he'd acquired, his training would be tested, he'd summon all his schooled creativity and he'd reach this slim dark-haired guest who pressed to her slender body a small quiet mystery – he'd tell her, without offending, he'd tell her – I love you.

He'd start with flowers – she loved flowers. There was a wedding in the hotel. Carefully, using his kitchen snips, he cut the top two blossoms from a stem of the mauve freesia making up the bouquet at the head table. In his kitchen he separated the two small flowers, set them in an ice cube form, filled the container with water and pushed it to the back of the freezer unit in his kitchen. It would be ready for their dinner tray. That night, checking their tray before it was taken to the sixth floor, he unmoulded the ice cube in which the two perfect freesia buds were congealed, dropped it into one of the water glasses and sent the uniformed young man on his way. 'Be quick,' was all he said.

Later that same night, surveying his kitchen before closing up, he found a champagne cork from one of the wedding's bottles. He picked it up, brought it to his nose, dropped it into his pocket and left.

The next night, after their dinner tray had been prepared, he checked it against the order and before handing it to the uniformed young man set a tiny, perfectly carved cork squirrel on one of the napkins.

Another night he noticed they'd ordered smoked salmon. Thinly sliced dark bread, lemon wedges and cream cheese usually accompanied the order. With his fine kitchen knife he cut one of the dense, dark slices into a dove and drew its feathers with the soft white cheese.

He was feeling better, a little less intense. Action had always suited him.

Then, at the Chinese market, he found quail's eggs. It wasn't something on the menu but he'd occasionally prepare them at home. Now he took one, pushed a hot needle into both ends, and blew the contents into a bowl to be scrambled with hens' eggs for his own breakfast later. He carried the weightless shell wrapped in layers of Kleenex, driving to work with one hand, afraid to set the thin-shelled, hollow egg down. At the chocolate shop in the hotel he asked for a length of pink ribbon and he tied it around the speckled egg's girth and set it on a napkin when he approved the tray for the sixth floor. He would keep this up as long as they stayed. He could be as inventive as their stay was long.

He didn't need to see her responses. He knew she recognized that the gifts were for her, from him. That was sufficient.

Goose was a regular item on the winter menu. He ordered his from a farmer he knew. He liked them to be a certain weight and he wanted to prepare them from the beginning, the way he'd been taught so many years before. He served them with oranges or with cherries if he could find the sour Hungarian kind – not always possible.

That night, for their tray, though they hadn't ordered fowl, he bound three perfect, soft grey tail feathers with a long curl of orange peel. He laid this across one plate and sent the tray upstairs.

Another night it was violets made from butter and pressed into an empty glass caviar jar, the following night one napkin bloomed as an elaborate damask chrysanthemum.

He found himself able to return to his accustomed routine. At times he even felt calm, although his thoughts often rose to the sixth floor. It would have been easy, in his senior position, to take the elevator up, to walk rightly down the hall, knock at 623 and inquire – 'Have the trays been to your satisfaction?' hear her voice, smell the expensive perfume, test the colour of her eyes, check the temperature of her pale cheek, lift a light, long-fingered hand to his mouth, smooth her hair back from her face, ask if she needed him to show her a way out, carry her books, lift her in her silver slippers and help her away from that room, away from the hotel. No. The hotel was a world. Who would leave it? He understood. She was fine and for that night he'd carve roses from dark chocolate. He'd pleat a paper doily and set them inside.

It had been the nicest two weeks she'd spent. She was rested;

he'd finished the work he'd come to do. She'd read, eaten well, so well, had even returned to her writing. There couldn't be a nicer hotel; the attention to details was remarkable. She'd never encountered its equal anywhere, nor had she felt so cared for in any hotel in which she'd stayed.

'Thank you so much,' she'd said to the hotel manager when they checked out, 'and please, my compliments to the chef.'

No More Denver Sandwiches

I t's cold. Dead cold. The middle of winter. They're sitting in Robin's Donuts looking at the Saturday paper. Holidays are discounted. The economy's lousy. Fly to Mazatlán, air and hotel, for less than it costs you to stay at home. Or Hawaii, Cuba, Jamaica, Palm Springs.

'Hey, you've been to Palm Springs,' he says to her. 'How about let's go there. It's cheap. What's it like?'

'It was another life,' she says. 'I'm not going back. Not only can't. Won't. Finished, final, over.'

'Yah, but what's it like?' he persists. 'Every year it's advertised. Bob Hope is there if he's still alive. Dinah Shore and the Dinah Shore Open. All the tennis greats and Elizabeth Taylor and Betty Ford and the drug people. There must be something there.'

So she tells him.

I was young, married. A good idea at the time; finally not such a great idea. His parents went to Palm Springs every winter. All their friends did. Dozens of couples, married for years, well off. The men would pack cardigan sweaters in light colours and their clubs in leather bags. The ladies had florals, pastel knits and bathing suits with skirts.

My ex-husband was sick with colds off and on all winter. His parents were concerned. They sent us tickets. Come down, we have an extra room. They always took a condo near friends. Why not, I figured. I hadn't travelled much. Palm Springs was where the movie stars went. They told me – sure

[229]

I'd see some. My father-in-law claimed he'd seen that guy who had a TV series, who owned a baseball team. The one with the pale eyes. Why not? I liked the idea of getting on a plane in winter and getting off in summer.

It was night when we landed and really late. The plane had been held up in Minneapolis and by the time we arrived it was maybe ten, maybe later. They opened the door of the plane and I remember walking through the opening onto the top step of those stairs they wheel up and the air just smacked me in the face. Dark and hot and wet. Soft with flowers and diesel and the smell of earth, rubber on warm asphalt and the flat sound of cars honking in the heavy air.

People moved around in short-sleeved shirts. The dark men unloading the plane had bare arms. To me, coming from winter, they looked naked. I couldn't breathe and I remember being so excited by all of it that I felt like running and running to say how great it was. Palm trees. I'd never seen palm trees. They were so exotic I couldn't believe they'd grow around an airport. And flowers, fat flowers everywhere. People were wearing sandals. My nylons were hot. My hair was back-combed and sprayed stiff and I could smell the lacquer softening in the humidity.

We had to rent a car and drive through Los Angeles to get to Palm Springs. We had no idea how far. The guy at the car rental said just follow this road to the turn-off and then left onto the highway, we'd see signs. I was hungry. I wanted a burger and fries. I wanted a chocolate milkshake. I wanted to take off my nylons and knit suit. I wanted to trot beside the car in the fluorescent green grass. I wanted to check those palm trees to see if they were real.

Why can't we stop for a burger first before we leave L.A., I wanted to know, but he said his parents would be worried, we were already late. We'd find something once we got on the highway.

Of course, neither of us had ever driven on an American freeway. If you have you know there's no getting off, there's nowhere to eat, there's just four lanes of cars each way and that's it.

Then he said we could eat once we got there, at a Denny's or a Sambo's. Can you imagine a restaurant called Sambo's today? I think, if you can believe it, they served pancakes in the Aunt Jemima tradition. But I knew what would happen. We'd go straight to his parents' place because you couldn't worry Mom and Dad and once we got there she'd offer to make us a Denver sandwich. It's gruesome. Scrambled eggs with little pieces of pink salami chopped in and green onion which never got fried, only warm. Warm green onion, wet eggs, pink meat bits. No one young eats that. Or she'd say cereal. A bowl of cereal. No one young eats cereal at night either.

That food did a lot of damage and in fact I figure it killed his dad. Colon cancer. Forty-seven years they were married and he never had roughage in his diet. Nothing fresh or whole. All those years she never let him near uncooked food. He loved fresh corn in the summer. She'd ration it, counting the cobs like he was on an allowance. Maybe she should have let him have all the corn he wanted. I bet she wonders.

Sure enough, 'I'll make you eggs. How about a Denver sandwich?' and he says, 'Okay, Mom.' The trip was like that.

We ate and unpacked and I changed and went outside to the patio. All the shrubs had lights under them and they floated in the dark like little clouds of vegetation. The pool was lit around the edges and the water was turquoise like in the movies. There were crickets or frogs and a TV was on in someone's condo. What I figured was a round kiddies' pool turned out to be a Jacuzzi. The sky was very dark and up in the mountains I could see the lights of houses which I knew belonged to movie stars. I figured this would be okay and I knew what I wanted.

I wanted to go to the restaurant where Frank Sinatra ate. I wanted to have drinks with fruit on plastic swords, a shrimp cocktail, Caesar salad, Chateaubriand, rare, a stuffed baked potato and something flaming for dessert. I wanted to sit in a leather banquette in the corner against the wall, facing out so I could see everyone and they could see me. I would wear my black dress with the low back and my shoulders would be tanned. I would have a pearl bracelet on one wrist. I would wear my hair up in a French twist and a few tendrils would escape at my cheek and neck and they would curl a little from the heat. Sipping cocktails, whoever I was with would lean near my ear and whisper that the man who'd just come in and taken a chair at the table near ours was a known Mafia figure.

'Right here, here in this restaurant right now?' and I wouldn't believe whoever it was telling me that, because even though he might have been wearing too much hair tonic he looked quite nice and handsome in a rough kind of way.

I knew, eating my shrimp cocktail, that this was a man who could order what he wanted in a restaurant and get it. I could tell, when I got up and excused myself and walked right past him to the ladies' room that he didn't have to raise his voice to be heard. I was certain, when I saw him ordering from the wine list, that when he was cruel it hurt him deeply and I couldn't finish my steak after he looked directly at me, smiled, and lifted his glass.

I wanted, at the end of my dinner, to get up and walk past his table again. I wanted him to stand up and be close enough so I could smell his hair tonic. I wanted him to take my wrist, the one without the bracelet, very firmly, but not to hurt me, and insist I sit down with him at his table, stay with him, be with him dark and dangerous, go with him where it was dangerous, quickly, and never be frightened, to a place with horses and fast cars and elegant casinos and maybe yachts, to turn night into day if we wanted, to be so quick and beautiful that New York composers would write songs about us and to never eat Denver sandwiches again.

Every day the men golfed. The ladies played cards which I didn't know how to do and didn't want to learn. I read in the sun by the pool, only me and some kids, somebody's grandchildren and their nanny, and after I'd had enough sun and done I don't know how many laps in the turquoise pool I'd change and walk the few streets over to Palm Canyon Drive, the street with all the shops and I'd prowl the stores looking for movie stars. I didn't see any, not one. I did see a lot of blond people, young and old, even one old woman pulling her own oxygen tank, poor soul, and everyone was really dressed. A lot of big flower prints which I knew I couldn't wear back home and never figured I'd be in Palm Springs again so while I tried on lots of clothes in those stores looking for movie stars, I didn't find anything much to buy.

A couple of times, at night, we went out to restaurants and I kept on the lookout for stars and my Mafia man. There I was, a kid really, anxious for everything. Life in gulps. I wanted the edgy stuff, the gentle stuff. I wanted to spin and never catch my breath, spin until I fell.

Most nights we ate in with his parents. After dinner their friends would come over for coffee, instant decaf and Sara Lee baking. I would sit between two people on the sofa, someone on either side of me, nice enough people, no, actually they weren't nice now that I'm telling it — small, dull, smug people is really what they were, the friends of my ex-husband's parents. I'd sit there with my wonderful tanned body. I'd sit there with my dark hair and my big eyes. I'd turn my head from one to the other to answer their questions. I'd look across the room at the wives and husbands of the friends of my in-laws, and language I'd heard but never uttered would bubble to my lips. I knew if I sat longer I'd shout 'Have you ever fucked someone you're not married to?' and I'd get up and clear dishes. I'd run water and look out at the hot green shrubs and the turquoise water and then I'd excuse myself and go to sleep.

I kept hoping I'd see someone famous. I hadn't given up on that. I wanted to know how tall were they. Did they have good skin or did they wear thick make-up? If I saw them in person I knew I could tell. I was curious about their mates. Did stars attract beautiful mates or could someone handsome be married to someone they just loved who might be plain. Did they drive their own cars when they were on vacation and did they pay cash? Did they in fact have to buy their clothes or did people give them gifts just to have them wear their things?

So late afternoons I'd be on Palm Canyon Drive and like I wanted to know everything and be everywhere, I wanted to be glamorous too. Why not?

I was trying on a pant suit and this one I could see myself wearing at home. It was a dark green linen. The jacket was sleeveless which I liked for my tanned shoulders and it buttoned down the front. The neckline was wide and cut a little low but if I had to I could pull it closed with a pin. I thought, with all the blondes, young and old, showing everything they had, day or night, I could wear a jacket with the neck cut in such a way that the tops of my very young breasts showed too. Why not? I was quite pleased and was close to buying the outfit, thinking I'd maybe come back for it when the saleslady said to me that it looked just as nice on me as it had on what's her name, the movie star from France who was involved with the skier.

She packed it for me and that night I insisted we eat out, alone. It turned out my in-laws were eating out too and had gone early. If you eat early there, there's a discount. All these wealthy people vacationing in an expensive resort lining up to eat almost before dark to save five bucks. My ex-husband was in the living room watching TV.

Here I come. I could see myself from where he sat. Young. Made crazy by the smell of orange blossoms in the air every night. Brown shoulders. Dark hair, big dark eyes. Excited. Wearing something new. Me and a French movie star in the same outfit. The air outside smells good. So do I. I walk into the living room slowly. I'm in high-heeled sandals to go with the outfit and I don't want to trip on the shag carpeting. He's going to be wild for this. The whole time we've been here he's been looking at everyone's cleavage. I'm offering the tops of my young breasts. Just a little showing. I walk in slowly, my heart pounding.

He looks at me. I smile. 'Do yourself up,' he says. 'You look like a tramp.'

I stayed with him for a couple more years.

Acknowledgements

To write and then see what you've written finally in print is to feel enormous gratitude. The act is a solitary one; the final work is most assuredly not. Thank you isn't sufficient but what else to say to John Metcalf for his astute editorial judgement, his patience and playful prodding; to The Porcupine's Quill for doing everything so well and making it all so easy – I am honoured to be one of their books; to David Arnason for his persistent encouragement and more – for his important sense of place – many literary things in this country would not have happened without him; to Robert Kroetsch for wisdom and grace; to Leon Rooke, oh to Leon Rooke, who was my best and always reader and to Connie Rooke who published me first and often in *The Malahat Review*. There might well have been no stories, no writing at all, without Robert Enright who said I could write and should write. What greater friend is there than one who sets aside his own work to help with yours.

Six of the stories in this collection were previously published in *The Malahat Review*, *Descant* and *Canadian Fiction Magazine*. 'No More Denver Sandwiches' was published in the anthology *Due West*, Coteau, Turnstone and Newest in 1996.

About the Author

MEEKA WALSH is a Winnipeg-based writer, critic and editor whose stories have appeared in a number of Canadian literary magazines, including *Descant, The Malahat Review, Canadian Fiction Magazine* and *Prairie Fire*. Since 1993 she has edited *Border Crossings*, an international arts magazine published in Winnipeg. She has received seven nominations for her writing at the Western and National Magazine Awards and has won two gold medals. In 1994 her story 'No More Denver Sandwiches' won second place in the Eden Mills Writers' Festival National Literary Competition.

Ordinary Magic: Intervals in a Life, a book of journals was published by Turnstone Press in 1989 and last year she edited *Don Reichert: A Life in Work* for the Winnipeg Art Gallery Press.

Meeka Walsh is also a member of the Canadian Artists' and Producers' Professional Relations Tribunal for the Status of the Artist.

The Garden of Earthly Intimacies is her first book of fiction.